PRAISE

INDIVISIBLE

"In a world divided by so many labels, this story is a reminder that there are no boundaries for love. It shines a light on the difficult choices people make for their family and community and reminds us that each family is a little world." —Yamile Saied Méndez, author of inaugural Pura Belpré Young Adult Medal winner *Furia*

"A heartening tribute to the power and endurance of familial love." —Adi Alsaid, author of *Let's Get Lost* and *North of Happy*

"*Indivisible* is a heartbreakingly poignant and timely coming-of-age story of the human cost of a morally bankrupt immigration policy." —Jeff Zentner, William C. Morris Award–winning author of *The Serpent King*

"Insightful.... The uncertainty and heartbreak faced by families separated by deportation is brilliantly displayed." —*SLJ*

"*Indivisible* somehow never loses its humor, its humanity, or its hope." —Kelly Loy Gilbert, author of Stonewall Honor Book *Picture Us in the Light*

"A total miracle of a book." —Adam Sass, author of *Surrender Your Sons*

INDIVISIBLE

BY DANIEL ALEMAN

Little, Brown and Company
New York Boston

Little, Brown and Company
Hachette Book Group
1290 Avenue of the Americas, New York, NY 10104
Visit us at LBYR.com

Originally published in hardcover and ebook by Little, Brown and Company in May 2021
First Trade Paperback Edition: August 2022

Little, Brown and Company is a division of Hachette Book Group, Inc. The Little, Brown name and logo are trademarks of Hachette Book Group, Inc.

The publisher is not responsible for websites (or their content) that are not owned by the publisher.

The Library of Congress cataloged the hardcover as follows:
Names: Aleman, Daniel, author.
Title: Indivisible / by Daniel Aleman.
Description: First edition. | New York : Little, Brown and Company, 2021. |
Audience: Ages 14 & up. | Summary: New York City high school student
Mateo dreams of becoming a Broadway star, but his life is transformed after
his parents are detained by immigration officials.
Identifiers: LCCN 2020041107 | ISBN 9780759556058 (hardcover) | ISBN
9780759554979 (ebook) | ISBN 9780759554153 (ebook other)
Subjects: CYAC: Family life—New York (State)—New York—Fiction. |
Separation (Psychology)—Fiction. | Illegal aliens—Fiction. |
Deportation—Fiction. | Mexican Americans—Fiction.
Classification: LCC PZ7.1.A4344 Ind 2021 | DDC [Fic]—dc23
LC record available at https://lccn.loc.gov/2020041107

ISBNs: 978-0-7595-5389-7 (pbk.), 978-0-7595-5497-9 (ebook)

Printed in the United States of America

LSC-C

Printing 1, 2022

TO MY MA AND PA, WHO HAVE
GIVEN ME EVERYTHING

ONE

MA IS ALWAYS TELLING ME HOW I *feel* too much.

"It isn't a bad thing, mijo," she reminds me every time this comes up. "It just means you carry around a little more than you should. When things are bad, it weighs you down more than it would most people. But when everything's good, you also get to feel a little more of the good stuff."

On days like today, I think she might be right. Maybe I *do* feel too much. I've been carrying all this weight inside my stomach for hours, and it just won't go away. It's heavier than these boxes I have to carry around, and I'm getting tired of the way it's bringing me down.

I look at the pile of boxes, trying to figure out which one weighs the most. Maybe if I grab the heaviest one, this feeling inside me will feel lighter in comparison, so I push a box of paper towels aside and pick up the one full of packaged tortillas.

It's lighter than I expected, but maybe that's just because my arms have gotten stronger. I've been helping Ma and Pa at the bodega for a couple of years now, but I only took over the task of restocking the shelves last summer. In the months since then, I've learned that no box is too heavy to carry.

I head toward the back of the store and set the box down in front of the half-empty tortilla shelf. This little corner of the bodega used to be nothing more than a few shelves with Mexican products, but ever since Pa decided to add items from other countries, we started referring to it as the Ethnic Foods section. As I begin to pile up the packages of tortillas on the shelf, that word starts burning my tongue. *Ethnic.*

"Too ethnic," I whisper to myself. *"Too ethnic."*

"Excuse me?"

I turn around to find a woman standing behind me. Her hand is frozen mid-movement as she reaches for a bottle of salsa.

"Oh, sorry," I say. "I was just talking to the tortillas."

She walks away quickly, throwing me a weird look as she disappears around the corner of the aisle.

A fresh wave of anger washes over me as I think about the day Adam came up to me at school a few weeks ago, saying he'd heard about an open call for an off-Broadway play that's beginning rehearsals this spring. They were looking for an actor who could pass as sixteen years old and who could sing and dance. We'd been dreaming about an opportunity like this ever since we first met. Suddenly, it felt as though all that time we'd spent running lines together, and training, and dreaming of being on a real stage had been for something, and this was it—our first real audition.

When Adam and I got to the theater earlier today and joined the long line of hopefuls, we were so nervous we could barely stand still. The line kept growing longer behind us, even as people started filing through the stage doors of the theater.

After half an hour of waiting, the guy in front of us turned around and asked, "So how did you two find out about this open call?"

He was tall, and blond, and older-looking. He couldn't really pass as sixteen, but from the way he spoke—so confidently, with his back straight and his chin lifted a little too high—I could tell this wasn't his first audition. When he told us that he was a drama student at Tisch, my stomach dropped. That's my dream program. Looking up and down the line, I couldn't help but wonder how many other experienced actors we were up against.

"How about you guys?" he asked. "Do you also study acting?"

Adam answered first, and I was grateful he did. He's always been so comfortable talking to strangers, always had that loud voice and big energy that makes it easy to imagine him on a stage or in front of a camera. "No, no," he said, flashing his perfect smile. "Well, I did the Teen Conservatory at the Stella Adler, but that was last summer."

Tisch guy answered with a satisfied nod, even as my stomach sank lower and lower. That was only one of the programs Adam has done. He didn't even mention all the weekend workshops he's been to, or the *other* conservatory he did last year at a different acting studio. Ma and Pa can't afford that kind of stuff, but I've been learning, too—from YouTube videos, from blogs, and from Adam himself. I've always liked to think I'm just as talented as him, but when he and Tisch guy turned toward me, I felt more insecure than ever.

"I, uh..." In that moment, it became so obvious—the fact that next to Adam, I'm quiet. Next to him, I'm short, less talented, less prepared. I cleared my throat. "I've never taken actual lessons, but I've learned in other ways."

"Yeah," Adam said. "Matt's super talented."

The blond guy's mouth twisted downward. "Well, don't be too hard on yourself if you don't get it," he said to me. "I don't think they're looking to cast an ethnic actor for this role anyway."

Adam froze beside me. *"What?"*

4

My hands started sweating. My mind went blank. I couldn't think of anything to say. I couldn't think of anything at all.

The blond guy slumped his shoulders, shifting awkwardly on the spot. "No offense," he said, looking down at his feet. "I mean, I'm sure you're talented. But, you know, you're a little too..."

"Too *ethnic*?" I spat.

"Listen, I'm sorry. I was just trying to make small talk to pass the time. We can all just go back to waiting."

He turned his back on us and crossed his arms.

"He's an idiot," Adam whispered to me. "Don't let him get in your head. You're gonna kill the audition. We both will."

But I didn't. How could I, when I was carrying all that anger inside me? I stumbled the second I walked into the audition room, and I was two lines into my monologue when I choked. I managed to remember the next line, to finish the piece, but when I was done, the casting director thanked me with a stone face, and I knew right at that second that I hadn't gotten it.

I take the last tortillas out of the box and slap them on the shelf. Then, I pat all the piles to make sure they look even. I know how much this store means to Ma and Pa. They opened Adela's Corner Store almost ten years ago, and it's the reason why we can afford to pay rent, and buy clothes, and put food on the table. I used to think I was destined to take over from them when the time came, but it's been a while since I started dreaming of something different, and I'd never looked back—until today.

What if it never happens? What if I can't make it as an actor because I don't look like the other guys standing in that line? Or because my parents haven't been able to pay for private lessons? Or because, even if my grades and SAT scores were good enough to get into Tisch on a scholarship, we might still not be able to afford the tuition?

My thoughts are interrupted by the sound of the bell at the front door. It rings so many times in a day that I've learned to tune it out, but there's something about the sound of heavy boots walking into the store—two pairs, at least—that captures my attention.

I hear muffled voices near the checkout counter. That's pretty common, too. When customers lower their voices like that, it's almost always because they're asking where they can find condoms, or laxatives, or hemorrhoid treatment. But then I hear something that sends a chill running down my back.

"We're looking for Ernesto Garcia."

Whoever is looking for Pa has a strong, deep voice. I move quietly toward the counter, wanting to see what he looks like. From behind the last aisle, I sneak a peek at the two men standing there.

Erika, one of the girls my parents hired to help out, is

behind the counter, staring back at them with a blank look on her face. "He—he's not here," she stammers.

"Do you know when he'll be back?" asks the second man. I know exactly what they are. They're wearing bulky black jackets with the letters *ICE* printed across the back.

Erika shakes her head. "No idea," she says. "He might not be back at all today."

There's a long moment of silence—or at least it seems long to me. It's as if time has stopped. I'm frozen, unable to move, unable to think, unable to even feel anything. I'm holding my breath, waiting—*praying*—for these men to just turn around and leave.

"Do you mind if I take a look around?"

Erika's eyes widen, but she doesn't say anything. I can tell exactly what she's thinking—she's wondering what these men might do if she refuses to cooperate.

I watch with my heart stuck in my throat as one of the agents takes a few steps toward the back of the bodega, where the tiny office is. Slowly, he stretches out a hand and pushes the door open, only to reveal a dark room.

"All right, then," he says, turning back toward the counter. "Thanks for your help."

Erika mumbles a few words as the men move toward the exit, and they are halfway out the door when something happens—a dozen bags of chips start falling on top of me.

I don't understand how I did this. I must've barely brushed the shelf with my shoulder, but a second later all the bags are on the floor around my feet, and the damage is done.

The agents stop in their tracks and turn to look at me. I stare into the eyes of one of them, and then the other. *What have I done?*

My heart starts beating hard against my chest, and there is nothing for me to do but wait—wait for them to come closer, to start asking me questions. I try my best to remember all the things I should do in this type of situation—I should ask them if they have a warrant. I should pull out my phone and start recording, because if they just strolled in here when they weren't supposed to, we might be able to use that in our defense.

As the seconds go by, though, my whole body starts feeling weak. I'm not sure I'll even be able to use my voice, or if I'll be strong enough to stand up to these men. But then, after what feels like forever, one of the agents gives a polite nod in my direction. I manage to return the nod, and then they walk out the door.

I let out a long sigh as Erika runs out from behind the counter and comes toward me. She starts picking up the bags of chips, putting them back on the shelf, and I slowly lean down to help her.

In the back of my mind, I realize that the weight I'd been

carrying in my stomach is gone. I can't even feel a trace of it. In fact, I feel nothing at all. Everything that happened earlier today is insignificant now that I know ICE is looking for my dad.

★ ★ ★

There's a heavy silence lingering around the table. I can't remember the last time dinner was like this. It's usually loud in the apartment, with Pa talking about what's new in the neighborhood, and who came by the bodega earlier, and Sophie telling us all about her day at school. Ma usually listens with a satisfied look on her face. I know she's too tired to talk much after working two jobs and making dinner, but I can tell she waits all day just for this—for the four of us to be sitting around the table.

Everything feels so wrong tonight. No one has said anything since we sat down to eat. The second Pa came home, I told him about what happened at the store, and he's been speechless since. He hasn't even said anything about the food, even though Ma made chiles rellenos, one of his favorites.

"We'll just have to be careful," he says suddenly. As if this were a final solution. As if we hadn't already been careful our entire lives. As if "being careful" wasn't the number one thing in the back of our minds at all times.

I must've been around seven years old when Ma and Pa sat

me down to have this conversation. At first, I thought I'd done something wrong, but Ma quickly said that wasn't the reason they wanted to talk. They explained everything to me—how they'd left Mexico, Pa when he was seventeen and Ma when she was twenty-one. They told me how they'd met once they were both settled in New York, how their families back home had been able to survive because of the money they sent them, how much better life had gotten since they had come to the United States. And how no one could ever know that they didn't have papers.

"If anyone at school asks, tell them your parents are from the South. They'll think we're from Texas or something," Ma said.

Pa nodded quickly. "Never, *ever* tell anyone more than they need to know."

They gave Sophie the exact same talk last year, when she was only six. Unlike me, she didn't just sit down and listen. She asked a million questions, which my parents answered patiently.

Sophie has always been a big talker. It's one of the things I love most about her—how easily she can make friends, how open and loving she is even with people she doesn't know. But it's probably also the reason my parents decided to have this conversation with her at such a young age.

Tonight, Sophie's quiet. She looks so tiny in her chair. She must've taken two bites of her food before putting her fork down, and now she's just staring at her plate. All I want to do is reach out to her, hold her hand, tell her everything's gonna be okay, but I can't find the strength to do any of that.

Ma clutches her stomach. Since her gallbladder surgery last year, she's been doing that a lot. She's not in pain—or at least she says she's not. I think it's just a reflex. The scar she now has on her belly is probably an important reminder to her—a reminder that we made it through what we thought was the worst that could possibly happen: getting sick without insurance, having to find a way to pay for the surgery, praying that no one at the hospital would alert the authorities that my mom didn't have papers.

"¿Cómo pudo pasar esto?" she asks. "They must've known—someone must've told them about you."

Pa presses his lips together, shakes his head without saying anything.

"ICE doesn't just come looking for people without a reason," Ma says.

Something strange happens in that moment. We all meet one another's eyes. I look at Sophie, then at Ma, then at Pa. The air feels heavy with the things we're not saying, but I know we're all thinking about it—what's been going on in the news lately. All that talk about Mexicans, and deportation, and the wall. But surely nothing bad could happen to us, right? *Right?*

That's what I look for in my family's eyes—some sort of reassurance that everything will be fine, that nothing's gonna change, but the only thing I find in their faces is fear.

Finally, Pa speaks up. "It's going to be okay. *We* are going to be okay," he says.

Almost at the same time, we all let out a sigh. Of course Pa is right. He *has* to be. He and Ma have been in this country for so long. They've built lives, built a business, built a family, and even though we've always been afraid, no one's come after them in all these years.

Pa picks up his fork again and keeps eating. Ma, Sophie, and I do the same. We all try to pretend that everything is normal, that there is nothing to worry about, but the silence from earlier comes back, and now it's even heavier than it was before we had this conversation.

2.

THE NEXT DAY STARTS LIKE EVERY OTHER day.

I wake up to the sound of my third or fourth alarm. I put on the shirt and pants I picked out last night, eat a bowl of dry cereal next to Sophie and Ma—Pa is already at the bodega—and leave home a little too late. I run across Fourteenth Street toward the nearest subway station, jump on the L train, and then transfer to the packed uptown 1 train. When I get off the subway at Columbus Circle, I rush through the crowds, looking at my phone every few minutes to check the time. Now that spring is here and the air is getting warmer, tourists have flooded the city like they do every year, which adds time to my commute. I make it through the school doors just before nine, sprint up the stairs all the way to the fourth floor, and walk into the classroom right on time for first period.

This is what school feels like most days—it's just a blur of running up endless flights of stairs, bumping shoulders with people as I rush through the hallways, a bit of class here and there, and then running up and down the stairs some more.

My locker is on the ground floor, which means I have to run back down after class is over to grab my books before second period. It is there, staring into the dark interior of my locker, that I finally have a second to breathe. Today has felt normal so far—no different than any other Thursday—but then a sinking feeling invades my stomach, reminding me that something is wrong.

I think about Pa. What if those men come back to the bodega while he's there? What will they do to him?

"Heya," a voice says from behind the open door of my locker. I swing it shut and find Kimmie standing there, with her black hair in a side ponytail. She keeps switching up the way she does her hair. It's one of the things she began doing last year, right around the time when she started introducing herself to people as Kimberly and talking about how she didn't want to blend into the crowd. Another one of her new things: scouring thrift stores for cool clothes. She's wearing a fluorescent-green jacket that makes her look like she works on the runway at the airport.

"Hey," I say, letting out a small smile. No matter what's

going on, seeing Kimmie always has a way of making me a little happier. She and I met in middle school, long before Adam came into the picture, and even though I'd never had many friends, Kimmie latched on to me and refused to let go. I've never fully understood why she picked me, of all people, but maybe there's something about the fact that she's half Korean and I'm Mexican that makes us see the world similarly— maybe both of us have always felt like outsiders in our own ways. Now I'm so grateful to have found her. She's been by my side through some of the toughest times—surviving that hellhole of a middle school we went to, and my chicken-legs phase, and Ma's surgery last year.

She loops her arm through mine as we join the slow crowd moving down the hallway. "So," she says, and just like that, I can tell she knows something. Most of the time, the way she's able to see right through me is a blessing—it means she's always there when I need her. Today, however, I wish I could put up a wall and not let her see what I'm thinking about. "Adam told me the audition didn't go so great yesterday."

The blow comes unexpectedly. With everything else on my mind, I'd managed to forget about the audition. I think longingly about twenty-four hours ago, when Adam and I were plotting our early escape from school—when I was still so hopeful, when ICE hadn't yet come looking for my dad.

"No," I say. "No, it didn't."

"Well, that's okay," she says, shrugging. "There'll be other auditions. Besides, I got something that'll cheer you up."

She lifts her free hand to show me her phone screen. The words *lottery* and *Hamilton* jump out at me.

"No way." I stop suddenly, so that the people who were walking behind us nearly bump into me. I take the phone from her just to make sure the email is real, and sure enough— *Hamilton*, orchestra seats, eight o'clock tomorrow. "How? I mean . . . *how*?"

"We won the lottery!" she yells, making a few people turn to look at us. From the way she's smiling, they might be thinking we won the *actual* lottery, but we may as well have. Kimmie, Adam, and I have been trying to get tickets for years. We've lost the *Hamilton* lottery so many times that we agreed to stop talking about it until one of us had good news.

Before she can say anything else, we hear Adam's voice coming from behind. "Hey!"

We turn around to see him swerving his way toward us. He's incredibly tall, so that his head sticks out above everyone else. He has dirty blond hair and the biggest smile you have ever seen, and when I meet his eyes, his entire face lights up.

"Did you tell him about the tickets?" he asks Kimmie as soon as he catches up to us. He's always carried a bright energy everywhere he goes, but today it seems to be shining brighter than ever.

"I just did!"

"Wait a second," I say, remembering something. Whenever we've won lottery tickets for a show, we've had to make the same tough decision about who gets to go. Whoever wins obviously keeps one of the tickets, but the second has to go to whichever one of us is most excited to see that particular show, or whoever didn't get to go the previous time. For *Hamilton*, though, I know this decision is gonna end up being painful. "How are we gonna figure out who goes?"

"That's the thing," Kimmie says, her face falling. "My aunt and uncle are in town for the weekend, so I have this family dinner tomorrow that I can't miss. The two of you can go."

"Are you sure? Kimmie, you—"

"I'll just meet you guys after the show. You two are way bigger *Hamilton* fans than I am anyway."

For a moment, I almost argue. I'm about to tell her that there's something she must be able to do—that she can't just give up her ticket—but in the end I stop myself, because I want to see *Hamilton* so freaking bad.

"So?" Adam asks me, lifting his eyebrows. "Are you coming?"

I laugh a little. With Kimmie and Adam both beaming at me, it's easy to let go of the weight I've been carrying in my stomach since yesterday. "Of course I am."

I look down at my phone and realize I have only a couple

of minutes before next period starts. "Gotta run. I have chem on the sixth floor, but I'll see you guys at lunch."

As I rush away from them, sneaking through small gaps in the crowd, I hear Adam's voice yelling after me, "*Hamilton,* baby!"

The run up the stairs to the sixth floor feels faster and easier than usual. I honestly don't know what I would do without Kimmie and Adam. They make everything better— they always have. I just wish I could tell them about what's going on at home. I'm sure that if I did, they would help me push all this anxiety aside, but this isn't just my secret to tell— it's my entire family's, so our "be careful" rule also applies to Kimmie and Adam. I've never told them that my parents don't have papers, even though I've told them a million other things about my life—that I'm gay, that I'm the biggest tele-novela fan, and that before I met them, I'd always felt a little lonely.

The second I sit down in the chemistry classroom, the heaviness returns to my stomach. It may come and go, but the truth is that I have no way to fully escape from it.

* * *

"Is everything okay?" Ma asks me as soon as I walk into the apartment that night. She's standing in the tiny kitchen, wear-ing her glasses and an apron that Sophie gave her last Mother's

Day, and the entire place is filled with the mouthwatering smell of her cooking.

"Yeah," I say as I close the door behind me. "Those men didn't show up at the store today."

I spent my entire shift listening for the bell at the door, dreading that it would be followed by the sound of heavy boots. The longer I spent at the bodega, the more jumpy I became. It got so bad that Erika offered to close the store on her own so I could go home and relax.

"Have you heard from Pa?" I ask my mom, stepping into the kitchen for a quick hug. Pa spends the afternoons meeting with suppliers, and picking up orders, and running errands for the bodega, but he usually makes it back well before dinner.

"He called to say he'll be home soon!" Sophie yells from the dinner table. She's sitting there with her books spread out in front of her, doing homework.

I look at Ma, who gives a small nod.

"Do you need help?" I ask, staring down at the counter. She's making flautas de pollo, another one of Pa's favorites.

"No, mijo. Go start your homework. I'll let you know when we're ready to eat."

"Okay, thanks."

I turn around to go into my room. Our apartment used to be a two-bedroom, but a couple of years ago Ma and Pa decided to trade rooms with me and Sophie. They moved into the smaller one, and we put up a fake wall to divide the master bedroom so that my sister and I would each have some space of our own.

I can't fit much in here, except for my twin bed and a small desk that is crammed against the wall. I have to keep my clothes and everything I own in storage boxes under the bed, and the fake wall divides the window in half, so it's pretty dark in here most of the time. I turn on a light, throw my backpack in the corner, and kneel down to pull a box out from underneath the bed.

I keep my money in the back pocket of an old pair of jeans. I don't get a wage for working at the bodega—I mostly just do it to help out my parents. Instead, they give me a small allowance every week, which I usually spend on Broadway shows, whenever my friends and I can get our hands on cheap tickets.

I grab a ten-dollar bill to pay Kimmie back for my *Hamilton* ticket, and then I start doing homework. I try to hurry up, hoping to sneak in a quick acting tutorial before dinner, but Pa comes home before I can get much done, and then Ma calls out my name.

"Mateo, ¡la cena está lista!"

When I don't answer after a few seconds, Sophie peeps into my room. "Are you coming?"

"Sí, Sophie. I'm coming."

I follow her to the dinner table, and we all sit down to eat. The air feels both similar and different from yesterday. Similar because the apartment is quiet except for the noise of four people eating, but different because we're all a little more relaxed. It's almost like the past day has been a test, and now that we know the ICE agents didn't come back to the bodega, it feels as though we've passed it.

"How was your day, mijo?" Ma asks me suddenly. I notice how she chooses to ask me and not Sophie or Pa. They usually don't need an excuse to speak up.

"It was good," I say, putting more rice on my plate. "Kimmie won the ticket lottery for a show. I'm going to the theater tomorrow night."

"Can I come?" Sophie asks, even though she already knows the answer.

"What show are you seeing?" Pa asks, and that's all it takes for me to start talking my heart out.

When I first started dreaming of Broadway a couple of years ago, I was a little scared to tell my parents about it. For months, I listened to Adam talk about his acting classes, trying to memorize every word he said, feeling a small glimmer of hope as I started believing that maybe I could also be on a stage one day. When I finally told my parents that I wanted to get into Tisch and become an actor, I thought they were gonna tell me I was crazy. I feared they were gonna be mad that I didn't want to take over the bodega, that I wasn't interested in looking after the business they've worked so hard to build, but that's not what happened.

"There's a reason your ma and I work as hard as we do, Mateo," Pa said to me that day. "Do you know what it is?"

"So we can pay rent?"

He laughed a little. "Well, yes. But there's an even bigger reason than that. *You.* We work hard so you and your sister can have a better life—a life that you choose for yourselves."

Since then, they've always been willing to listen to me when I talk about Broadway, even though they don't have an artistic bone in their bodies, and they've never even seen a show themselves.

"Is that the one with all the diverse actors?" Ma asks when I mention *Hamilton.* She may not be able to keep track of everything I say, but at least she tries.

I nod, and as I begin to ramble about what a genius Lin-Manuel Miranda is, this starts to feel like a regular night. After a few minutes, Sophie interrupts me to tell us how Leslie, her best friend, got a nail polish set for her birthday, and she promised to bring it to school tomorrow so she can paint both of their nails during recess. Then Ma tells yet another crazy story from work. A couple of years ago, right around the time a 7-Eleven opened in the neighborhood and the bodega started struggling, she took up a few shifts as a housekeeper at a hotel in Midtown to earn some extra cash, so now she splits her time between the hotel and the bodega. She tells us how today, right in the middle of her shift, she knocked on the door of a room and there was no answer, so she used her key to enter. She started doing her work: changed the sheets, emptied the trash cans, swept the carpet.

"And the second I walk into the bathroom, I find an older couple in the bathtub."

My mouth falls open. "What did you do?"

Ma's face turns a bit red. "I ran," she says, covering her mouth with one hand. "I ran faster than I've ever run in my life." She tries to say something else, but then she starts laughing and her words are impossible to make out.

Sophie and I start laughing with her, and when I turn toward Pa, he's chuckling as well. The lines around his eyes deepen, but he looks younger somehow. That's what makes me realize he hasn't smiled this way in a long time.

When we all stop laughing and go back to eating, a feeling of peace settles around us. Even though we don't say much for the rest of dinner, the silence that surrounds the table isn't as heavy as it was last night. We can hear the warm spring air whistling as it sneaks in through an open window in my parents' bedroom, and the sound of our fridge, and Pa humming softly to himself every time he bites into his flautas de pollo. There's something else, too—something that we can't hear as much as feel. Staring at the half smiles that are still on Ma's and Sophie's faces, I truly believe that everything is going to be okay.

★ ★ ★

"Mateo, hurry up! It's starting!"

Every night at ten, Ma and I sit down on the couch to watch *Pasiones de tu Corazón*—or *The Passions of Your Heart*. The title is completely meaningless, of course, but at least it has dramatic effect. It started as a telenovela about a guy who was trapped on a deserted island after a plane crash. Since then, he has gotten rescued, fallen in love, had his heart broken, fallen in love again, had a baby, found out the baby wasn't his, met his lost twin brother, and discovered that the plane crash was a plot to murder him.

I walk into the living room just as the theme song starts playing and sit down close to Ma. This is our thing. Watching the telenovela with her is one of my favorite parts of each day.

"Wait, who's that guy?" she asks me.

"He's Amara's sister's ex-lover."

"Oh, right," Ma says. "What is he doing?"

"I don't know, Ma."

The telenovela is always accompanied by extensive commentary and questions from my mom, which is another reason I love watching it with her.

There's something else about this show—a reason it means so much to me. Halfway through the second season, the main character's former-enemy-turned-best-friend came out as gay. It was a few episodes later, on a night a lot like this, that I finally found the courage to turn toward my mom and say, "You know Roberto? How he's into other men?"

Ma nodded quickly.

"Well, it's just that, sometimes . . . I feel the same way as he does."

Coming out to Ma was faster and easier than I ever imagined it would be. I don't know how much *Pasiones de tu Corazón* had to do with that, but I think it may have made it a little easier for Ma to understand how I felt. And seeing someone fall in love with another man on-screen somehow made me feel less alone.

"Why is he putting all that money into the bag?" Sophie asks from behind the couch.

"Sophie, go to your room!" Ma says without taking her eyes off the TV.

Sophie turns around reluctantly, but she leaves her bedroom door open. She knows she's not supposed to watch *Pasiones*—Ma says it's too grown-up for her—but she finds ways to keep up to speed with the story without us realizing.

We're holding our breath, watching as the guy on the screen swings the bag of money across his chest, when something happens. There's a knock on the door. *Our* door.

Ma and I turn to look at each other. Her expression quickly

shifts from shock to fear. No one ever comes knocking at this time.

Pa walks out of his room. He's wearing his pajamas, and he looks just as scared as we feel. I know we're all thinking the same thing. We're imagining ICE agents out in the hallway, here to take my dad away.

Another knock comes, more desperate than the first.

My whole body feels paralyzed. I don't move. I can't even breathe. I don't know how Pa finds the strength to move his legs, one small step at a time, toward the door. Slowly, he leans forward to look through the peephole.

He sighs so loudly that the sound of his lungs deflating fills the entire apartment. "Es la Señora Solís," he says, undoing the latch.

He opens the door, and sure enough, Mrs. Solís, the neighbor from down the hall, is standing there. "Ernesto," she says. She's wearing a white nightgown and has rollers in her hair. "Qué bueno que sigues despierto. Mi tele no sirve, y estoy tratando de ver *Pasiones*."

She always comes to my dad whenever one of her electronics isn't working—her microwave, her iron, her stove. Tonight, it's her TV, and she needs it to work so she can watch the telenovela.

Pa nods once. "Let me take a look," he says. "In the meantime, why don't you watch here?"

Mrs. Solís joins Ma and me on the couch, and Pa walks

out of the apartment to go check on her TV, because that's just what he does. It doesn't matter that he spent all morning at the bodega and all afternoon running around the city, meeting with suppliers, paying the bills. It doesn't matter that he's exhausted and needs to wake up at five thirty tomorrow morning. He goes to check on Mrs. Solís's TV because she needs him, and he's not going to let her down.

* ★ ★

As I sit watching *Hamilton* with Adam beside me the following night, I can't help but feel all the same things I felt the time we went to see *Wicked*, my very first Broadway show—the chills, the tingling in my hands. My chest swells with the music, and deep down, I feel a desperate need to be up on a stage. I also love hearing the small gasps Adam lets out every now and then, and feeling the way he tenses in his seat whenever a singer hits a high note.

"So?" Kimmie asks the second we walk out of the theater. She's standing right beside the doors with a big smile on her face. "How was it?"

"It was *unbelievable*," Adam says.

I nod. A part of me wants to tell her every last detail about the show, but I also don't want to rub in the fact that we got to see it when she didn't. Instead, I ask, "How was dinner with your family?"

"It was all right," she answers with a small shrug.

We stand on the sidewalk while people continue to file out of the theater through the doors behind us. The air feels a little warm for March. If there is one thing I like about winter, it's that the cold air somehow neutralizes the smells of the city, but when I take a long breath, I'm pretty sure I catch the stench of trash somewhere nearby.

"So," Adam says.

"So?" I ask.

"McDonald's?"

"Let's do it."

Every time we go see a show, we go to the McDonald's in Times Square afterward for Chicken McNuggets and ice cream cones.

We walk half a block toward Broadway and find ourselves in the middle of all the lights and billboards. I only like Times Square when it's late at night. It's when the crowds aren't as bad and the lights look their brightest.

Kimmie leads the way into McDonald's, and Adam and I follow. After waiting for an excruciating ten minutes, the three of us walk out, each of us holding a brown bag in one hand and an ice cream cone in the other.

We go sit on the red steps, as usual. We eat the ice cream first so it won't melt, and then we each open our boxes of

McNuggets. It's what we've always done—since the time we went to see our first show together, back in freshman year, this has been our thing.

"You guys know Darryl Williams?" Kimmie says suddenly, looking down at her box of nuggets.

Adam snorts. "Do we *know* Darryl Williams?"

I mean, we don't *know* know him, but we know *of* him. Everyone does. Among the twelve hundred students at our school, Darryl might as well be a celebrity. He has dark brown skin and big eyes, and there's some sort of charm about him that I can't even explain. It's also true that, while other people have tried and failed to start bands, Darryl has done it. His songs have tens of thousands of streams on Spotify, and people actually show up at parties whenever they hear he's playing.

"I got paired up with him for an essay."

"I didn't even know you had a class with him."

"AP English lit," Kimmie says. "We're meeting up next week, and . . . I think I'm gonna ask if I can show him some of the stuff I've written."

Kimmie has never had the same Broadway dreams that Adam and I have, but she's always loved music. Back when we first met, she used to sing at her church on Sundays, and when her parents got her a keyboard for her birthday last year, she found it impossible to stay away from it. She would stop talking midsentence to type lyrics she'd just thought of into her phone, and she'd be late to meet Adam and me because she'd gotten caught up writing songs.

"You should definitely do it," I say.

"It's just terrifying, you know? But I feel like this could be my chance to *do* something. I mean...if he likes my music, maybe I'll even ask if I could play with his band sometime."

For a moment, I can't believe what just came out of Kimmie's mouth. Even though she's dreamt about starting a band for the longest time, she's always been too scared to do it. Tonight, though, there's something different about her. There's light in her eyes that's never been there before.

"I think he's gonna love your songs," I say, dipping a chicken nugget in my barbecue sauce.

Suddenly, I catch something from the corner of my eye. Adam is staring at me, and there's something different about him, too. He looks as though he's deep in thought, and there is a nervous smile on his face that I don't recognize.

"What are *you* thinking about?" I ask.

"I just..." He looks up, and his face glows in the light of Times Square. "I'm picturing these billboards a few years from now. Our names are gonna be on them, you know?"

"If we're lucky."

"I know we will be."

I smile at him, and then I pick up another nugget. I love

doing this—talking about our dreams as though we're certain that they're gonna come true. But then, out of nowhere, I think of something that makes me feel as though a bucket of cold water has been dropped on top of me.

"Do you think you'll get a callback?" I ask.

"What?" Adam says with his mouth half-full.

"For the audition," I say. "Do you think you'll get a callback?" I already know I won't get the part, but I hadn't had a chance to ask Adam this question until now.

"I—I don't know. I mean, I didn't think it went great," he says. "I don't think I will."

"I hope you do," I say, and I truly mean it. From the start, we both knew only one of us could get it, and if it's not me, then I sure as hell want it to be Adam.

"Well, we already got lucky with the *Hamilton* tickets," Kimmie says. "Who's to say we all can't get lucky again?"

Just like that, my doubts go away. She's right. Maybe tomorrow I'll have to go back to worrying about the million things that have been on my mind lately, but tonight, as I sit in the middle of Times Square next to my two favorite people in the world, it really, truly feels as though anything is possible.

On Monday, English literature lets out early, so I run down to my locker to drop off my books before lunch. The second I swing the door open, familiar images stare back at me—photo-booth pics of Adam, Kimmie, and me, a magazine cutout of Idina Menzel, and a *Dear Evan Hansen* Playbill that I managed to get signed by a few members of the cast after waiting in the cold for hours.

I shut the door and turn to walk in the direction of Kimmie's locker. I almost never get to see school like this. There are usually so many people in the hallways that it's hard to move. There's always the buzzing sound of hundreds of voices talking, and laughing, and yelling at the same time, but right now it feels like an entirely different place. I'm not sure I like it. As the sound of my own shoes bounces against the walls, my mind is filled with images from this weekend—Ma clutching her stomach, Pa letting out long sighs every now and then, Sophie hiding her bright pink nails under the table, until I noticed them myself and decided to ask why she'd picked that color, and all four of us sitting together at dinner, surrounded by a heavy silence that seems to have come back to stay.

The bell rings just as I lean against Kimmie's locker. People burst out of their classrooms, swarming the hallways, and I search the crowd for a familiar face.

I see her before she sees me. She's walking in my direction, holding books against her chest, and she's giggling. It takes me a moment to realize that she's not alone—that Darryl Williams isn't walking past her, but walking *beside* her.

I've never seen Kimmie like this. There's a spark in her eyes as she looks up at Darryl, and there's something in his face, too. The corner of his mouth twists into a smile as he says something to Kimmie that I'm too far away to hear.

The second she sees me standing by her locker, she turns awkwardly toward Darryl to say a few last words. He nods, smiles at her, and then walks quickly down the hallway.

"So..." I say as Kimmie approaches me.

She spins the dial of her locker and opens it. "So?"

"What was that?"

"Nothing."

"You were talking to Darryl."

"Yeah," she says, not looking at me. She takes books out of her bag and shoves them into her locker.

"And..."

"And?"

"You were acting all...*giggly.*"

Kimmie turns sharply toward me. "No, I wasn't," she says, but the smile on her face gives her away.

I press my lips together to stop myself from laughing. "Yeah, you were."

She closes her locker and clears her throat as we begin walking. "Over the weekend, we started—"

"What happened over the weekend?" We turn around to find Adam right behind us. I have no idea when or how he appeared.

"Kimmie and Darryl became a thing," I say.

"What?" Adam's eyes go wide. "You and Darryl Williams?"

"Shhhh!" Kimmie hisses, looking over her shoulder. "Don't yell out his name! And we're *not* a thing."

"Then what are you?"

"What I said we were—partners for an essay. We were texting all weekend to talk about how we wanted to split up the research, but then..."

"What?"

"We started texting about non-essay-related stuff."

Adam lifts his eyebrows. "Like what?"

Kimmie gives him a small punch on the arm. "Music," she says pointedly. "He told me about his band, and I told him about the kind of stuff I write."

"And what did he say?"

"Well, he couldn't really say much. Not until I actually play something for him."

In that moment, we walk through the front doors of the school and are hit by a strong ray of sunlight. After being in dimly lit classrooms all morning, walking outside makes me feel like we've been freed from prison.

"So what are you gonna do?" Adam asks as we walk down the block toward the halal cart. We try to avoid eating in the school cafeteria as much as we can, so Mondays are halal cart days.

"There's not much I *can* do," Kimmie says. "I mean, he's Darryl Williams. What if he doesn't like my songs? What if I—"

I turn toward her. "You like him."

"I mean, I like his music, but I—"

"And he likes you," I say as we reach the corner and join the line for halal. "I could tell he does."

Kimmie shakes her head. "I don't know what you think you saw but—"

"Kimmie," Adam says. "At least one of us should get a boy-friend already." He came out back in freshman year, before I did, and he's had a crush on a guy that lives in his building for the longest time. I remember walking in on a conversation that he was having with Kimmie long ago and hearing him say how hard it was to see this guy every day and not be able to tell him how he feels. That was the first time I ever heard about him, and it was one of the main reasons I felt safe telling Adam and Kimmie I was also gay. Adam doesn't talk much about his neighbor anymore, and he's never even shown us a picture of what the guy looks like, but I have a feeling he's still hung up on him.

I've never really met someone who makes me feel that way—someone it's hard to be around, someone who makes me giggle the way Kimmie was doing earlier. At most, I can say I had a short-lived thing for Adam when we first met back in freshman year. There was something about his long hair, his deep voice, and his Herschel backpack that was so...cool to me. But soon enough, the three of us started hanging out, and it felt like we could never be anything more than friends, so I went back to waiting—waiting to feel something, to find the right guy. I just hate thinking that I might have to wait until college to meet someone.

"Let's not talk about Darryl anymore," Kimmie says when

we reach the front of the line. "Come on, what are you guys getting?"

★ ★ ★

Dinner is different on Wednesday night. It has been a full week since the ICE agents came to the bodega looking for Pa, and there's been no sign of them since then. Ma makes a bigger meal than usual, which feels almost like a subtle sign that we're celebrating something. Sophie won't shut up about the school trip she went on yesterday—she and her second-grade class went to the Museum of Natural History—and Pa seems happier, more relaxed.

"You know who I bumped into on Eighth Avenue?" he says. "Carlos Acevedo."

"And how is he doing?" Ma asks.

"He's good, but he said his little girl is recovering from the flu." I don't know how he does it, but Pa has a way of making the city feel small. He seems to know everyone. "He asked me to say hi to all of you."

All week, it has felt like we've been *waiting* for something. I just wasn't sure what it was. Now I realize this is what we've been waiting for—a sign that everything is going to be all right. Because if the agents haven't come back in a full week, why would they come back now? It may just be false hope, but at least for the remainder of dinner, we choose to pretend that everything has gone back to the way it used to be.

It isn't really until later, when I'm watching *Pasiones de tu Corazón* with Ma, that I realize just how much lighter I feel. The weight I've been carrying for a full week is completely gone. I hadn't noticed just how heavy it was until now that it's no longer weighing me down.

During the opening credits, Ma turns to look at me, and I see it in her eyes—she feels lighter, too. She may say I feel too much, but she doesn't always admit how similar the two of us are. She's also used to carrying a little more than she should.

We're halfway through the episode when Alberto, a character who had a dramatic death scene earlier in the season, is revealed to be alive, and it isn't two, but three sighs of surprise that fill the air around us.

"Sophie, go to sleep!" Ma says.

"But I—"

"*Go.*"

Even though I'm still in shock about Alberto, I manage to laugh. And as Sophie steps back into her bedroom, I rest my head on the couch, breathing easily.

★ ★ ★

I wake up the next morning to the sound of Ma knocking on my bedroom door.

"Mateo," she says. "Mateo, are you up?"

My eyes snap open. I reach for my phone, look at the time, and my stomach drops. I slept through my alarms—all five of them.

I throw the covers off me and get up. Within a couple of minutes, I'm fully dressed and all the schoolbooks I left scattered across my desk while I was doing homework last night are safely inside my backpack.

I walk out of my room, and the first thing I see is a flash of black hair rushing past me. Sophie is running around the apartment, sticking her hands between the cushions on the couch and looking under the coffee table.

"What are you looking for?" I ask.

Ma answers before Sophie can. "Her math homework. She doesn't remember where she put it—oh, Sophie! I found it!"

Sophie comes running toward her.

"You hung it on the fridge behind your art project. Go put it in your bag."

I step around the two of them to open one of the kitchen cabinets and take out the box of cereal. I don't have time to sit down and eat an entire bowl, so I just pour some cereal on the palm of my hand and shove it into my mouth.

"*Mateo*," Ma says.

"Sorry, Ma," I say with my mouth still half-full. I look at the time on the microwave and realize I won't even be able to brush my teeth. "Gotta run."

I give her a quick hug and turn toward the front door. My hand is on the doorknob when I remember something.

"I have SAT prep after school today, so Erika's covering—"

"Yes, I know," Ma says while she helps Sophie put her backpack on. "Now go. We'll see you at dinner."

I nod once, and a moment later I'm running out the door.

I make it to school just as the bell rings. By the time I've run up the stairs, walked into first period, and found an empty desk, I can feel myself sweating through my shirt.

The second Mrs. Jenkins closes the classroom door, my eyes start shutting. I'm exhausted from the run, and the trig classroom is the worst. The windows are small and have bars on them, so the dim light makes this feel like the perfect place for napping. There are some people who actually do it—if you listen closely, you can sometimes hear soft snoring—but I always resist the temptation. I make every last effort to pay attention, and take notes, and hang on to every single word that comes out of Mrs. Jenkins's mouth.

When the last bell of the day finally rings, I watch jealously as people rush toward the front doors of the school, even as I try to push my way in the opposite direction. Like most weeks, SAT prep drags on, but I just keep telling myself the same things I always do—that I have to try my best, that I have to focus, that my GPA and SAT scores are the first steps toward NYU and my Broadway dreams, and that one day, I'll look back and realize all of this was worth it.

As soon as I walk out of school and head toward the subway a few hours later, my stomach grumbles. I wonder what Ma is making for dinner tonight. I can't wait to eat and change out of these clothes, but I shouldn't leave Erika to close the store by herself when she's been covering for me all afternoon. And so, when I get off the subway, I make my way down Avenue A as quickly as I can, until I finally reach the bodega. When I try to push the door open, though, it doesn't budge. I try again, thinking maybe it's just stuck, but no—it's locked.

Taking a step back, I realize the CLOSED sign is up. My heart starts beating fast. The bodega *never* closes early. Erika wouldn't have done this unless something terrible had happened.

I press my hands against the glass, looking in, but I see nothing. All the lights are off.

"Hello?" I shout, hitting the door with the palms of my hands. "Erika?"

From the corner of my eye, I see movement behind the counter. A second later, Erika appears. She turns the lock, undoes the top and bottom latches, and lets me in.

I step inside with a knot in my throat. I know right away that there's no one else here—there's emptiness all around us, filling every corner of the store.

"Erika," I say softly. "What happened?"

She opens her mouth to speak, but no sounds come out. She shakes her head, first slowly and then desperately. "They came back," she manages to say.

"They?" I ask. "The ICE agents? Did they take my dad?"

Erika nods, but none of this makes sense. I don't understand how this could've happened. Only last night, we were starting to think we might be able to survive this.

"How?" I ask. "How did..."

Erika swallows hard and then starts speaking, not looking directly at me. "Your dad came back to the bodega this afternoon. He said he thought I might need a hand without you here. Everything was normal, until—until the agents came in and asked for him. I wanted to protect him, to tell them that he wasn't here, but they said they had a warrant. And then they saw him and asked to see his ID."

Tears start welling up in my eyes. I picture my dad standing exactly where I am, looking into the eyes of the agents. I feel the helplessness he must've felt, the numbness that must've come to his legs. "And then what happened?"

"They...they put him in handcuffs."

"And my mom? Have you heard from her? Has she—"

"They already had her," Erika says, her voice breaking. "There were other agents outside the store—three or four of them. They must've found her at your apartment."

I feel weak. All I want to do is stop fighting—I want to stop carrying the weight of my body and just crumple to the ground. I wish I could pass out right here and never wake up, but then a word leaves my lips, no louder than a whisper. *"Sophie."*

"What?"

"My sister," I say, taking a step closer to Erika. "What happened to her?"

"I—I don't know."

Panic comes flooding my chest. They couldn't have taken her, could they? An image flashes before my eyes—Sophie in tears, yelling at the ICE agents as they took our mother away. Was she at the apartment when they came for Ma? Is she safe?

"I have to go," I whisper to Erika. She says something else, but I don't hear what it is. Maybe she's asking what to do. Maybe she's wondering whether she should just lock the store and go home, or if she should even bother coming back to work tomorrow. Whatever Erika is wondering isn't important right now. I don't care about anything but my sister.

I run out of the bodega. The bell rings loudly as the door bounces back into place, but I don't turn around.

Our apartment is only a couple of blocks away, but tonight, the street seems to stretch on for miles. When I finally reach our building, I storm inside and sprint up three flights of stairs. I put the key in the lock with a shaking hand, praying that my sister will be home, but when I push the door open and step inside the apartment, the air feels cold and still.

I know right away that Sophie isn't here. The first thing she always does when she gets home is turn on every light, because she hates being in the dark, and right now the windowless kitchen and living area are pitch-black. I turn to my left, feeling the wall for the light switch, and when I find it, I have to blink a few times to get used to the brightness.

"Sophie?" I call out just in case, but there's no answer.

I don't realize I've been holding my breath until I start to feel like I'm choking, and that's when I let out all the air in my lungs. I would've thought that my stomach would feel heavy, but the truth is that I feel nothing at all. I feel empty. It's as if I'm barely even here, as though this is nothing but a strange dream and I'm going to wake up any second.

I'm not sure how long I stand there, looking at the empty apartment in front of me, but suddenly, the emptiness is replaced by a hundred questions that start spinning inside my mind. What happened to Sophie? Where is she? What do I do?

I know I can't just stand here. I need to go out there and find my sister, but I have no idea how to do it. Where do I start? How am I even supposed to find the strength to move my legs and go look for her?

It starts in my hands—a tingling sensation that quickly shoots up my arms and spreads to the rest of my body. It feels a lot like restlessness, like desperation. I turn on the spot and run out the door without another thought.

I'm not even sure where I'm headed. As panic continues to rise in my chest, I try to push it aside so I can think clearly for a second. Ma would've come back from work and stopped by the apartment for a while before going to pick up Sophie from school. So maybe—*maybe*—Sophie wasn't home when they came to take my mom away. But she couldn't still be at school after all these hours, waiting all by herself, could she? Either way, I have nowhere else to go. I need to start there.

I burst out the door of our building and start running south, in the direction of Sophie's elementary school. Before I can get very far, however, I realize something. If Ma never came to get her, there's someone else she could've gone with.

I stop at a red light and pull out my phone. With shaking fingers, I scroll through my contacts until I find Maria's name. Ma insisted that I save her number on my phone in case of an emergency, but I never thought I'd have a reason to need it.

A woman's voice answers after the first ring. "Hello?"

"Maria?"

"Mateo? Is that you?"

My voice cracks as I try to answer. "Y-yes. It's me."

Maria sighs into the phone. "We've been trying to reach you, but Sophie couldn't remember your phone number. And neither of your parents are picking up."

"So—so she's there?" I ask. The pedestrian light turns white, but I remain frozen on the spot, clutching my shirt. "Sophie's with you?"

"Yes, she is. Mateo, what's going on? Your mom didn't show up at school, so I brought Sophie home with me."

I bend over, sighing in relief. "I'll explain later," I say. "What's your address?"

When she tells me, I turn left. She lives east of where I am right now, so I run down Third Street toward Avenue D and don't slow down until I've reached the right building.

Even though Maria is Sophie's best friend's mom, I've only met her a couple of times. When she opens the door of her apartment, though, that doesn't matter. I don't care that she barely knows me, or that she has no clue what's happening. I fall into her arms and give her a hug. For a second, she remains frozen, but then she hugs me back like only a mother can.

"Matt?" Sophie's voice comes from behind her. I let go of Maria and turn toward my sister. She runs into my arms, and I lift her up, my tears spilling into her hair. And right there is where I find the comfort I need. The familiar smell of her strawberry shampoo, the warmth she radiates, the way she hugs me back with all her strength—everything about her feels like home.

"What's happening?"

"I'll tell you as soon as we get back to the apartment," I

say, putting her down. I turn around quickly to look at Maria, not wanting Sophie to see that I'm crying. "Thank you—for bringing Sophie here. For taking care of her."

Maria stares back at me with wide eyes. I can tell she knows something is terribly wrong, and I'm almost sure she knows what it is, but for the longest time, she doesn't say anything.

While we stand there in silence, Leslie, my sister's friend, slowly gets up from the couch and goes to stand next to her mom. In the background, I can hear the TV and two boys fighting.

"Is everything okay?" Maria asks finally.

Even though all I hear inside my mind is my own voice yelling *no*, I manage to nod and say, "Yes."

Maria blinks a few times. "Where's your mom and dad?"

I shake my head. I'll need to explain to Sophie what happened, and I'll need to do it soon, but now is not the time. Her life is about to change, and I need to think a little about what I'm going to say.

"We need to go home," I say, putting a hand on Sophie's shoulder and leading her toward the door. "Thanks again for everything."

Maria opens her mouth, draws air in as though she's about to say something, but the second I meet her gaze, she presses her lips together. Maybe there's something in my eyes that makes her change her mind about arguing with me. Maybe she can see all the exhaustion, all the shock, all the anxiety from the past hour. Maybe she can see the uncertainty that's plaguing my mind, the paralyzing fear I have of going back home and opening the door to find the apartment empty once again. Or maybe she can see that I'm preparing for something important—that I need to save my energy for the talk I'm about to have with Sophie.

Whatever her reason for staying quiet, Maria doesn't look away from my eyes. She nods once, as if saying, *Do what you need to do.*

As Sophie and I turn to walk down the hallway, I nod back. I'm hoping that my nod will say, *I know what I'm doing. I can take care of Sophie. We'll be okay.* But I can tell Maria doesn't believe it. How could she, when I don't even believe it myself?

I'D HAVE THOUGHT SOPHIE WOULD START ASKING me questions the second we leave Maria's apartment, but she doesn't. She remains silent, walking slowly by my side, as we make our way back home.

At first, I'm a little relieved. At least I'll have a bit more time to think about what I'm going to say. But after a few blocks, her silence starts making me uneasy. It's so unnatural for her to be this quiet, especially when there are so many unanswered questions about what happened today.

She knows, I think to myself, and with that thought comes a sharp pain that hits me in the chest.

I sneak a glance at her from the corner of my eye and see that she's walking with her shoulders slumped. Her backpack looks too big for her, as it always does, and her face doesn't reveal even the slightest trace of emotion. It's as if she's just walking, putting one foot in front of the other, but she's not really there.

In that moment, the tears threaten to come back. They sting my eyes, forcing me to blink quickly to make them go away. I'll have time to cry later, when Sophie has fallen asleep and I'm all alone in my room, but right now I need to hold it in.

We stop when we get to our building. I don't reach for my keys, and neither does she. We turn to face each other and just stand there for a minute, breathing quietly through our mouths.

"Sophie, I—"

"Did they come back?" she interrupts me, her voice barely there. "Those men who wanted to take Pa away?"

Slowly, I nod, and I can no longer hold back my tears. They just spill from my eyes, falling everywhere—on my chest, on my bare arms, on the sidewalk. And through the blurriness, I watch as my sister's heart breaks. I watch as her world crumbles and her eyes fill with tears, and there's nothing I can do except stand here in front of her. I want to say something to comfort her, but I can't find my voice. I want to wrap her in my arms, but I can't even move my legs enough to close the distance between us.

"And..." I manage to say eventually, even though my chest is heaving so badly I can barely even breathe. "And they came for Ma, too."

Sophie bends over, and I worry that she's going to throw up right there on the street. I instinctively reach for her, putting an arm over her shoulder. The tears stop falling from my eyes, and all I can think about is that I need to get her into the apartment. I need to get her somewhere safe.

"Let's go inside," I say. "Come on."

She nods, retching a little as she follows me up the front steps of the building. I have to half carry her all the way to the third floor, and when we walk into the apartment, we don't even stop to think about the eerie emptiness that surrounds us. We go straight for the living room and collapse side by side on the couch.

For what feels like a really long time, we don't say anything. I listen to Sophie's quiet sobbing, but then, all of a sudden, she turns to look at me.

"What's going to happen now?" she asks.

I have no idea, I think. What are we supposed to do? I don't even know where our parents are right now. Where have they been taken? We have no way to contact them, to ask them for advice.

"We're gonna have to stick together," I say. That's the only thing I'm certain of. "And we're gonna have to be patient until we find a way to talk to Ma and Pa. They'll know what to do."

I'm sure they'll be allowed to make a call at some point. I reach for my pocket to take out my phone, and I grasp it tightly in my hand, begging it to ring.

"I'm hungry," Sophie says. I realize suddenly that I am, too. All the stress and the tears had made me forget, but the second I think about it, my stomach starts growling.

"I'll make us something to eat."

I get up from the couch and go into the kitchen. Looking inside the fridge and cabinets, I find several things we can use: corn tortillas, onions, tomatoes, lettuce, and a can of refried beans. Ma must've been planning to make tostadas for dinner at some point this week.

I grab all the ingredients and get to work. Soon enough, I realize that having something to do is helping me push all my thoughts away, if only for a few seconds at a time, so I ask Sophie to come help me tear up the lettuce.

When we're done making the tostadas, we each grab our plate and walk out of the kitchen. We're halfway to the dinner table when we stop, turn to look at each other, and silently agree to go eat on the couch instead. Eating at the table without Ma and Pa would feel wrong right now.

We bite into our tostadas, and the room is filled with loud crunching sounds as we chew. They could never be as good as Ma's, but we're so hungry that we finish them in no time.

"Do you want another one?" I ask Sophie, and she nods.

I pick up both our plates and go back to the kitchen to make us a couple more tostadas. While I spread the beans over the tortillas, I tell myself that if I'm able to feed us both and get Sophie ready for bed tonight, I'll have succeeded. And tomorrow, when I have to do it all over again, at least I'll be able to find a bit of strength in the fact that I was able to do these things the day before.

★ ★ ★

Sophie's bedtime routine isn't very complicated, but Ma usually takes care of it while I'm in my bedroom doing homework after dinner. She always gets Sophie into bed right before *Pasiones de tu Corazón* starts, so I'm never really involved in the process.

Sophie takes a shower every night. She tells me she'll be okay doing that on her own, but I stand outside the bathroom door just in case she needs anything. After a few minutes of hearing the shower running, she comes out wearing her pajamas. Her hair is dripping wet, so I help her wrap a towel around it, and then I watch as she brushes her teeth. I close the curtains in her room, and then I tuck her into bed.

"Mateo?" she says just as I turn around to walk out of her room. She never calls me by my full name. Only Ma and Pa do that.

I stop to look at her. For a moment, she stares at me with a frown on her face, but then she lets her head fall back on the pillow.

"Good night."

I press my lips together into what I hope looks like a smile. "Buenas noches, Sophie."

After closing her bedroom door softly, I slip into my own room. I grab fresh underwear and head into the shower.

I don't even know how long I stand under the stream of water, pressing my hands against the tile on the walls and letting my tears fall freely. When my eyes start feeling dry and I have no more tears left to cry, I reach for the shampoo. I see the one Ma uses, which is meant for long, curly hair. I see Sophie's, which comes in a bright pink bottle. And then there's the one I share with Pa—the no-frills kind.

My heart hurts when I think about the fact that they might never come back. They might never shower here again, never have to hear desperate knocking on the door. We always complained about having only one bathroom for the four of us. Now I'd give anything to go back to a time when waiting for the bathroom was one of our biggest concerns.

I don't turn any lights on after I finish showering. I walk quickly across the dark apartment and sneak into my bedroom. It's almost time for *Pasiones*, but I don't feel like watching tonight. I don't think I'd be able to get through the entire episode without collapsing on the side of the couch where Ma should be.

I crawl into bed and close my eyes. The sounds of the city outside my window are there to comfort me, but I already know I won't be able to get any sleep tonight, so I resign myself to just lying there quietly.

I'm breathing slowly, trying to push away the image of my parents being put into handcuffs, when I hear soft knocking on my bedroom door.

I jump into a sitting position, my heart beating fast. Sophie's silhouette walks in.

"Sophie, what's wrong?" I ask.

"I couldn't sleep." She takes a few slow steps toward my bed. "Can I sleep here?"

I nod, even though she probably can't see me. I move over to make room for her, and she curls up near the corner of the bed, the way she used to when she was younger and she'd ask if she could sleep next to me because she was having nightmares.

For a while, all we can hear is the city and the sound of our own breathing. But then I hear sniffling coming from Sophie's side of the bed.

I have nothing left to say that will comfort her, so I just listen to her cry, feeling more helpless than I've ever felt in my life.

★ ★ ★

After what feels like hours, Sophie falls asleep next to me, and I start to wish that I could get some sleep myself. Once or twice, I almost doze off, but then I snap back awake, and I'm hit by a brand-new wave of grief as everything that happened earlier starts replaying in my mind.

At some point, the sky outside my window begins to turn lighter. My mind starts feeling foggy with lack of sleep, and I take a deep breath, hoping I'll be able to at least get some real rest before my alarm goes off.

When I close my eyes, my mind is filled with images of a woman. She's pretty, with long black hair and big eyes, and she looks just like my mom. I never met my abuela in person, so it's easy to imagine her as the woman from Ma's old photographs. Even though we would Skype with her every now and then, in my mind she never aged. I've always liked to think of her as that young woman with deep eyes and a shy smile.

Suddenly, I hear her voice—or is it my mom's? They sound so similar that I can't tell the difference, but I do know these are my grandmother's words—one of her many old sayings, which Ma has repeated to us since we were little: *Si es para ti, ni aunque te quites. Si no es para ti, ni aunque te pongas*, which loosely translates to, *If something is meant for you, it'll come even if you try to avoid it. If it's not meant for you, it won't come even if you're waiting for it.* Of course, it sounds better in Spanish. Almost everything does. But I start to wonder if that is true—if this was always meant to happen, if there was no way we could've prevented it. I wonder if there's anything we could've done to save my parents.

There's a deep sadness that comes flooding my chest every time I think about Abuela. I can't help but remember that morning a few years ago when the phone rang during breakfast. I remember the look on Ma's face as she listened to what my aunt was saying, the way she bent over in pain. I remember how she could barely even speak after she hung up, how she had to take a million deep breaths just to be able to explain that Abuela had passed away. I also remember the way Ma just vanished—vanished into her room for days, vanished into a different version of herself. And I remember how, a couple of weeks after the news came, I overheard her talking to my dad while they were cleaning up the kitchen after dinner.

"I haven't seen my mother since I was twenty-one," she said. "And now I never will."

The silence that followed was heavy with grief, with pain, with uncertainty of what to say next.

Ma gave a long sigh. "I guess, deep down, I always thought we would be reunited. I thought Mateo and Sophie would get to meet her. I thought I'd get to hug her, and smell her perfume, and look into her eyes again."

That was the first time I really understood everything my parents had given up when they left Mexico. I'd always known they'd made sacrifices, but I had never really seen or felt those sacrifices firsthand. After that, something shifted deep inside of me. When Ma and Pa got home from work looking exhausted, I offered to help with dinner. When they suggested that I apply to a specialized high school, I went to the public library and checked out a dozen books to help me prepare for the admissions test. When they asked about my Broadway dreams, I'd promise them I was gonna make it big one day, hoping that at the end of the day, everything they've done would be worth it.

But now, as I weave in and out of a weird state of sleep, I start to worry that my parents' sacrifice will have been for nothing, and I can feel it more than ever—the pain my mom felt when she said those words. *I haven't seen my mother since I was twenty-one, and now I never will.* I feel the helplessness she felt when she realized that the reunion she had always dreamt of was never going to happen. I understand why she reacted the way she did—why she was unable to leave her room for days, why she refused to face reality, because that is all I feel like doing right now. I want to fall into a deep sleep and not have to wake up.

Since I found out our parents were taken, I've been so focused on comforting Sophie that I've completely forgotten that I also need some comfort. I need someone to tell me that everything is going to be okay. I need Ma to remind me that I feel too much, and that I shouldn't be carrying all these horrible feelings when there's nothing I can do about them. I need to see Pa's smile, always so calm, so I can believe that we are going to make it through this.

Sophie stirs beside me, and my eyes snap open. I remember that I can't afford to withdraw into my own grief. My sister needs me, and now I'm the only person she has.

And so, when the sun rises, bathing my room in soft light, I manage to find enough strength to lift my head from the pillow. I plant my feet on the floor and get up from bed, because Sophie needs to get ready for school. She needs to eat breakfast, and pack up her books, and get to class on time, and she can't do these things without me.

★ ★ ★

Breakfast is a messy event. I try to do all the things Ma would usually do—pour a glass of milk for Sophie, cut up a piece of fruit, put a bowl of cereal in front of her—but my brain is so foggy with exhaustion that I can barely function.

"Will you pick me up right at three?" she asks me when we finally make it to her school.

I texted Maria earlier to ask if she could pick up my sister today, and she agreed right away. I promise Sophie that I'll head down to Maria's right after I finish class, and as soon as she disappears through the school doors, I start running toward the subway. I already know I'm gonna be late, but if I hurry, I might still be able to sneak into first period.

I walk into school just as the bell rings. I swipe my student card in front of the security guard, and then I sprint up the stairs to the fourth floor. I'm breathless by the time I reach my classroom, and the door is already closed. I'm officially late.

I push the door open slowly, peering in just to be able to make eye contact with Mrs. Jenkins. She presses her lips into a straight line for a second, but then she gives a small nod. I close the door behind me quickly and rush toward a desk in the back of the room.

We're technically not allowed to use cell phones in class, which makes it hard to keep an eye on it at all times. I set my phone carefully on my lap, so I can just look down and check the screen without anyone noticing, but even after the full forty-five minutes of class, there are still no voicemails, no missed calls, no sign that either of my parents has tried to reach out. They couldn't have been put on a plane to Mexico yet, so why haven't they been allowed to make a call? Where are they?

By lunchtime, I start to get desperate. I go to my locker and stare inside for the longest time, not taking books out of my bag, not even moving, not doing anything at all. My mind starts to fill with images of my parents in dark cells, when all of a sudden, I hear someone behind me.

"Heya."

Something lights up inside of me. "Kimmie," I say, closing my locker door.

"Are you okay?" she asks the second I look into her eyes.

My parents might get deported. Those words burn my tongue. They threaten to escape from my lips, but there's something that's stopping me from telling Kimmie the truth. It's an alarm—the same one that always goes off in my head whenever someone asks where Ma and Pa are from, or where my extended family lives. I can hear it, repeating the same things as always: *Don't say anything. No one can know. Remember the "be careful" rule.*

The thing is, my family's secret is out. The worst has already happened, so the "be careful" rule doesn't apply anymore. If I'm being honest with myself, a part of me is relieved. I'm free to let Kimmie in on this secret, to tell her about what's happened to Ma and Pa, but I can't bring myself to say the words out loud.

Maybe I just need a little more time. Thinking that I'll tell her as soon as we walk out of the building, I force myself to nod and say, "Yeah. Let's get out of here."

We start walking in silence. For a couple of minutes, I'm too lost in my own thoughts, but then, inevitably, I notice that Kimmie is practically glowing, and not just because of the electric-yellow top she's wearing.

I turn toward her and see it in her eyes—she's *dying* to tell me something, but for some reason, she's also choosing to wait. We walk out of school and stop right next to the doors, where we usually wait for Adam to come out and join us. *This is it*, I think to myself. This is the perfect time to tell her. It's just the two of us, and there's no one close enough to hear what I'm about to say.

It takes all of my strength to draw air in and say, "Kimmie, I—"

"Darryl asked me to rehearse with his band!"

"What?" Adam appears behind us in that moment, and my chest deflates. The muscles in my back and shoulders loosen up a little, and as we start making our way toward the small pizza joint on Columbus, my entire body feels heavy.

In the back of my mind, I'm grateful that at least Adam is here, so I don't have to be the one to ask Kimmie all the questions she's dying to answer.

"How did this happen?" he asks.

"We stayed late at school yesterday to try and work on our essay, but we ended up just talking about music the entire time. And then he just threw it out there—that I should come to his band's rehearsal, try playing a few songs with them. Is this even real?"

"Well," Adam says. By now, we've reached the pizza place and are waiting in the long line for dollar slices. Fridays are always pizza days. "I don't wanna steal your thunder or anything, but something happened."

"What is it?" Kimmie asks.

"I got a callback."

She frowns. "From who?"

"A *callback*," Adam says pointedly. "To the audition we went to last week."

I turn sharply toward him. "Y-you did?"

Adam nods slowly, and I know exactly what's going through his mind. I know how badly he wants to be excited, to jump up and down because he got a callback, but I also know he's trying hard not to make me feel bad because I didn't get one.

Kimmie squeals before I can even think of something to say. "That's amazing! When do you have to go back?"

"Thursday," Adam says, smiling as wide as his lips will go.

"Congratulations," I say, and I want to mean it. I *really* do. I want to be happy for Kimmie because she may have just gotten herself a spot in Darryl's band, and excited for Adam because he's worked so hard for this opportunity, but I just can't. I can't feel anything at all.

When we get to the front of the line, I order a plain slice. I'd normally get toppings, but they're an extra dollar, and I'm not sure I should fork it over. If there's one thing I've learned from Pa, it's that when money is tight, every dollar counts, and I don't know how long the money I have is gonna last.

When I turn toward my friends, I try my best to act normal, to erase from my face any sign that might tell them something's wrong. I follow Kimmie to the exit, and we sit on the window ledge with the sun hitting us right in the eyes.

For a while, I don't pay attention to what Kimmie and Adam are saying. I'm thinking about Sophie, wondering how her day at school is going, but then Adam turns toward me. Staring at me with narrowed eyes, he folds his slice in half and takes a big bite. "Are you okay, Matt?" he asks as he chews. "You're quiet today."

"Yeah," I answer quickly. Maybe my attempt at acting normal isn't as successful as I thought it was. Or maybe he and Kimmie know me too well for me to be able to hide anything from them. Either way, I somehow manage a smile. "I just didn't sleep well last night." Even as I say it, my eyelids twitch, threatening to close. I take a bite of my pizza, trying to think of a way to change the subject. "So what did they ask you to prepare for the callback?"

Adam's face lights up, but while he answers my question, I only half listen. And as the truth about what happened to my parents boils inside my chest, I just keep eating without saying anything at all.

I PICK UP SOPHIE FROM MARIA'S APARTMENT right before three, just as I said I would. I thank Maria countless times for taking care of my sister, trying to avoid her stare at all costs, and we get out of there as quickly as possible.

While we're making our way home, I debate whether or not I should go to the bodega. I know Nelly, another one of the girls who helps us out, must've opened it this morning and been shocked to find my dad gone. In the last ten years, he hasn't missed a single day of work. I also know Erika must be there already, in time for the start of her shift. I just don't know if I can do it—if I can go in there and take responsibility for all the things my dad would usually do. I don't know if I want to face Erika and explain to her that I haven't even heard from my parents yet.

As we turn onto Avenue A, I decide to stop by after all. It's what Pa would want me to do. And what excuse am I gonna have if he ends up returning one day and I have to explain to him that the bodega went out of business because I wasn't looking after it?

The second we walk in, Erika stares at me with wide eyes.

"Has anyone come by the store?" I ask her.

She shakes her head. "It's been quiet around here."

"Has anyone called?"

She shakes her head again, and the weight I've been carrying in my stomach becomes a little heavier.

"Come on, Sophie," I say, leading the way to the office in the back. I set her up at the desk so she can do her homework, and then I get to work. As I start picking up boxes and restocking the shelves, I keep waiting for my phone to ring in my pocket, but it never does.

Where are they? I ask myself again and again. *Why haven't they called?* During last period, I did a few Google searches under my desk. I ended up on a government website where you can find information on people who have been detained by ICE, but when I typed in Ma's and Pa's names, I found zero results.

I pick up a box of soap and head toward the Personal Care

section, telling myself that maybe they're busy fighting to stay in the country. Maybe they've managed to get a lawyer, and they're doing everything they can to come back home.

A small ray of hope appears somewhere inside of me, and I hold on to it for as long as I can. Surely they'll be given a chance to fight deportation, won't they? They've been in this country for more than twenty years. They have American children. They've never gotten in trouble, and their love for America is so deep that it runs through their veins. Surely ICE wouldn't be in a rush to kick out people like Ma and Pa.

They might be able to come home. The thought brings lightness to my chest, makes me feel as though I can breathe for the first time in twenty-four hours. Even when a million doubts start appearing in my mind, I use all my strength to push them away. I have to believe this is true. I have to believe that my parents still have a chance, that I won't have to raise Sophie on my own, that they'll be here to help me get through college, and watch me become an actor, and share all the good and bad moments we haven't lived yet. I have to believe that not everything is lost, because if I don't, I'm going to lose my mind.

Those thoughts are what help me get through the rest of my shift, and Erika and I close the store at eight, just as we do every other day.

"Thank you, Erika," I say to her right after we walk out the front door. "For everything."

She gives me a small smile that I can't figure out. On the one hand, it looks like she feels sorry for Sophie and me, as though there are things she wants to say to us but isn't brave enough to speak out loud. On the other, there's doubt in her eyes. It takes me a second to realize that she's wondering what's going to happen with the bodega. We may have made it through a full day without my parents' help, but what's gonna happen when the time comes to pay back suppliers? To place orders for more products? To sign Erika's and Nelly's paychecks?

My uncle Jorge crosses my mind. I tried calling him early this morning, but he didn't answer his cell. We've barely seen him since his baby was born. I know he's been busy, and a part of me doesn't want to go bothering him, but I also know he's the only person we can turn to at this point.

"I'm here to help," Erika says. "But . . . if you think I should start looking for other jobs, could you please let me know? I have to pay for school, and—"

"I know."

"—nursing equipment is expensive, so I need to—"

"We'll figure things out," I say as confidently as I can, but the doubt in her eyes doesn't go away.

I touch the pocket of my jeans, tempted to pull out my cell phone and try Uncle Jorge's number again, but I decide to wait until later, when we're home and I've had a little more time to think about how I'm gonna break the news about my parents to him.

Erika nods once. "See you tomorrow," she says, and then she walks away with her hands in her pockets.

★ ★ ★

When Sophie and I walk into the apartment, it hits me all over again—the darkness, the emptiness, the air of abandonment. And just like that, all the hope that's been building up in my chest for the past few hours goes away.

"Go finish your homework," I say softly to Sophie, unable to keep my voice from shaking. "I'll start making dinner."

I walk into the kitchen with a hole in my stomach. I open the fridge, see what's inside, and the hole grows a little bigger. There really isn't much.

Whenever we grab something from the bodega, Pa writes down exactly what we took in a big book he has inside the office. I thought about doing that before we left the store earlier—just grabbing necessary supplies and writing them down. The problem is, I've never really known what happens after things get written in the book. Does Pa pay for them at the end of the month? Does he just take them out of the store's earnings? In the end, I decided not to mess with the system, but now I wish I had.

I close the fridge and open the cabinets instead, to find a box of macaroni and cheese that Ma must've been saving for an emergency. She always says how this type of food doesn't have the nutrients that two growing children need, but even she can't deny that it's convenient to have at least one box in the kitchen. And today, it feels like a lifesaver.

I fill a pot with water and set it over the stove with shaking hands. I'm just starting to realize how much I'll have to do now that Ma and Pa are gone. We may still have food in the kitchen, and some clean clothes, and the apartment is still in decent shape, but pretty soon it'll be up to me to take care of all those things. I'll have to stock the fridge, and do our laundry, and clean the apartment, on top of everything else I already have to do. How am I gonna find the time for all that? How will I manage to pay for food and rent?

My legs start feeling weak all of a sudden, but I keep my feet firmly planted in front of the stove as the water comes to a boil. *What are we going to do?*

"Mac and cheese?" Sophie squeals when she walks into the kitchen a few minutes later.

I turn toward her and smile. At least it isn't too hard to make Sophie happy. She finds joy in the smallest of things—the squirrels in Washington Square Park, petting the downstairs neighbor's cat, sneaking a glance at *Pasiones* every night while Ma and I are watching it. Tonight, it's macaroni and cheese.

We carry our bowls to the couch and sit down to eat. Even though this hardly compares to the Mexican food Ma makes every night, we're both hungrier than we'd like to admit. At first, I eat quickly, paying little attention to anything but the grumbling in my stomach, but then I look up from my bowl and realize something. There are tears sliding down Sophie's face, and her hand is shaking so much that she's having a hard time bringing her fork to her mouth.

My heart splits open. I don't say anything. I can barely even think. I put my bowl down on the center table and reach for my sister. My fork slips and falls to the floor with a loud clank, but it doesn't matter. Nothing matters, really. Nothing but Sophie. I hug her, patting her softly on the back while she sobs into my shirt. I wish desperately that I could offer her more than this—that I could promise her Ma and Pa will find a way to come back, that I could do something, but this hug is all I can give her.

"I want Ma and Pa," she says.

"Me too, Sophie," I answer through the knot in my throat. "Me too."

We remain there for what feels like hours, holding each other. Then, I pick up our near-empty bowls and go into the kitchen to clean up. Like yesterday, I give Sophie a job to keep her distracted—I pass her the clean dishes and she dries them with a towel.

We're almost done, and I'm about to turn off the water, when someone knocks on our door.

I turn sharply toward Sophie. There's pure terror on her face as she drops the towel to come wrap her arms around my waist.

I make a shushing sound. "Stay here," I mouth at her, and she nods once, loosening her hold on me as I start moving toward the front door.

Whoever is out there must've already heard noise inside the apartment. We weren't exactly being quiet while we were washing the dishes, but I still step carefully over the wooden floors, so as not to give them any more reason to know we're home.

Even though I'm only a few steps away from the door, it feels like I have a mile to go. I'm hoping it'll be nothing. It could just be Mrs. Solís again, but deep down, I know I can't be that naive. Whoever knocked must've come for a good reason.

When I approach the peephole, I see the blurry shape of a man's head. I cower away from the door, alarmed by the fact that it's definitely not Mrs. Solís. But when I gather the courage to look again, the man's face comes into focus, and my chest deflates like a balloon. It's Uncle Jorge.

I open the door to find him standing there, tall and strong. For a second, we remain frozen. I stare at him, and he stares back. There's a shocked look on his face, as though he can't believe I'm really there—as though he hadn't been quite sure who would open the door.

And then, suddenly, I hear Sophie's voice behind me. "Uncle Jorge!"

She comes charging at him, and he picks her up easily. He has warm brown eyes, a buzz cut, and a well-groomed beard, and he looks nothing like anyone in my family. That's because we're not related by blood. Even though we've called him Uncle Jorge for as long as I can remember, his last name isn't Garcia. It's Reyes, and he isn't really my dad's brother.

"I came as soon as I could," he says, stepping into the apartment.

"How did you find out?"

"I got a few calls," he says as he closes the door behind himself, still holding Sophie firmly with one arm.

"Calls?" I ask. "From who?"

"Tus papás. Your dad called first, asked me to come check on you. And then your mom, a few hours later, asking me to do the exact same thing." So that's what Ma and Pa did with the phone call they were each allowed—they both decided to call Jorge instead of me. "Erika called me as well, told me what happened."

I'm surprised Erika thought of reaching out to him. It makes sense, I guess, especially if she's worried about her job. Even though it's my dad's bodega, Jorge is the owner on paper. It's his name on all the legal stuff, his signature on all the important documents. He agreed to sign on behalf of Pa as a way to thank him for everything my parents did for him when he was younger.

"Mateo, I—I'm so sorry," he says. "I'm sorry this is happening."

I nod, wiping tears away. I don't have time to feel all these emotions right now. I have too many questions I need answers to. "How are they?"

Uncle Jorge puts Sophie down before answering. He remains kneeling on the floor in front of her for a second. "They . . ." He sighs. "They're holding up. They're mostly just worried about you and Sophie. You're all they talked about."

Again, I nod. It's so ironic that all I've been doing is worry about them—where they are, how they're doing, what's going to happen to them. It hadn't occurred to me that they would be asking themselves the exact same questions about Sophie and me.

"Where are they?" I ask.

"Your mom was taken to a detention center upstate. Your dad is in a jail in New Jersey."

Jail. The sound of that word seems to echo in the apartment. We all freeze for a moment, listening to it in our minds.

How is this even possible? Pa belongs right here, at home with his family, not in a jail in New Jersey.

"Can we talk to them?" I ask, at the same time that Sophie asks, "Can we go see them?"

Uncle Jorge shakes his head at both questions. "Not now. We might be able to go visit them at some point, but I can't say for sure."

"How about calling?" I say. "They *have* to be allowed calls."

"There are numbers we can try," says Uncle Jorge. "But I already tried them, and I didn't have much luck."

"So ... what now?"

"I'm not sure how this is going to work," Uncle Jorge says, running a hand through his hair. I can tell he's trying hard to be calm, to be strong for Sophie and me, but the trembling sigh he lets out gives him away—he's just as terrified as we are. "Your parents will probably have to go in front of an immigration judge at some point. I'm trying to find a lawyer for them, but I have no idea how much that'll cost."

I think of the money I have saved up in the pocket of my old jeans, and I feel a sharp pain in my heart when I realize that's probably enough to cover only an hour or two of a lawyer's time.

"We should be learning more in the next few days," my

uncle continues. "In the meantime, you and Sophie will come stay with me and Amy."

"What?" I say. "We can't—"

Uncle Jorge shakes his head. "We'll take care of you while we figure things out."

"But this is our home, and I—"

"It'll still be here when you're ready to come back."

"What about the baby?"

Jorge has no answer to that. We both know he lives in a tiny two-bedroom apartment, and a new occupant just took over the second room.

"We—we'll move her crib into our bedroom. We can make space for the two of you."

I turn to look at Sophie. In her eyes, I can tell she's torn. Going to stay at Uncle Jorge's sounds tempting. At the very least, there'll be food on the table and someone to tell us everything's gonna be okay. But she also looks scared. I know she doesn't want to leave our apartment—she wants to wait here for our parents to come back.

"Why do you think your parents called me?" Uncle Jorge says when I've been silent for too long. "They asked me to take care of you and Sophie. They *want* you to come stay with us."

I have a hard time believing Pa said that—or at least that he used those exact words. Would he really want us to inconvenience Jorge and Amy like that? Does he really think that moving the baby's crib is a good idea, when he knows it'll probably not even fit in their tiny room? Is he really willing to ask them to put their whole lives on pause for Sophie and me? I don't think this is something Ma would want, either. She wouldn't want us to leave our apartment. She would want us to stay here, to look after the home she and Pa built for us, to be in a place that feels familiar and safe.

"We can't," I say. Even as the words leave my mouth, I look at Sophie for confirmation that this is the right thing to do. "Not now. We need to stay here—to keep things as normal as we can for as long as we can, until our parents find a way to come back."

Sophie blinks a few times. Her silence tells me everything I need to know, because if she didn't like what I was doing— if she really wanted to go stay at Uncle Jorge's—she would speak up. I'm sure of it.

She comes to stand by my side, and we both look up at Jorge for a few seconds. He also looks torn—between the promise he made to my parents and what he knows makes the most sense for him and his family.

In the end, he gives a small nod. "You don't have to come if you don't want to," he says. "But I'm here. I am here for you. If you need money, or food, or anything at all, you can come to me. Don't forget that, okay?"

I know, I want to say. *Thank you. Knowing you're here for us means everything to me.* But I can't bring myself to say any of those things, because there are too many other thoughts rushing through my mind: how much I hate this—how much I wish we didn't have to rely on Uncle Jorge, or anyone else, for that matter. How much I wish my parents were still here, that they had never been taken away, that we weren't living this nightmare.

★　★　★

Uncle Jorge leaves after a while, but not before writing down four numbers on a notepad. The first is his cell phone, which we obviously already have, but he felt the need to write down just in case. The second is Amy's cell phone. The third and fourth are the numbers to the places where Ma and Pa are being detained.

We try the number for the detention facility where Ma was taken first. I know Uncle Jorge said we won't be able to reach my parents right now, but we have to at least try. Sophie sits very still next to me on the couch as we listen to a recording: *"You have reached the Buffalo Federal Detention Facility. Our office hours are eight AM to four PM, Monday through Friday. If you are—"*

I hang up angrily, and a second later I feel a surge of anxiety over my mom. Have they really taken her all the way to Buffalo? What's that detention facility like? Is she okay?

Trying to push those thoughts away, I lift up my cell phone

with a shaking hand. We try Hudson County Jail next, where Pa is supposed to be, and this time, a human answers the phone.

"This is Hudson County Jail. Officer Jones speaking."

"Uh—hi," I say quickly, pressing the phone harder against my ear. Sophie leans closer to me, trying to listen in. "I'm looking for Ernesto Garcia. I'm his son, and I was hoping I could just—"

"I'm unable to give out any information regarding inmates at this time," the officer says in a bored voice. "Please call back during the hours listed on the website."

I resist the urge to throw my phone against the wall. I picture Officer Jones sitting at his desk with a computer in front of him. He's probably doing nothing, just browsing social media while he sips coffee. He could've helped. He could've just typed Pa's name into his computer and told me something—anything. He could've told us if my dad is really there, if he's doing okay. He just didn't care enough to help.

When I look up the hours online, my fears are confirmed. They only take calls from Monday to Friday, so we'll have to wait the whole weekend.

"I'm sorry, Sophie," I say. "We'll try again tomorrow."

She frowns a little. "But tomorrow's Saturday."

"I know," I say. "We'll try anyway."

★ ★ ★

Sophie and I quickly realize that there isn't much to do without our parents around. We each take a shower and get ready for bed, but we're both feeling antsy and not at all in the mood for sleep.

Luckily, I can think of something to keep us distracted. *Pasiones* is on tonight, and we already missed yesterday's episode, so we need to catch up.

I let Sophie sit on the couch next to me. There's no point telling her to go to bed, and I really don't want to watch on my own. I'm sure Ma wouldn't care, considering the circumstances.

My heart hurts a little when I think of Ma. What is she doing right now? Does she realize what time it is—that it's time for the telenovela? Is she thinking about us, wondering if we're watching?

Focus, I tell myself. *Don't get distracted*. Because when she comes back home and tries to catch up on *Pasiones*, I'll need to be able to bring her up to speed with everything that's happened.

"Did I dream it?" is the first thing Sophie says when she wakes up on Saturday morning.

I hesitate. A part of me doesn't want to answer. I want to let her think that she did—that it was all a dream and Ma and Pa are out there, making huevos rancheros for breakfast like they do every weekend. I want her to hold on to that hope, if only for a few seconds, but then I shake my head.

"No, Sophie," I say. "You didn't dream it."

She slept in my room again last night. After watching *Pasiones*, we both realized our exhaustion was greater than our anxiety, and we fell asleep easily.

"Come on," I say to her. Just as I wanted her to feel hope for as long as possible, I don't want her to hang on to this feeling of disappointment any longer than she has to. "We have things to do."

We eat a bit of dry cereal for breakfast, and I wash our bowls quickly. Then, I ask Sophie to grab the bag of dirty laundry while I go into my room to grab some money. I pull out one of the storage boxes from under the bed, dig into the back pocket of my old jeans, and count the bills: two hundred and eleven dollars. I don't know how long this is going to last us, but it'll have to do for now. I grab sixty bucks and put the rest of the money back in its place, praying that when the end of the month comes and it's time to pay the rent, we'll have figured out a way to cover our expenses that doesn't involve just taking money from Jorge.

First, we go to the laundromat on Thirteenth Street, and Sophie helps me fill up two washing machines. Once I insert the coins and our clothes start spinning, we turn around and walk out of there. We have forty-five minutes before we have to come back to take our clothes out of the washers, so we might as well get started on everything else we need to do.

We walk in the direction of the West Village, toward the fruit cart Ma likes. After having tried dozens of fruit carts throughout the city, she claims that this one has the best fruit and the best prices in all of Manhattan—not to mention that she always likes to linger for a nice long chat with Lety, the woman who works at the stand.

When Lety asks how Ma is doing, I mumble, "She's good," and look away. I'm not ready to tell people about Ma and Pa yet.

We get some apples, bananas, and even a pack of strawberries, just because they're Sophie's favorite. With arms carrying heavy bags of fruit, we run back to the laundromat and get there with several minutes to spare.

Sophie and I watch anxiously as the washing machines slow down and come to a full stop, and then we transfer all the wet clothes to a dryer. We now have a full hour before the timer goes off, so we go to the supermarket on Fourteenth Street.

There are some things that we just never get from the bodega—things like meat, and veggies, and eggs. We pick up enough food to last us for a couple of days, and once we have everything we need, we head to the bodega.

Nelly is working today, as she does every morning. Even though she's been helping us out for a couple of years now, she's always been a little shy. She's older than Erika and me—in her late twenties, maybe—so she probably just cares a little less about socializing at work. All I know is that she has a young son and she lives in Queens.

The second Sophie and I walk into the bodega, she turns toward us, and her expression falls. "Mateo," she says under her breath. "I thought you weren't coming in until two."

"I'm not here for my shift. Just here to grab something."

I push Sophie gently toward the back of the bodega and start listing out the things we need, while she picks them up from the shelves.

"What kind of dish soap?" she asks me, pointing at all the different ones.

"Uh...the blue one."

Once we have everything we need, Sophie follows me into the office in the back. I take out Pa's heavy book from the top drawer on the desk and list out every single item we took. I guess we'll figure out what happens with the things that get written on this list at the end of the month. Or maybe I'll ask Jorge. He might know.

Sophie and I stop by the apartment to drop off all of our shopping bags, and then we head back to the laundromat to get our clean laundry. By the time we return home, we're too tired to fold clothes, but we do it anyway. And once we're done and we go lie on the couch, at least we feel like we've accomplished something.

★ ★ ★

We keep trying to call Ma and Pa all morning, but it's the same as yesterday. We don't get past recordings and bored-sounding officers who refuse to help us.

I go back to the bodega at two for the start of my shift,

and I bring along some of Sophie's coloring books to keep her busy while I'm working.

I'm standing behind the cash register, bagging a customer's purchases, when I hear a phone ringing, and my heart stops. It's coming from my own pocket. *My* phone is ringing.

I use one shaking hand to give the plastic bag to the customer, and the other to take my phone out. Gesturing to Erika to cover for me at the register, I rush into the office in the back.

"¿Bueno?" I answer, closing the door behind me. I'm expecting to hear one of my parents' voices on the other end, but instead I get a recording: *"You have a collect call from Hudson County Jail. If you wish to accept this call, please press one."*

I lower my phone to press one. Immediately after, I hit the speakerphone button, so Sophie and I can both listen in.

My sister stares at me with a shocked look on her face as I move closer to the desk, where she has all her stickers and markers. And then, when Pa's voice comes from the speaker, we both give small jumps.

"Mateo?"

"Sí." My voice comes out shrill. "Sí, aquí estoy, Pa."

"¡Yo también!" Sophie shouts beside me. "I'm here, too, Papi."

"Mijos." He sighs loudly. "How are you? Are you okay? Has Jorge come get you?"

"We—we're okay, Pa." I'm having a hard time putting words together. My heart is beating too fast. "And yes, Uncle Jorge came looking for us."

"Are you staying with him and Amy now?"

"No," I say. "We didn't want to leave home. We didn't want to bother them, with the baby and everything."

Pa doesn't reply. My guess is that he wants to argue—he might want to tell us to accept Jorge's help, but he also knows that if he had been in my shoes, he would've made the exact same decision.

"I asked for his help," he says slowly. "This was always the plan—years ago, he and I made a deal that if we ever got detained, he would take care of you."

"You had a plan?" I ask. "Why didn't you tell us? You should've—"

"I wanted to," he says. "There just...there never was a right time. I didn't want to scare you, or prepare you for something we weren't even sure was going to happen. No one ever likes to think they're gonna need the plan."

Hearing him say that makes me feel like I'm choking. I can't even imagine Pa going to Jorge to have this conversation. He has never found it easy to ask for help, even though he's always ready to jump into action if someone else needs him.

"You should listen to Jorge. He'll know what to do."

"We'll wait," I say. "We'll wait until all of this is sorted out. If they let you and Ma come back home, maybe we won't need to go to Uncle Jorge's at all."

"Yeah," Pa replies, his voice weak. "Maybe."

We all breathe silently for a minute. I can't be certain, but I think Pa and Sophie might be imagining the same as I am—the worst-case scenario, where Ma and Pa would have to leave the country, and my sister and I would be left here all alone.

"How are you, Papi?" Sophie says.

"I'm..." he begins, but it takes him a while to find the right words. "I'm praying for a miracle."

My parents used to be devout Catholics. We used to go to Spanish Mass every Sunday and say a prayer before dinner every night, but all of that changed when I came out. Ma and Pa felt like they had to choose between their gay son and their religion, since they couldn't find a way to reconcile both. Luckily, they chose me, but if Pa's praying now, it's a sign that things are not looking good. It must mean that there's nothing left to do.

"What's that place like?" I ask.

"It's, uh... not great."

"What's gonna happen now?"

"I don't know, mijo," he says. "A deportation officer has been explaining the options to me."

"What are they?"

"Well, I could leave the country voluntarily."

"No," I say immediately. "You have to fight. *We* have to fight so you and Ma can stay."

Pa remains quiet, but I can imagine him nodding slowly to himself.

"What are the other options?" I ask.

"They could release me on bond—if we hand over some money, they might let me go home while they decide whether they'll let me stay in the country or not."

"Okay," I say, letting out a small sigh. "Okay, that's good." I'm not even sure it is, but at this point, I'm prepared to take any positive news we can get.

"Mateo, listen carefully," Pa says. "There's some money hidden away in the office. There's a safe in the bottom drawer of the desk. The combination is the last two digits of your birth year, followed by the last two digits of Sophie's. You got that?"

"Y-yes," I say. "Got it."

"Good. Use that money for emergencies. And if you need anything—anything at all—go to your uncle Jorge. He's there for you. He promised me he would be."

"Okay, Pa."

"I have to go, but I'll get in touch as soon as I can. And if you talk to your mother, tell her I love her."

A knot appears in my throat. From the corner of my eye, I notice that Sophie has started crying. "Papi, no! Don't go yet."

"I have to, mi amor," he says. "Listen to your brother. Be good, okay?"

Sophie doesn't answer. She wipes away her tears, but more come.

"We're gonna find a way," Pa says right before he hangs up. "We've always found a way. I love you."

★ ★ ★

When my phone rings again on Sunday morning, my heart stops just as it did yesterday. I answer, click one when a recording asks me if I want to accept the call, and this time, it's Ma's voice coming through the phone.

"Mateo?" she says. "Mateo, is that you?"

"Sí, Ma. Soy yo."

She lets out a long exhale, and it almost sounds as if she's in pain. "¿Cómo están? ¿Están bien? ¿Dónde está Sophie?"

Before I can even think about answering all her questions, I pull the phone away from my ear. "Sophie!" I yell, running out of my room. "Sophie, it's Ma!"

She comes crashing out of her own room. We stand in the middle of the apartment, both of us shaking a little, as I hold out the phone in front of us.

"Mami!"

"Sophie," Ma says. "Mi niña, are you okay?"

"No, Ma," Sophie answers, which brings an added load to the weight in my stomach. "We miss you. Where are you?"

"I'm in Buffalo. Have you talked to your dad? How is he?"

"He called yesterday. He's in New Jersey," I say. "Ma, how did they even find you?"

"I . . . I'm not sure, mijo." She swallows so loudly that I can hear it through the phone. "I'd just gotten home from work, and suddenly someone knocked on the door."

"You shouldn't have opened. Did you at least look to see who it was?"

"I did, but there was no one in the hallway. But then someone yelled out saying it was the police, so I thought I *had* to open. And when I did, they were there—three ICE agents."

I shake my head to myself, thinking of the stories we've heard—the raids that have happened around the city in the last couple of years, the ways ICE tricks people into letting them into their homes. I want to tell Ma that she should've been more careful, that she shouldn't have opened the door, that maybe if she'd thought twice, she would still be here with us, but I manage to hold it all in. There's no point beating ourselves up now. "Ma, what do we do? How do we get you out of there?"

"Just take care of Sophie," she says, panting a little. "That's your main job, okay?"

"Yes! Yes, I know."

"Mateo," she adds pointedly. "Sé fuerte y sé valiente."

A chill comes running down my back. *Be strong and be brave.* That's another saying we've been hearing for years.

"Voy a tratar, Ma." There's not much more I can promise her right now, but I mean it when I say I'll try. I *have* to—if not for me, for my sister.

When Ma asks about Uncle Jorge, I tell her the same thing I told Pa—that I'm hoping we won't have to go stay with him at all. That we want to stay home. That we're holding on until they find a way to come back.

"Are you eating well? What have you had for dinner?" she asks, because that's always been one of Ma's main concerns—making sure that we're well fed.

"I've been trying to make some of the things you make, but they're not as good."

She lets out a breath that sounds almost like a chuckle. "Well, I hope I'll be back soon. And I can make you anything you want. *Anything.*"

"Sounds good, Ma. Just focus on coming back."

We stay on the line in silence for a bit, holding on to this moment for as long as we can—this small moment of togetherness—until Ma tells us that she needs to go.

And, just like Pa, she makes one last promise before she hangs up. "We'll all be together soon," she says. "I know we will be."

For a moment, I don't say anything. But then I reply, "Okay, Ma. We'll see you soon," because right now hope is all we have, and we need to hold on to it no matter what.

★ ★ ★

I'm standing behind the counter at the bodega on Sunday afternoon, trying to stay awake, when the bell at the front door rings and Graciela Muñoz walks in. She's one of my parents' old friends from church, and by the look of her outfit, that must be where she's coming from now. I haven't seen her in a while, but she looks just as I remember—her hair piled on top of her head, her big emerald earrings catching the light as she walks toward me.

"I heard about Ernesto and Adela," she says to me, putting a hand on her chest. "How terrible!"

Graciela is one of the people we lost touch with when we stopped going to Sunday Mass. After Father Esteban started going off about how gay marriage was ruining society during service one day, Ma and Pa felt like a little distance from our church wouldn't be the worst idea. They weren't really sure what anyone else in the community would think if they found out I was gay, but I guess they were just afraid—afraid that someone might believe what Father Esteban had said, that people would make me feel unwelcome, that I'd feel different somehow. But now, here she is—Graciela, one of the many people we feared might judge me—talking about my parents as though no time has passed. Maybe we were wrong to leave the church. Maybe we didn't have to put ourselves through that, but I guess it doesn't really matter at this point.

Before I can even think of something to say, Graciela grabs my hand from over the counter and squeezes it. "How are you and your sister holding up? Come let me give you a hug."

I almost tell her that I'm okay, that I should get back to work, but then, when she narrows her eyes at me, I come out from behind the counter and we hug. She holds me so tight that I'm unable to breathe for a second, and then I tell her everything. She nods along with a concerned look on her face, and just before she leaves, she tells me how much everyone at church was talking about Ma and Pa after Mass today.

"I hope they come back home," she says. "When they do, you should all stop by the church. We miss you."

The bell at the front door rings again as she walks out, and this time, it doesn't seem to stop ringing. An endless flow of people comes in and out of the bodega all afternoon. Some of them pretend that they're here to buy something, and then they start a casual conversation when they're at the checkout counter. Others walk in for a short talk and leave without buying anything. And then there are others who bring stuff with them—people like Carlos Acevedo and his wife, Laura, who hand me a Tupperware full of empanadas.

"It's a quick and easy dinner," says Laura. "Just put them in the oven for ten minutes, and you're done!"

We also get food from Lola Suárez, who works with Ma at the hotel, and from Ceci Romano, who's a cook at a restaurant in Little Italy and makes the most mouthwatering lasagna.

Antonio González, who's one of the first friends Pa made when he arrived in New York, puts a hundred-dollar bill on top of the counter.

"Antonio, we can't take this," I say, sliding the bill back toward him.

"Yes, you can," he says. "When I lost my job a few years ago, your pa gave me a discount on every single thing I bought from the bodega. He never asked me to pay him back, so this is it—it's not much, but this is how I can repay him."

Mr. Torres from the flower shop down the block brings a pamphlet for an immigration lawyer. "These are the people we called when my brother-in-law was detained," he says.

"And did it work? Were they able to help him stay in the US?"

"Well...no. But it's worth a try."

Before we know it, Sophie and I are bathed in food containers, and advice, and stories of people who were and weren't able to stay in the country, and good wishes for our family.

By the end of my shift, I'm happy to be able to finally turn the OPEN sign at the door to CLOSED and get some peace and quiet. But even though my mind is racing, there's a little light shining deep inside of me.

As Sophie and I walk up the stairs of our building toward the third floor, I realize what the light is—it's a feeling of comfort. I think of everything Ma and Pa have built—all the people they've touched, and helped out, and become friends with since they first came to this city twenty years ago. And when I open the door of our apartment to reveal the emptiness we've started to get used to, I'm reminded that there's a whole community that has our backs. I'm reminded that despite everything that's happening, we are not alone.

"Matt?"

"Oh, yeah. He's definitely no longer with us."

"Hello? *Matt!*"

When I snap back to the present, it takes me a few seconds to remember where I am and how I got here. I'm sitting in the school cafeteria with Kimmie and Adam. I have a tray in front of me, and there's an untouched cheeseburger waiting on it. Mondays are usually halal cart days, so one of them must've gotten word that they were serving cheeseburgers in the cafeteria today. This is one of the only decent things you can get at school, so we wouldn't have come here if we hadn't been completely certain there were gonna be cheeseburgers.

We must've met right after class, walked up here, and gotten our food, but when I try to remember doing all these things, it feels like I'm looking back on a distant dream. It's easier to remember the images that were flashing before my eyes a second ago—images of my mom and dad sitting in dark cells, afraid and alone.

I realize that Kimmie and Adam are both staring at me with raised eyebrows, and I know I'm supposed to say something, but I have no idea what they were just talking about.

"Uh...sorry, what?" I say.

"Oh, so he *is* awake."

"Welcome back to the real world."

"Stop," I say, and even though I try to make it sound like I'm joking, my tone comes out a little harsh. Even now, the images in my mind seem more real to me than what's in front of my eyes.

"What were we talking about?" I ask.

"Adam's callback. It's on Thursday."

"I just asked if you're free after school," Adam says. "You know, to run lines and stuff. I could really use your help."

Was it really only two weeks ago that we went to that audition? Was it last Friday that Adam told us about the callback? Without warning, a nasty feeling rises in my throat. If what that blond guy hinted at was true—if I didn't stand a chance at getting that part because I'm *too ethnic*, then what chance do

I stand now that Ma and Pa have been taken away? If they get deported, who is gonna help me pay for college? How will I find an opportunity like the one Adam has now?

I have to look away from Adam's brown eyes, because he's staring at me hopefully, with a half smile on his face. A part of me wants to say yes. Deep down, I want nothing more than to go to Adam's after school, and run lines with him, and mess around like we always do, but I can't. Sophie will be waiting for me at Maria's. I have to pick her up, and then I have to be at the bodega for the rest of the afternoon. I can't afford to be the same old Matt—the one who could run off after school to hang out with his friends, who could spend his time dreaming about making it on Broadway.

"I can't today," I say, and a heavy silence falls around our table. "I—I mean, I have to work at the bodega."

"Can't you tell your dad that you need the afternoon off?" Kimmie asks, and suddenly, there's a spark in her eyes that intimidates me as much as the hope in Adam's. "We all know I'd be no help running lines with Adam. And we could do something fun after you guys are done rehearsing—maybe go to the movies, or something."

Adam nods. "I *really* need you."

My hands start feeling sweaty. In the back of my mind, I realize I could do it right now—I could tell them the truth about my parents. I may not have been brave enough to do it last Friday, but this is the perfect opportunity. If I told them, Adam wouldn't pressure me into rehearsing with him after school. They would understand why I've been acting weird, why I've barely spoken since we sat down to eat.

I open my mouth, but no words come out. *Why can't I do it?* Why can't I tell my best friends—the two people I trust most in the world—that my parents have been taken away? With a sinking feeling, I realize what it is. There's shame deep inside of me—shame because my parents have been taken away like criminals, because they might get kicked out of the country, because my family and I are not as American as we've always liked to think.

Kimmie and Adam frown at me, still waiting for my response. I know this shame is pointless when it comes to them, because they wouldn't judge me. They'd be there for me. I can just picture them jumping into action, asking me what they can do to help, and maybe even finding a way to make everything better . . . but they'd also start seeing me differently. Things would change between the three of us, and I can't have that—not now.

"Let's do tomorrow," I answer finally. Even as I smile, I realize I shouldn't have said that. Tomorrow I'll have the exact same responsibilities that I have today, but I can't take it back now.

"Awesome," Adam says, flashing his perfect teeth at me, but Kimmie stays still—too still.

She narrows her eyes at me. "Matt, are you okay?"

Of course she knows something is wrong. Kimmie is able to tell when I'm feeling sick, when I've done poorly on a test, and even when I'm upset because one of my favorite characters died on *Pasiones*. She can tell when I'm happy, when I'm sad, when I'm anxious . . . and also when I'm lying.

"Yeah," I say. Maybe I'm a better actor than even I give myself credit for, because I manage to make it sound convincing. I shrug, trying to loosen up my back. "Just a lot going on—you know, with school and work at the bodega."

Adam's smile becomes bigger. But as he launches into a full description of what he wants to prepare for the audition, Kimmie keeps staring at me. I can tell she doesn't believe me, but she knows me well enough to realize that I don't want to talk about what's bothering me, and she's a good enough friend not to ask any more questions.

* * *

That evening, Sophie and I head home after my shift at the bodega with even more food, pamphlets, and handwritten notes. Once again, Ma and Pa's friends showed up nonstop, to the point where I started to feel a little overwhelmed. What are we supposed to do when everyone keeps telling us to do different things? Who are we supposed to call when everyone claims to know who the best option is?

As I look for my keys in my bag, I tell myself that I'll let Uncle Jorge deal with these types of decisions. He'll know who to contact. He'll know what to do. I just need to call him as soon as we get home.

"Do you need help with that?" I ask Sophie as I push the front door of the building open. She's holding a heavy plate of lasagna that Ceci Romano dropped off, even though we've barely made a dent in the one she brought us yesterday. Sophie has managed to carry it a full two blocks from the bodega, but going up three flights of stairs is a different story.

"No, I got it," she tells me, and she leads the way up the stairs.

We're about to reach the first landing when we start to hear voices bouncing against the walls of the stairwell. We stop, and Sophie turns to look at me. It's not unusual for the hallways of our building to get loud, but there's something about these voices that makes me a little uneasy. Staring into Sophie's eyes, I can tell she's thinking the same thing. I know right away it isn't Jessie from the fourth floor speaking loudly to her mother on the phone, or any of our other neighbors talking among themselves. These voices are hushed, cautious. They're voices that don't belong here.

Slowly, we start climbing the stairs again. The closer we get to the third floor, the easier it gets to understand exactly what they're saying.

"But this is the right address?"

"I mean, yes," Mrs. Solís answers in her heavy accent. "But I haven't seen anyone since the Garcias were detained. Haven't even heard a sound coming from the apartment. I'm almost sure it's empty."

"What happened to the kids, then? Mateo and Sofía?" asks a different voice. It's just as serious as the first one.

"I don't know," says Mrs. Solís, and I'm confused. Why is she lying? Of course she knows Sophie and I are still living here. We ran into her in the hallway just this weekend.

"Do you know how to get in touch with them?"

There's a short silence, and I can just imagine Mrs. Solís shrugging. "They must have family somewhere else in the city. But no, I don't know how to find them."

"All right," sighs the first of the two strangers. "Thank you for your help."

The second we hear steps coming down the stairs, I signal to Sophie to get moving. We run down as quickly and quietly as we can, sneak out of the building, and immediately start walking across Fourteenth, trying to blend into the crowd.

We've walked only a few feet when I get the urge to look back, and I can't resist it. I sneak a quick glance over my shoulder and see two people walking out of our building, a man and a woman, both of them wearing regular clothes. I can tell this much: They're not ICE agents . . . but then, who could they be? What do they want? How did they know where to find us, and how did they know our names?

From the corner of my eye, I see them turn the other way, toward the subway, and I let out a sigh of relief. But even when I'm certain that they're not following us, we don't turn back home. We loop around the East Village slowly, still carrying all the things we got from the people who came by the store earlier.

Only when the sky gets completely dark do we turn back in the direction of our building. We make our way cautiously up the stairs, listening for any voices that shouldn't be there, and when we reach the third floor, we sneak into our apartment as quickly as possible, trying not to make a sound.

★ ★ ★

It feels like a second after I turn the lock and do the latch that someone comes knocking on our door.

"Mateo? Sophie? Are you there?"

Even though I know exactly who it is, I still look through the peephole to make sure she's alone.

"Gracias a Dios que están bien," says Mrs. Solís when she sees us. She walks into the apartment without an invitation and quickly closes the door behind herself.

"Mrs. Solís, what was that? Who were those people?"

She frowns. "You saw them?"

"We did. We were coming up the stairs, and we heard them asking about us."

"They said they were from Child Protective Services. I heard them knocking on your door, and when they wouldn't go away, I stepped out of my apartment to see what they wanted."

"What else did they tell you?" I ask.

"I couldn't get much out of them. I'm surprised they even showed up. I've seen it happen before—kids being left to their own devices after their parents are detained." Mrs. Solís swallows hard. "Mateo, I can't be sure what they came here to do, but if they had tried to take you and your sister away, I could've never just stood by and watched. Ending up in the system can't be much better than—"

"Thank you," I say. I don't even want to think of what might've happened if we'd been home, or if our neighbor hadn't been there to lie for us. "Mrs. Solís, thank you so much. You saved us."

"Mateo," she replies, "I can't imagine what you two are going through right now, but . . . do you really think that being here on your own is the right thing to do? Wouldn't it be better if there was someone else to take care of the two of you? Someone you trust?" Even as she says that, I can see her eyes wandering toward the kitchen, where the dirty dishes are piling up and the garbage is starting to smell.

"We have nowhere else to go, Mrs. Solís."

"There is one thing I said to those people that was true—you do have family in the city. Your uncle Jorge? Didn't he offer to let you stay with him?"

I guess I shouldn't be surprised that she knows about this. Word travels quickly in our community.

When I don't answer, Mrs. Solís takes a step closer to us. For a moment, she stares at me without blinking, but then she frowns, her chest trembling as she lets out a long breath through her nose.

"I shouldn't meddle," she says softly. "I'm sorry. But I do want to say this: I have never regretted asking for help when I needed it. Sometimes, the only way to be strong is to let someone else carry some of the weight with you. Just something for you to think about."

She turns around and opens the door of the apartment slowly. Right before she closes it behind her, she whispers, "Don't forget to lock this."

"What did all of that mean?" Sophie asks me right away, but I don't answer. I'm too busy making sense of everything our neighbor just said.

All these years, I've always thought of Mrs. Solís as the old lady from down the hall who couldn't figure out how to use an electronic device to save her life. I can't believe it's taken me this long to see this other side of her—her wisdom, the genuine way she cares about my family.

"Those people might've wanted to take us away."

"Take us where?"

I shake my head slightly. "Nowhere good, Sophie."

"Are we safe?"

"I think so." I don't believe they'll be coming back—not if they think they're never going to find us here anyway. "Thanks to Mrs. Solís, we might be."

As I turn on the oven to heat up some of Laura Acevedo's empanadas, I start to wonder if our neighbor is right—if we're just delaying the inevitable by staying here. Despite everything Sophie and I did on Saturday, the laundry hamper is already getting fuller and the fridge emptier, and I haven't even had time to wash the dishes, or take out the trash, or sweep the floors. I have no idea how Ma and Pa managed to get these things done without us realizing, because just the thought of doing it all again this weekend makes me feel exhausted.

But when I call Jorge a few hours later, I don't mention Child Protective Services. We talk about the lawyer he found, and about how Pa said he might get released on bond. In the end, I don't ask him if we can come stay with him and Amy. I guess I just want to feel like I still get to call the shots—as though I still have a say in what happens with our lives—if only about this one thing.

THE NEXT DAY AFTER SCHOOL, I MEET Kimmie and Adam right outside the front doors.

"You guys ready to go?" Adam asks, readjusting his backpack over his shoulder.

All I've been able to think about since this morning is the look on Sophie's face when I told her I'd be picking her up from Maria's a couple of hours later today. When she asked me what I was doing, I didn't have the guts to tell her I was hanging out with my friends, so I just said it was something important.

"Hurry up as much as you can, okay?" she said to me.

"I will, Sophie. I promise." In the back of my mind, I told myself that maybe this was for the best anyway. If Child Protective Services decides to return, we won't want to be anywhere they might think to look for us, so Sophie will probably be safer at Maria's.

But now, as I stare into Adam's face, I think about Sophie waiting for me to come get her, and about Erika handling the bodega all by herself, and I feel the urge to blurt out an excuse. I try to think of a way to apologize, to explain that I can't come over anymore, but then Kimmie speaks up.

"Let's get outta here."

I swallow hard as we walk together toward the subway station. I tell myself that it might do me some good to step away from everything for a couple of hours and just be with my friends, hoping that if I repeat this enough times, I'll stop thinking about Sophie and Erika.

The subway ride feels long. Adam's family lives in Brooklyn, in a duplex apartment that has been in his family for generations and hasn't undergone any major renovations in decades. Everything from the wallpaper, to the tile in the bathrooms, to some of the appliances in the kitchen seems to be straight out of the sixties, but it's big, with enough space to fit his parents, his two brothers, and his nonna.

Her voice is the first thing we hear when we walk through the front door.

"Alessandro, is that you?"

"No, Nonna. It's me!" Adam yells back, closing the door behind us.

"Where's Alessandro?"

"I don't know, Nonna."

"Can you call him?"

"Why don't you call him yourself?"

There's a pause. "I left my phone downstairs."

Adam rolls his eyes at us, and then he runs into the kitchen. He comes back a second later holding an old cell phone in his hand, and then we follow him up the stairs.

I can't help but smile a little to myself. Adam's nonna always reminds me of what life used to be like freshman year—us coming over to his place after school every other day, his nonna telling us to be quiet again and again, and then, after a while, popping her head into his room to ask if we were hungry.

Things changed when I started working at the bodega the summer after freshman year, which meant that I wasn't free after school anymore. Kimmie and I usually come over only once every few weeks now, but this apartment still feels familiar, almost like my second home. Being here usually gives me a warm, cozy feeling, but today, all I can think about is the way my own apartment has stopped feeling like home.

"That's new," Kimmie says as soon as we walk into Adam's bedroom, pointing at a *Hamilton* poster. His room is like mine on steroids—there's so much Broadway memorabilia that you can't even see the color of the walls.

Adam smiles at her. "I ordered it online the day after we went to see it."

Kimmie lies down on the bed, and I turn nervously toward Adam. The sooner we're done rehearsing, the sooner I'll get to be with my sister. "You said the producers sent you a scene to practice for the audition, right?"

"Yeah," he says. "I printed it out."

He hands me the pages, and I look down at them. Adam has highlighted all the parts I'm reading. Only a couple of weeks ago, I was practicing for the same part as he was. Now I'm taking on a small supporting role. Trying not to think about it too much, I clear my throat and start reading, but even though I recite the words, my mind is elsewhere.

Whenever I look up from the pages, I see a spark in Adam's eyes. He's a natural—I've always known it. He also printed out the pages for himself, but he barely even looks at them. He's got them memorized already, and everything about him—from the way he delivers the dialogue to the subtle way he uses his hands, is unbelievable to watch. I would usually be amazed at his talent, try to learn something from him, but now I find myself feeling a little bitter, because he's so much better than me, and he always will be.

I choose to focus on Kimmie instead. She's still curled up on Adam's bed, with her phone right in front of her nose. At first, I assume she's writing a song. She keeps tapping her knee with her index finger, which tells me she's counting beats, but then she starts letting out small smiles every now and then.

"Who are you texting, anyway?" Adam asks after we've finished running through the whole scene for the fourth time.

Kimmie turns to look at us, her fingers frozen over her phone. "Darryl," she says, and then her fingers start moving quickly again as she finishes writing her text.

"How are things going with him?" With everything that's been on my mind, I'd forgotten to ask about her rehearsal with his band. She might have even told us about it yesterday, when I wasn't listening.

"Good," she says, sitting up on the bed. "We, uh...we kissed."

"What?"

"You *kissed*?"

"Are you kids hungry?"

The three of us turn toward the door at the same time. Adam's nonna is standing there, smiling at us.

"Nonna, we're—"

"I made cannoli this morning."

Adam looks at me, and then at Kimmie. We've never been able to say no to cannoli, so we end up following Adam's nonna to the kitchen. She was the one who taught us that you can have one "cannolo" or many "cannoli." One "panino," or two "panini." The words "cannolis" and "paninis" just don't exist.

I've always loved learning Italian from her. It's not all that different from Spanish, which is the only language I spoke at home for the first few years of my life.

Nonna stays in the kitchen long enough to witness our first bites, and once she's certain that we all like the cannoli she made, she heads back upstairs.

"So," Adam says, looking at Kimmie. "You kissed Darryl."

She nods, her mouth crunching as she eats her cannolo.

"How did this happen?"

Kimmie smiles. "Well...we went to Starbucks after school yesterday, you know, to work on our essay. And the second we were done and walked out, he kissed me. It was *amazing*."

Adam's mouth falls open. "You kissed *the* Darryl Williams, and you waited until now to tell us? I'm honestly offended you didn't pick up your phone to text us the second it was over."

"Well, I don't kiss and tell," Kimmie says, even though she just did.

"Is he a great kisser? He looks like he would be a great kisser."

"The best I've ever had," Kimmie says, which makes me laugh a little. Like me, she doesn't really have any points of reference.

"So what now?" asks Adam. "Have you talked to him since yesterday?"

Her smile widens as she says, "Yeah. I saw him in class this morning."

"And?"

"And he asked if I wanna hang out tomorrow."

"What are you guys gonna do?"

"Rehearse with his band again."

"*Kimmie!*" Adam shrieks. "Why haven't you said anything? You—"

We're interrupted by the sound of the front door of the apartment opening and closing. Adam's dad appears at the kitchen door an instant later. Mr. Caruso looks just like Adam, except that his hair is brown instead of blond. His eyes widen when he sees us sitting at the table, but then he smiles.

"Kimmie, Matt! How are you two doing?"

Before either of us can answer, Adam speaks up quickly. "We're just hanging out."

He should know by now that Kimmie and I would never tell his dad we're here to help him prepare for an audition, but I can't blame him for being a little nervous.

Either way, Mr. Caruso seems distracted. "Good, good," he says. "Is your nonna home?"

"She's upstairs."

Judging by the look on Mr. Caruso's face, he just might be in trouble with Nonna. "I'll see you all in a bit," he says, and then he turns to run up the stairs.

The air around us shifts all of a sudden. The excitement from a moment ago is gone, and the silence that fills the kitchen feels heavy somehow.

Kimmie speaks up first. "You haven't told your parents about the audition, have you?"

Adam shakes his head, looking down at his plate. "I'll only tell them if I get it . . . which means they'll probably never have to find out!" He laughs as though it was funny, but I know what's going on behind his smile.

Adam's parents have never been very supportive of his acting dreams. No matter how many times he's tried to tell them how much he loves Broadway, his dad insists that he and his two brothers will take over the family business one day. What started with his grandfather bringing back suitcases of Italian goods to New York turned into an import company. Now they bring food, and leather, and all sorts of other stuff over from Italy, and acting and singing aren't relevant skills for the job.

"You're gonna kill the audition," I say, because I know he needs to hear this. "You know the script so well, and they already liked you. Just do what you did last time."

"Matt's right," Kimmie says, turning toward him. "I think you're gonna get the part."

Adam blushes in that moment, looking away from both of us.

"You're gonna have to invite us to opening night if you do get it," Kimmie adds, which makes Adam blush even more.

Suddenly, my phone buzzes. Looking down, I see a text from Maria: *Are you coming to get Sophie soon?*

My legs start shaking under the table. According to the clock on the wall, it's almost five, which means I'm already late.

I feel wide awake all of a sudden, as I realize I can't waste any more time. While Adam recites dialogue to himself and Kimmie smiles down at her phone, reading a text from Darryl, my sister is waiting for me, Erika is alone at the bodega, and my parents are in detention centers. I have more important things to do—things that actually matter.

"I have to go."

Kimmie and Adam turn to look at me with deep frowns.

"What?" says Adam. "Why?"

"Don't you wanna go see a movie or something?"

My heart starts beating fast against my chest. I remind myself that I have to stay cool, that I can't let them see through me this time.

"I really want to, but my mom just texted me. She got caught up at work, and she needs me to pick up my sister from a playdate." There—an excuse that they'll find easy to believe, no matter how much it hurts to throw out a casual mention of Ma.

As disappointment grows on my friends' faces, I see it more clearly than ever: There's always been an invisible line drawn between us. Even though Adam's grandparents are Italian and Kimmie's mom immigrated from South Korea as a child, their families are nothing like mine, because they don't know what it's like to worry about deportation. Adam and Kimmie can both say that they have deeper roots in this country than I do—they're so *American*. They got to be on the lucky side—the side where having your movie plans ruined is a major disappointment, and where you get to make things like boys, and friends, and achieving your wildest dreams your top priorities.

My side has always been different—it's one where my family and I have always had to "be careful," one where our existence has always been up for debate, where my dreams are less valid, no matter how hard I might be willing to work to achieve them.

I swallow down a knot in my throat. I can't believe it's taken me so long to realize this—that I was able to fool myself into thinking that I was just like them all these years. But even as these thoughts spin around in my mind, tearing me up on the inside, all Kimmie and Adam can see is the smile that I've made sure to keep on my face.

"I'm sorry," I say, pushing my chair back. "I really do have to go."

"Okay," Adam says. He looks confused, but he doesn't argue with me.

"Don't overprepare for the audition," I say to him, smiling even wider. "It's gonna be great."

He smiles back at me, but I try not to look at Kimmie. If she's narrowing her eyes at me, I don't want to know. I don't want to answer any questions she may have about why I'm jumping up from my chair, or why I'm in such a rush to get out of here.

As I run toward the subway, I hear a familiar voice inside my mind. *Quien con otros siempre se está comparando nunca sale ganando.* It's another one of Abuela's old sayings: *If you're constantly comparing yourself to others, you'll never win.*

I know it's true. I know Kimmie and Adam aren't to blame for any of this. They didn't get to choose their lives any more than I got to choose mine. It's not their fault that their families don't have to worry about their immigration status, or that mine has been separated. The problem isn't with them at all. But as I hurry down the steps of the subway, I feel bitterness inside me that I've never felt before, and now that it's shown up, I have no idea how to make it go away.

9

By the time I finally make it to Maria's, I'm completely out of breath. I'm not sure if it's because I ran all the way from the subway, or because of all the guilt that has been building up inside my chest, which makes me feel like I'm choking.

"I'm sorry, Sophie," I pant, wrapping my arms around her as soon as I see her. "I'm so sorry it took me so long to get here."

A part of me expected to find her in tears, desperate for me to come get her, but when I pull away and look into her eyes, there's none of that. "It's okay," she says.

After I thank Maria and we start making our way back home, it occurs to me that maybe Sophie needed this as well— to be away from home, away from the bodega, if only for a little while.

My phone starts ringing the instant we walk into our apartment. When I answer, Pa's voice comes from the other side, and I can tell right away that he's calling with bad news.

"The bond was set at fifteen thousand dollars," he says.

"But we don't have that kind of money." A couple of days ago, I locked myself inside the office, opened the safe, and counted the money inside. I just needed to know how much there was, so I can be prepared for when we actually need it.

Pa gives a long sigh into the phone. "I've been thinking about voluntary departure."

"No!" Sophie and I yell at the exact same time.

"You can't leave, Papi," my sister says.

"You have to at least try. *Try* to come back home."

Pa remains silent for a long time. "The lawyer your uncle Jorge found says we might be able to build a case so they'll let me stay in the US, but there's no guarantee that it would work."

"But you—"

"Escucha," he says. "You have to listen first. We have to think about the long term. If I leave the country on my own, it means I'm technically not being deported. It might be easier to come back in the future. But if a judge orders me to leave, they might not let me come back for a very long time—or maybe ever."

Even though my heart is beating fast, I try my best to breathe slowly, to make sense of what my dad is saying.

"Isn't it worth it, though? Isn't it worth it to see if the judge will let you come back home?" I ask. "I mean—do they know Sophie and I were born here? Did you tell them your children are American?"

"I did. And that's one of our options—if we could prove that you and Sophie would be really affected by my deportation, they might let me stay."

"Well, we can do that. We can show them how—"

"Mateo, it's not that easy." Pa sounds exhausted all of a sudden. "*Exceptional and extremely unusual hardship*—those are the words the lawyer used. That's what we would have to prove, and just telling them that you and Sophie would have to grow up without us is not enough." He lets out another sigh, and the words *exceptional and extremely unusual hardship* seem to echo in the air around us. Coming from the man who used to pronounce *lounge* as *lunch*, and who could never remember that *limón* means *lime* and not *lemon*, the words seem heavier somehow. I can just imagine Pa hanging on to his lawyer's every word, trying hard to memorize what he said, repeating this to himself for days. "It's not looking good, mijo. Everyone I've talked to thinks your ma and I won't be allowed to stay."

For a moment, we're all silent. We can hear Pa's ragged breathing and the sounds of the city outside the apartment, but none of us is able to speak.

Finally, it's Pa who breaks the silence. "Have you spoken to your ma? What has she told you?"

120

"We—we spoke to her on Sunday," I say, and my stomach feels heavy, because we haven't heard from her since. "She's hopeful. She thinks you might be able to come back home." I hope hearing this will give Pa a bit of strength, because I can tell he needs it.

"I can't imagine her case would be too different from mine," Pa says. "If you talk to her, ask her what she thinks, what options she's been given."

"Okay, Pa," I say. "I'll ask her."

When we get a call from Ma the next day, however, I forget about those questions. From the moment we first hear her voice, she sounds weak, desperate. She barely sounds like herself.

"Sophie," she says. "Sophie, ¿cómo estás, mi niña?"

"I'm okay, Mami," my sister replies. "I miss you."

"I miss you too, mija. *So* much," Ma answers. "¿Y tú, Mateo? How are you?"

I honestly don't know what to say. I want to say how scared I've been, how even the smallest sounds out in the hallway bring panic to the deepest part of my stomach as I imagine Child Protective Services standing outside our door. I want to say that watching *Pasiones* without her just isn't the same, that I've barely been sleeping, that the sound of Sophie's soft sobbing keeps ringing in my ears every night, even hours after she's fallen asleep. I also want to tell her that I need her and Pa to come back because even though I've tried, I can't picture a future without them here.

Instead of saying those things, I choose to lie. "I'm all right, Ma. How are you?"

She also stays silent for a long time, but I imagine all the things she wants to say. She must want to tell us about the detention center in Buffalo—how miserable it is, how much she misses her home. She must want to tell us about the other women there, how they've all been holding their breath since they were first detained, to the point that the air around them feels old and still. She must want to say how hard it's been to be away from Pa, how empty life feels without having Sophie and me to take care of. But we've always been more similar than either of us cares to admit. She also chooses to lie. "Estoy bien," she says. "Have you talked to your dad?"

"Yes," I say. "Yes, we have. He called us yesterday."

"What did he say?"

I consider lying about this as well. I don't want to put the wrong ideas in her mind, but then I realize this is one thing I can't lie about. "He said he's thinking about voluntary departure. Have—have you thought about that?"

"Some of the women here have mentioned it, but I don't really understand what it means. Everyone has told me not to sign anything, not to answer questions if my lawyer's not there, because sometimes they do that—they get you to sign papers you don't understand, and all of a sudden you've given up your chance to fight."

"What about your lawyer?" Sophie asks, and I turn sharply toward her. Suddenly, it hits me that she's a part of this conversation—that she has to worry about immigration hurdles and lawyers. She's way too young to have concerns like these, but there's nothing I can do to protect her from them. "Has he said anything?"

"I've only talked to him once," Ma says. "I barely had time to ask him questions."

In that moment, I can't help it. I start to beg. "Ma, no matter what they tell you, you can't just leave the country. You have to do everything you can to stay."

"Sí, mijo," she answers quickly. "I haven't given up hope. I'll find a way to come back to you."

I nod quietly to myself. Even though she's said this before, today I believe it a little less than I did last time.

★ ★ ★

When I see Kimmie walking down the hallway holding hands with Darryl the next day, I have to do a double take to make sure my eyes aren't playing a trick on me. I knew everything was going well, but I had no idea things between them were hold-hands-in-the-hallway official.

"Heya," Kimmie says.

"Hey," I say, staring at Darryl. He's taller than he seemed from far away, but just as good-looking.

"Kimmie keeps telling me about you, but we haven't really met," he says, flashing a big smile at me. I'm grateful that he speaks first, because I had no idea what I was gonna say. I shake his hand, and when he looks right into my eyes, I feel a little weak in the knees.

"Nice to meet you." In the back of my mind, I notice that he said "Kimmie" instead of "Kimberly." Sneaking a glance at her, I wonder what made her decide not to introduce herself to Darryl by her full name, as she's been doing with everyone else lately.

We start moving down the hallway slowly, in the direction of Kimmie's locker. Even though she and Darryl are walking right next to me, I feel more alone than I've felt in a long while.

I can't help but think about two days ago, when we were eating cannoli in Adam's kitchen. It's hard to ignore the fact that, while Adam is off at an audition and Kimmie is walking hand in hand with a boy—and not just any boy—I'm here with a knot in my throat because of the conversation I had with Ma yesterday. All morning, I've been asking myself the same questions that kept me up for hours last night—whether she'll survive the detention center, whether she's even being given proper food and a bed to sleep on, whether she'll ever be able to come back home.

"So Kimmie tells me you're thinking of applying to NYU next year?" Darryl says suddenly.

I try my best to smile. "Yeah, uh . . ."

"Darryl just got his acceptance letter," Kimmie tells me as we reach her locker.

"Oh, wow," I say, my eyebrows shooting up. "What program are you doing?"

"Music composition at Steinhardt," Darryl says. "But you wanna get into Tisch, don't you?" He throws a sideways smile at me, and despite everything that was going through my mind a second ago, my knees feel weak again. I don't know how he does it—how he's able to make me feel this way with such little effort. Maybe it's his cool posture, or his deep voice, or maybe just the fact that he's so freaking cute.

"Yeah, but . . . but I'm not sure yet. I'm not nearly as good as Adam. He—"

"Darryl and I are feeling like pizza for lunch," Kimmie interrupts me, slamming her locker door shut. She's not gonna let me talk myself down, and I love her for it. "Wanna come with us?"

I almost say yes, but then I remember that today isn't Friday. Fridays are always dollar-slice days, and Kimmie knows that, so pizza on a Thursday must've been Darryl's idea.

Slowly, I open my mouth to answer. "I have to—"

"Adam already left for his audition," Kimmie says before I can make up an excuse. "So the two of us will meet you on the front steps of school after next period, okay?"

She and Darryl give me one last smile before walking away, and I turn in the direction of the stairwell. As I climb the steps toward my next class, I start to feel weight in my stomach that has nothing to do with Ma and Pa and everything to do with Kimmie and Darryl. Maybe it's because I'm jealous that Kimmie has found a guy, when I haven't even kissed anyone all through high school. Or maybe I'm just scared that Kimmie having a boyfriend will drive her further away from me, and the distance between us will become a little wider.

I walk into the history classroom, and while I try to find an empty spot near the back, I feel longing deep inside of me. I want to go back to a few weeks ago, when everything was still normal—before Kimmie got a boyfriend and Adam and I went to that audition. I want to go back to when Ma and Pa hadn't yet been taken away, when my biggest concern was moving around my shifts at the bodega so I could go hang out with my friends. I want to go back to then and there and freeze time.

★ ★ ★

Uncle Jorge comes over that night. The first thing I notice when I open the door is that his beard, which he usually keeps perfectly trimmed, looks a little messy and uneven. Between work, a crying baby keeping him up at night, and trying to

126

find a way to help my parents, I can't imagine he's had much time for grooming.

"Sorry I'm late," he says. "I was dealing with some stuff."

"What kind of stuff?" I ask as we sit down in the living room.

Jorge frowns. He seems to be having a battle with himself, trying to decide if he should say this or not, but in the end he chooses to speak the words that are hanging from his lips. "You know how I technically own the bodega, because I signed the legal papers, and all that?" he says, and I nod quickly. "Well... because your mom and dad were working there without a permit, the feds came after me."

"No," I say. Not Uncle Jorge. My parents have done so much to help him, to keep him out of trouble ever since he was a teenager. It's because of my dad that Jorge broke away from the local gang. Thanks to Pa, Jorge straightened up and went back to school. If he got in trouble now, after all these years, after he's gotten his life together and built a family, my parents would be destroyed. We would all be.

"It's okay," he answers quickly. "It's not like they would throw me in jail for giving them jobs. I had to pay a fine... that's it. It's all sorted out."

I wonder how much he had to pay, but I don't ask. It's probably more than we can afford to pay him back right now, and we already owe him plenty of money. When Ma had to have surgery last year, Jorge was the only person we could turn to. He agreed to give us a loan, and as far as I know, Pa hasn't finished paying him back.

"Have you eaten yet?" he asks.

Sophie and I shake our heads. "We were waiting for you to have dinner."

He nods once, and then we all get up from the couch and go into the kitchen to get everything ready.

We still have half of one of Ceci Romano's lasagnas left. I kept it in the freezer so it wouldn't go bad, but I still take a quick whiff of it before I decide that it is good enough to eat. I shove it in the oven, and while we wait anxiously by the kitchen counter, Jorge's eyes slowly search the apartment.

"I can come over this weekend to help you clean up a bit," he says.

I feel my face turning a little red. I wish I'd hidden the mess before he got here—at least rinsed out a few dishes, taken out the trash, wiped the kitchen counter. "I was planning to do it myself. I—"

"Mateo," he interrupts me. "We can clean up together."

Not looking directly into his eyes, I nod. Cleaning the apartment and keeping Sophie and myself fed shouldn't be too hard, but I'm starting to feel weak, and I don't have the energy to argue with Jorge right now.

When the timer goes off, I take the lasagna out of the oven, and Jorge helps me carry the plates to the table.

"Have you been eating well?" he asks as soon as we sit down, and I can almost hear my mom in his tone.

"Yeah," I say. "People are still bringing us food—less than before, but we've managed just fine."

"Do you need money?"

I put a bite of lasagna in my mouth and shake my head. "We're good for now. Thanks."

"And have you thought some more about coming to stay with Amy and me?"

I put my fork down. Suddenly, I can't remember the reasons we decided to stay here in the first place. "I still think we should wait," I say. "We have to see if our mom and dad find a way to come back."

Sophie nods quickly, but I wonder if she's also getting tired of having to do it all on our own.

Jorge presses his lips together. I can tell he's not going to argue. When it comes to important things, he's always treated us like adults, always been willing to listen to us, and it's no different now.

"The offer still stands," he says. "You're always welcome in our home. No matter what."

I pick up my fork again and keep eating. I hope Jorge knows how grateful I am to him for being here, for trying to look after us, but I just can't find the right words. Instead, I hope the gentle silence that has fallen between us will tell him all the things I'm unable to say out loud.

★ ★ ★

After Uncle Jorge leaves, I help Sophie get ready for bed, and then I hop in the shower. Once the hot water is falling over me, I'm able to think a little more clearly.

With Jorge's words still spinning inside my mind, I can't help but feel as though I'm gonna have to make a decision about our future soon. Sophie and I can't live like this forever. The thing is, if we moved in with Uncle Jorge, what would happen to our apartment? It wouldn't make sense to keep paying rent if the place is empty, but if we end our lease, we'll never be able to come back. Ma and Pa found this place before I was even born, and they always talk about how ridiculous rents are in Manhattan, how we would never be able to afford an apartment like this if it wasn't rent controlled, how lucky we are to live here. If Ma and Pa find a way to stay in the US and we've given up our apartment, what would happen to us then? Where would we live?

I think about the phone conversations we've had with my parents. Looking back, it's hard to even remember what we've talked about. I wish I could just call them right now and ask for their opinion. Or better yet, I wish I could see them, talk to them face-to-face and figure out the answers to these questions together.

I'm lathering my arms with a sponge, my hair covered in shampoo, when all of a sudden I hear it—a loud, piercing scream. My sister's scream.

I shake my head desperately, running my fingers through my hair to get the shampoo off. My sister screams again, and a horrible image appears in my mind—Child Protective Services at our door, taking Sophie away. I can't think of anything else that could be making her scream like this.

The entire world starts spinning. I don't know which way is left or right, or where to even find the knob to shut off the water. When I find it, I turn it all the way and let out a scream of my own. I must've turned it the wrong way, so for a second a stream of scalding water hits my back. I turn it around quickly and step out of the shower in such a hurry that I almost slip.

"Sophie!" I yell out as I wrap a towel around my waist. "Sophie, I'm coming!"

I rush out of the bathroom, prepared to face whoever has come to take us away from our home, but I find no one. There's only Sophie, and she's standing on top of a chair.

"Sophie, what's wrong?" I ask.

"A cockroach," she says. "I just saw it. It crawled under the stove."

I let out a small sigh. A *cockroach*. Normally, that thought would've made me jump on a chair just like Sophie did. But today, I welcome it, I'm glad that's all it is. At least the intruder in our home isn't here to take us away.

"Wait there," I tell her. "I have to go get dressed."

"N-no!" she stammers. "Don't go!" My sister's always been scared of bugs, but she has a special terror reserved for spiders and roaches.

"I have to. I can't kill it like this." I gesture at the towel around my waist, and she nods quickly.

"Just hurry."

I turn around to walk back into the bathroom, and a minute later I come out wearing my pajamas. Sophie is now kneeling on top of the chair, looking as though she's about to faint.

Ever since Mr. Chávez upstairs got a roach infestation a few months ago, we've had to deal with the stragglers. But then we started seeing only one or two each week, and it had been a while since we'd seen any at all. It was usually Pa who killed them, but Ma always stepped up whenever he wasn't around. Tonight, I have no choice. It has to be me.

I tiptoe into the kitchen and open the cabinet under the sink, where Ma keeps the insecticide.

"Be careful," Sophie says as I point the can at the crack between the stove and the floor. I nod once, but when I press the button, nothing comes out.

"Dammit." The can is empty. We've probably gone through two full cans since this whole thing started, and Ma must've forgotten to buy a new one. "Okay, Sophie, we're gonna have to do this the old-fashioned way."

I hear her moan in disgust as I walk toward the front door and look down at all the shoes lined up next to it. My heart hurts when I see Ma's good shoes, and her chanclas, and Pa's loafers, but I don't have time to get nostalgic.

In the end, I go for my old Converse. They're worn, and dirty, and broken around the soles. A little more misuse won't make much of a difference.

Carrying the shoe in one hand, I go back to the kitchen and bang my free hand against the door of the oven. Nothing happens.

I bang again, and out comes the cockroach, running for its life.

"Aaaaaaah!" I let out a scream so shrill that it barely sounds like my own. I stumble backward to get out of the roach's way, until I hit the refrigerator. For a second, it looks confused, but then it starts running in Sophie's direction.

The screams that fill the apartment—both Sophie's and mine—are piercing. They're gonna make the neighbors think we're getting murdered, but I don't care. I run after the cockroach, unable to contain the scream that just keeps leaving my throat, until I get close enough, and I stretch out my hand, and *bang*!

"It's gone," I pant, feeling as though all the energy has left my body.

Now my biggest concern is cleaning the floor and the bottom of my shoe, but before I can go grab paper towels, Sophie jumps off the chair and wraps her arms around my waist.

"It's over," I say, touching her hair. "We're okay. Everything's okay."

But Sophie doesn't let go. She doesn't loosen her grip around me. And in that moment, it all becomes so clear to me. We can't stay here. If I can barely protect Sophie from a cockroach, how will I take care of her if she gets sick, or if we run out of money, or if anything unexpected happens? How will I protect her if Child Protective Services comes knocking on our door again and tries to take her away?

We stand there for I don't know how long, until we finally realize that we have to do something about this mess. I grab stuff from the kitchen to clean the floor and my shoe, and then Sophie turns on the TV. *Pasiones* is about to start, but I have something more important to do. I pick up my phone and call Uncle Jorge's cell.

He answers at the first ring. "Hello?"

"I've thought about it," I say slowly.

"Y-you have?" He sounds sleepy, and I wonder if he was already in bed. "So you'll come stay with me and Amy?"

"Yes," I say, and for the first time, there is no doubt in my mind that this is the right thing to do. "We need your help. We need you."

10

UNCLE JORGE COMES TO PICK US UP at noon on Saturday. Sophie and I packed our bags last night with all the essentials—clothes, and shoes, and towels, and everything else we think might be important to have at Uncle Jorge's. At the last minute, Sophie also tries to bring along all of her coloring books and half a dozen stuffed animals, but in the end her suitcase won't close, so she's forced to make difficult decisions.

Once our bags are waiting by the door, I turn to look at the apartment—at the home my parents built. I look at the round dinner table, which has stains and scratches and chipped edges from years of holding heavy dinner plates, and hot cups of tea, and hours upon hours of conversation. I look at the photos on the wall of the living room, which show all of our best moments—me as a kid feeding the ducks in Central Park, Sophie as a little pink ball on the day she was born, my parents looking young and relaxed somewhere in Brooklyn, and a photo of all four of us grinning on the Coney Island Boardwalk. When I look at the small living space, I think of the day Pa ran into the apartment with a big smile on his face, saying he had found a couch on the sidewalk that was much better than the one we had. I remember how much he and Jorge struggled to get it through the front door, and how we all sat down to watch TV on our new couch that night.

I never thought I'd be leaving this place. In the back of my mind, I pictured my parents growing old in this apartment, Sophie and me coming back to visit as adults. It's always been so . . . *ours*. It's the only home I've ever known.

"The rent is due next week," I say under my breath.

Behind me, the wooden floors creak as Uncle Jorge shifts his weight from one foot to the other. "We'll make sure it's paid. You don't have to say goodbye to the apartment just yet. We can hold on to it for as long as it takes, until we find out if your parents will be allowed to stay."

I nod slowly, and then I turn around. Suddenly, all I want is to get out of here, and I'm not sure how it happened—how I went from never wanting to leave to desperately needing to get out.

Sophie is already waiting by the door. I go join her and put a hand on her shoulder.

"Are you ready to go?"

She nods, but her face doesn't give anything away. I'm starting to worry that she's losing a part of herself. She barely looks like the girl from the photos on the wall—the smiling, carefree girl she used to be. Then again, I probably don't look the same, either. Maybe both of us have changed for good.

I hold her hand tight as we walk down the stairs of our building. I hope my firm grip will tell her all the things I'm not strong enough to say right now—that I'm here for her, that we're in this together, that we're gonna be okay. That despite everything that's happened, she's allowed to be a child, to not have to worry, because there's someone here to take care of her.

The taxi ride to Jorge's apartment is mostly silent. He lives on the edge of the West Village, not far from our own place. We could've walked, if it wasn't for our heavy suitcases.

Growing up, Uncle Jorge used to live in the same building as us. He's never talked much about his childhood, but I do know his family came to New York from Puerto Rico a long time ago. His mom passed away when he was young, so it was his grandmother, Doña Alba, who raised him, but she was always so sick. When I try to remember her, all that comes to my mind is coughing—lots and lots of coughing. There came a point where she just couldn't take care of Jorge anymore. She couldn't keep track of where he went after school—or if he was even going to school at all—and he got involved with Los Verdes.

That's what the Verdes have always done—they go after kids like Jorge, who feel a little lost, who aren't sure where they fit in. Everyone says that once you get in with them, you can't get out, but my dad didn't believe that. The second he realized Jorge was selling drugs and going out at night to do who-knows-what, he decided to put a stop to it. This happened before Sophie was even born. I must've been only five or six, but I remember how angry Jorge was at first, all the ways he tried to tell my dad to mind his own business. I also remember how Uncle Jorge started looking healthier all of a sudden, how he started coming over after dinner every night and sat down at the table to do his schoolwork, with my dad right next to him.

For a while, we were all scared—we had to look over our shoulders for months before we were certain the Verdes weren't gonna come after us. We've never really understood why they let Jorge go. I think it might've had something to do with my dad, because if they knew who he was, and all the ways he'd helped people out, they may have chosen to give him and Jorge a chance to walk away unharmed.

Now, as the taxi pulls over in front of Jorge's building, it's hard to believe any of that ever happened. After those difficult years, he managed to finish high school. With a bit of help from my dad, he got into Hunter College, where he met Amy. Now they're married, and have a baby daughter, and they live here, in a brownstone building in the West Village.

We get out of the cab, and he helps us carry our bags up the front steps of the building and to the second floor. The door to his apartment opens as we're approaching it, and Amy appears, wearing a flowery summer dress.

"How did everything go?" she asks. She has a sweet voice and long, reddish-brown hair. Even after all this time, I have a hard time understanding what she and Jorge saw in each other in the first place. They could not be any more different. She grew up in Brooklyn and has always had a soft spot for antiques, and the ballet, and stuff that Jorge couldn't care less about. Maybe what brought them together was just the fact that he needed a little more order in his life, and she needed a little less.

"All right," I answer, but I quickly realize she wasn't talking to me. She's looking at Jorge, who's coming behind Sophie and me.

"Good," he says, grunting a little as he carries the heavy bags the last bit of the way. "Locked up their place, and we got all the stuff they need right here."

Amy's gaze travels toward the suitcases. For the briefest second, her eyes widen, and I know what she's thinking—where are we gonna fit them? I asked myself the same question, but there was lots of stuff we needed to bring, and we didn't have any smaller bags anyway.

Their apartment is tiny but nicer than ours. There are tall windows in the living room, which let in a surprising amount of light—by New York standards, that is. They have a nice kitchen, a big, cozy couch, and the entire place is covered in floral artwork—Amy's doing, of course. She works at an art gallery in Chelsea, so she's always had an eye for these things. If it were up to Jorge, the place would probably be covered in pictures of motorcycles and sports team logos.

"Do you need anything?" Amy asks Sophie and me. "Are you hungry?"

"N-no. I'm fine. Sophie, are you fine?"

My sister nods quickly.

"All right, then." Amy flashes a smile at us, but I'm not sure it's genuine. Ma and Pa have always said that Amy can come off as a little fake. Once or twice, my mom even said Amy makes her think of a robot. "Why don't you take your things to the baby's room?"

Uncle Jorge nods. "Come on," he says. "Let's get you settled in."

He leads the way down the narrow hallway and through the first door on the left. The room is even smaller than I remember. The walls are painted light pink, and there's baby stuff everywhere. In the space where the crib should be, there's an air mattress, which I figure Sophie and I will have to share.

"But where will Ellie sleep?" Sophie asks.

"In our room," Jorge says. I guess he and Amy found a way to make her crib fit in their bedroom after all.

None of this is ideal, but it'll have to do for now. We hang a few of our clothes inside the tiny closet and shove our suitcases in at the bottom. They stick out, so that the closet door won't even close, but again, it'll have to do for now.

Before we know it, it's almost two o'clock, and I need to head to the bodega for my shift.

"You don't have to go," Uncle Jorge says. For the past week, he's had to keep an eye on the store. With my dad gone, it's he who's been scheduling shifts, and paying back suppliers, and making sure we're well stocked on everything. Ever since he graduated, he's worked at the same tech company downtown, and now I can't understand how he's been able to go to his day job and still find time to do all those things at the bodega.

"Of course I do." I can't let Pa down. He would want me to go. We all know how busy the store can get on Saturdays, and I can't leave Erika to deal with it on her own. She's been working so hard lately. "Sophie, are you okay staying here?"

"Yeah," she says, and I feel a little relieved. At least now she has a safe place to be while I'm working, and she won't have to just wait inside the tiny office, bored out of her mind.

"Okay. I'll be back for dinner."

Even though I run, I'm still late for the start of my shift. It'll take some time to get used to not living two blocks away from work.

The first couple of hours at the bodega feel faster and easier than I would've expected. *We're safe now*, I keep repeating to myself. Even if Child Protective Services comes knocking on our door again, they'll have no idea where we've gone, and so far there's been no sign of them at my school or Sophie's, which makes me hope that they've given up on us. We won't have to worry about putting food on the table, or running out of clean laundry, or making sure that we have everything we need.

I just wonder how long this is going to last. It's not a forever thing—I know that much. If anything, it feels like we're just putting a Band-Aid on the problem. My sister and I won't be able to sleep in the baby's room for long. Ellie will eventually outgrow her crib and need to move back into her own bedroom, not to mention the fact that Sophie and I will get tired of sharing that tiny space, of sleeping on an air mattress, of not having a place to call our own. Jorge and Amy will also get tired of having to take care of us. They'll want to go back to their normal lives, to raising their kid in peace, to having their apartment to themselves again.

We're safe now, I remind myself once again, trying to push all those negative thoughts away. I try to hold on to that feeling of relief long enough to get to the end of my shift.

When I get back to Uncle Jorge's, the food is already on the table, and they're just waiting for me to have dinner.

"I made tacos tonight," Amy says. "I thought it might make you feel a bit more at home."

Something inside me melts. I don't think we give Amy enough credit sometimes.

"Thank you," I say to her. "That's so nice of you."

When we sit down at the table, however, I realize these are not tacos like the ones Ma would make. Amy used hard-shell tortillas, ground meat, lettuce, and cheddar cheese. *Fake tacos*, my mom would call them.

"Is everything okay?" Amy asks Sophie right away. My sister is having a harder time hiding her disappointment than I am.

"Yes," I answer quickly, before Sophie can say anything. "These look amazing."

I pick up a taco and do my best to pretend that I'm enjoying it. I give my sister a look that only she will understand, begging her to do the same, and she takes a bite out of her own taco.

With a sideways glance at Amy, I realize she's loving the tacos so much that she's literally licking her fingers. I can't imagine any of this is easy for her, but she opened the doors of her home to Sophie and me, she welcomed us without a word of complaint, and she even made a dinner she thought we would like. She really is trying her best, and I could not be any more grateful to her for that.

* * *

The rest of the weekend feels painfully slow.

Ellie cries all night on Saturday. Maybe she knows something is different. Even though she's only a few months old, she can probably tell that her routine has been disrupted, and she doesn't like it. Either way, I don't think anyone in the apartment gets any sleep. Sophie and I don't leave our room, but we lie side by side on the air mattress, wide awake and staring at the ceiling, while we listen to endless wailing and Jorge's and Amy's desperate attempts to get the baby to quiet down.

Even after all that, Ellie seems to be in a bad mood all day on Sunday—probably from lack of sleep—and, by extension, Amy's in a bad mood as well.

The only bit of good news comes when Ma calls in the middle of the day, saying that she's now allowed to have visitors, but since she's out in Buffalo, we'll have to wait until next weekend for Uncle Jorge to be able to drive us there.

We have chicken and broccoli for dinner that night, which

again, is impossible not to compare to Ma's cooking. I can't help but miss the salsa, and the lime, and all the things Ma will never serve dinner without.

By Monday morning, a part of me is glad to have to go to school. The second I walk through the front doors, I'm no longer Mateo, the kid whose parents might be getting deported. I'm no longer the kid who has to look after his seven-year-old sister, or the one who doesn't even have a permanent home anymore.

"Heya." For the first time in several days, the sound of Kimmie's voice coming from behind the open door of my locker brings a feeling of relief to my chest.

I turn toward her. "Hey."

Maybe the relief also comes from the fact that she's on her own. It feels like I haven't had one-on-one time with Kimmie in a while.

"Where's Darryl?"

"He had to go to the study room to work on a group project," she says. Today, she's wearing her hair down, which she almost never does. She wraps her arm around mine, and we start walking toward the front doors of school.

"So?" I ask.

"So . . . it happened." She squeezes my arm, letting out an excited squeal.

"Sorry, *what* happened?"

"Darryl asked if I wanted to join the band."

"*What?* When?"

"Last night. I went to the rehearsal, and it was *so good*. And then he and I stayed late writing a song, and he told me that the other guys had begged him to get me on board as a backing vocalist."

"That's . . . *wow*."

"*I know,*" she says. We walk out into the bright sun, and we stop to wait for Adam to come out, like we always do. "How are *you*? Lately, you've been so . . ."

"So what?"

"*Different*. Is everything okay, Matt?"

I get that urge again—the urge to admit everything to her. Maybe it won't ever go away, but when I think about what I felt when I walked into school this morning, I stop myself. As long as I don't say anything out loud, school can remain a safe place—a place where I get to escape from what's going on at home.

"I think I know what's bothering you," she says after I've been silent for too long.

I narrow my eyes at her. "Y-you do?" Maybe she's figured out what's going on somehow. After all, she knows me better than anyone.

Kimmie nods confidently. "You're upset about the audition you and Adam went to."

I let out a long breath through my nose. It all makes sense now—the weird way Kimmie has been looking at me lately, the fact that she hasn't dared to ask what's bothering me. While I've been busy worrying about Sophie, and fearing the possibility that Ma and Pa might never come back home, and watching as my entire world crumbles, this is what's been going through Kimmie's mind—that I've been acting weird because I'm jealous.

"Kimmie, that's not—"

"I get it," she interrupts me. "You wanted the part, too, and what happened with that guy while you were waiting in line was awful, and so unfair, but . . . Adam didn't do anything wrong. The casting director just liked him for some reason."

"I know. And I'm happy he got the callback. I just—"

"That's the thing. He didn't just get a callback," Kimmie says, and her face turns very serious. "He got the part."

"What?" Maybe it's just the fact that the light of the sun is blinding me, but all of a sudden, everything starts looking a little artificial. "He—he got it?"

Kimmie nods.

"Wow. I don't even—"

Adam's voice appears suddenly. "What are we talking about?"

Kimmie and I turn around at the same time. I meet Adam's eyes, and my whole body stiffens. I want to say something, but even my jaw has tightened. No matter how hard I try to speak, the words just won't come out.

Adam puts his hands in his pockets. "I guess Kimmie told you."

I nod. All of this feels so wrong. He shouldn't look ashamed. He should be excited, and I should be hugging him, and we should be jumping up and down. I mean, he got a part in an off-Broadway play! We've been dreaming about something like this from the moment we first became friends.

"When did this happen?" I ask when I finally find my voice.

"Friday afternoon. The producers called and offered me the part."

"And when do you start rehearsals?" I ask, because if I keep asking questions, at least there won't be awkward silence between us.

"In a few weeks," he says.

I can't think of anything else to say. I'm trying hard to come up with something, to find a way to make Adam understand that I'm not jealous, that I'm happy for him, that the audition isn't even the reason I've been acting weird. But as the silence stretches on, and Kimmie and Adam keep staring fixedly at me, I start feeling very hot, and I can't stop myself from blurting out the first thing that comes to my mind.

"I—I'm happy for you. I mean, it's only a stupid role."

Adam's eyes go wide. "What is that supposed to mean?"

I know exactly what it meant, but now all I can think about is how it must've sounded to Adam.

"I didn't mean it that way," I say quickly. My heart starts beating fast, and my face keeps getting hotter and hotter. I can feel my friends' eyes on me, and I'm starting to worry that if I don't get this right, my wall will crumble and I'll have to lay it all out in the open. "I was so wrecked after I screwed up my audition—you know I was. What I'm trying to say is: It was only *one* role—one of many that we're gonna audition for. It's not like I can't be happy for you because you got this one and I didn't."

Adam doesn't say anything. He's staring at me with raised eyebrows, and I can just tell he doesn't believe me. I turn toward Kimmie instead, hoping that she'll speak up and say she understands what I meant, but her lips are pressed together, as though she's trying hard to keep herself out of this.

"I'm sorry, Adam. I—"

"It's okay," he says, blinking repeatedly. "I get what you were trying to say."

"Adam, I'm so happy for you. I don't—"

"You don't have to explain," he says. Putting his hands in his pockets, he turns toward Kimmie. "Should we go get food?"

Even as we walk down the front steps and head toward

the halal cart, Adam doesn't bring up the role again. None of us do. I keep wishing I could go back to a few moments ago, that I could take back what I said, that we could find a way to celebrate. But I also choose not to say anything, and before we know it, we're all trying to pretend that this is just another normal day, even as I feel the distance between us growing wider and wider.

THE NEXT DAY, I MOVE QUICKLY THROUGH the hallways at school, trying not to make eye contact with anyone. I don't really feel like facing Kimmie and Adam, so when lunch hour comes, I stop by my locker as quickly as possible, thinking I'll head up to the study room on the sixth floor to get some work done. I've only taken a few steps toward the stairs, however, when I see Kimmie and Darryl walking in my direction. I turn around right away, hoping that they hadn't seen me yet, but then Kimmie calls my name, and I freeze on the spot.

"Hey," she says as soon as she catches up to me.

"How's it going?" Darryl asks.

"I'm just—"

"We're gonna go get lunch," Kimmie interrupts me. "They're serving cheeseburgers in the cafeteria."

I shake my head. "I'm not that hungry. I should—"

"Adam's not coming," she adds quickly. "He had to go... *somewhere.*" From the way she looks down, it's not hard to guess what that means. He must've had to go meet with the producers or something.

"All right," I say finally.

Kimmie gives a satisfied nod, and she leads the way to the cafeteria.

"So," she says once we're sitting down with our food in front of us. I'm vaguely aware of the fact that people are looking our way. It might be because they've heard Kimmie joined Darryl's band, but then again, they could simply be wondering what he's doing sitting with two nobodies.

I force myself to look up at her and say, "So?"

"What's going on?" she asks me. "You keep saying you're fine, that you're tired, but I know you're not. You say you're happy for Adam, but I'm pretty sure that's not true. So... what is it?"

"I've just... been feeling weird lately."

"Because of what happened at the audition?" she says. "If that's what it is, it's okay. You're allowed to be upset, and I know that the last thing you needed was to watch Adam get the role when you didn't, but I think you should just talk to him. Tell him what you're actually thinking."

When I don't answer, Darryl leans forward on the table, staring deep into my eyes. "I don't know you guys very well," he says. "But if you're mad at Adam for some reason, just tell him. That's the way we do it in the band. If something's not working, we fix it."

I bite into my cheeseburger, just to have an excuse not to say anything. I don't disagree with any of what they're saying, but I don't feel like dealing with this right now. I don't have the energy to worry about Adam's hurt feelings, or the time to focus on anything other than my family.

"So?" Kimmie says. "Will you talk to him?"

I swallow hard. "There's nothing to talk about." What would I say to Adam, anyway? No matter how much I try to tell him that I'm happy for him, he's not gonna believe me at this point. And maybe Kimmie is right—maybe I *am* allowed to be a little upset, because Adam and I have never been on a level playing field when it comes to our Broadway dreams.

Kimmie nods once, staring down at her food. "I'm gonna go get more fries," she says. As she picks up her tray, a part of me wants to say something else, to stop her, but I don't. I just sit there, watching her walk away.

Darryl clears his throat. "Kimmie's worried about you," he says.

I don't reply. As she joins the line for food, something starts hurting deep inside of me. I get this urge to get up from my chair, go up to Kimmie, and just wrap my arms around her, but I stay put.

"And if she's worried, *I'm* worried, you know?"

I meet Darryl's eyes. He's still leaning slightly toward me, his arms crossed over the table and his smile bright.

Somehow, I manage to find my voice. "You really like her, don't you?"

"I do," he says, nodding once. "I *really* do. And if there's one thing I've learned about her, it's that there are two things she loves most: music and you."

"Me?"

"Well, you and Adam. But mostly you."

I look down, the feeling in my stomach growing more and more painful.

"Listen, creative industries are just super hard to break into," Darryl says. "I've spoken to so many people in music, and they've all said the same thing—that you can't let the rejections stop you."

"I know. I'm just—"

"People think my band was an overnight success, but we've worked so hard to build it up. And we're not even halfway to where we want to be. So, all I'm saying is: I'm not gonna stop, and you shouldn't, either."

"It's not that simple," I say, and for a moment, I feel tempted to blurt out something else. A part of me wishes I could tell him about everything that's going on with my family. I wish I could say that the audition isn't even the reason I'm upset. In the back of my mind, I can't help but think of how much easier it would be to tell the truth about my parents to someone who doesn't know me that well, someone who wouldn't start seeing me differently, but I stop myself when I remember how much things have already changed with Kimmie and Adam since last week. I can't ask Darryl to keep a secret from Kimmie, so if I told him the truth, I'd only be making things more complicated.

Darryl's eyes shift, and when I look over my shoulder, I see that Kimmie is making her way back toward us.

For the rest of lunch, I try not to look at her too much. I already know I haven't exactly been a great friend lately. I don't need to remind myself of all the ways I've been letting her down.

★ ★ ★

During breakfast on Friday, I see my own exhaustion reflected on Jorge's and Amy's faces. Amy, who usually looks so put-together, has dark circles under her eyes and tangles in her hair. Jorge just looks like he's about to pass out from lack of sleep. Ellie hasn't stopped crying at night, so we've all been running on only a few hours of rest for the past few days.

The thought of seeing Ma tomorrow is what's gotten me

through this week. It's what I've been thinking about every night while I stare at the ceiling, with Ellie's crying ringing in my ears, and what I've tried to focus on at school to keep my mind off Adam.

My day goes by slowly. Every class seems to drag on for hours and hours, and I keep checking my phone, only to find that no more than a few minutes have passed since I last looked at the time. When school is finally out and I need to head to the bodega, I tell myself that this is the last thing I have to do—I only have to get through my shift today, and before I know it, I'll be seeing Ma.

I'm standing behind the counter, counting down the hours until closing time, when Graciela Muñoz walks in.

"I heard you're going to see your ma tomorrow," she says to me. Again, I have no idea how word got out about this, but I don't ask who told her.

I swallow hard. "Yeah."

"Please tell her I'm thinking of her, praying for her," she says, and then she pulls something out of her purse. It's a bag of magdalenas from Don Alfonso's, the bakery next to the church.

"I'm not sure if you'll be able to give this to your ma, but I bought it for her. I know how much she loves these."

I take the bag and thank Graciela, not bothering to explain

that they definitely won't allow something like this inside the detention center.

A small while later, Carlos Acevedo shows up. "Do you need anyone to drive you up there?"

"N-no. We're fine."

"Okay, then. Good luck, Mateo. Tell your mother we're waiting for her to come back."

I nod, but again, I don't say anything. The more I hear people say that they're counting on the fact that my parents will return home, the more terrified I am at the possibility that they won't.

When Saturday morning finally arrives, Jorge, Sophie, and I wake up at the crack of dawn, even though we were all wishing we could sleep in. Ellie had a better night, but she still kept us up for a good hour or two.

Jorge borrowed Amy's parents' car so he could drive us up to Buffalo. I take the passenger seat, and Sophie rides in the back. We get out of the city quickly—there's no traffic at this time on a Saturday—and soon enough we're on the highway.

We're silent most of the way. Sophie keeps busy in the back with the stuffed penguin she chose to bring, and I sneak glances at her every now and then, trying to make sure she's okay. It's been at least a year since Mr. Frizzle has made an appearance. I wonder what made Sophie bring him back out, if there's something Mr. Frizzle can offer—company, or hope, or comfort—that I've been unable to give to her.

Trying not to overthink it, I turn to stare at the blooming trees outside the window, preparing myself for what's about to happen.

I'm scared of what we're going to find when we get to the detention center in Buffalo. I think of the way Ma has barely sounded like herself when we've spoken to her on the phone, and I wonder if being in that awful place has changed her. I have no idea what she's been through, what she's seen. What if we get there and find that Ma is no longer the person she used to be?

"I have to pee," Sophie says softly from the back seat, interrupting my thoughts. I look at the time on the dashboard and realize we're halfway there.

"We'll pull over at the next rest stop," Uncle Jorge says, and so we stop at a gas station near Endicott. Sophie and I run into the tiny convenience store, and Jorge stays behind to fill up the tank. While Sophie is inside the bathroom, I walk around the store, grabbing chips, and donuts, and bottles of water. I hadn't realized until now that we'd forgotten to bring snacks for the road. I guess none of us thought of it. You bring snacks on a road trip to go somewhere fun, not when you're going to visit your mom in a detention center upstate.

The second half of the way feels a little quicker. It's almost one o'clock by the time we see a sign on the side of the road announcing we've made it to Buffalo, and we're all exhausted from the drive.

When we see the detention center ahead, however, I straighten my back in my seat. I take a deep breath and run a hand through my hair. We need to look as nice as possible for Ma.

Uncle Jorge finds a parking spot and turns off the engine. As he unbuckles his seatbelt, he turns to look at me, and then at Sophie.

"You okay?"

Neither of us answers. When the lingering silence in the car starts to suffocate us, I push the passenger door open and step out. Jorge and Sophie join me a second later, and we walk side by side toward the entrance of the building.

My hand finds Sophie's, and I squeeze hard. She might think I'm comforting her, but it's really the other way around. I need to hold her hand to make sure I won't trip, to keep myself putting one foot in front of the other even though my legs are shaking so bad that I fear they might give out under my weight at any second.

★ ★ ★

Everything that happens next feels like a blur. Maybe it's the lack of sleep, or the long drive, or the anxiety swelling up in my chest, but I can barely keep track of what's going on. One second we're walking through the front doors of the building, and the next we're putting all our belongings back in our pockets after walking through metal detectors. I'm vaguely aware of following a group of people down a long hallway, and then, all of a sudden, I find myself sitting in a room next to Sophie and Uncle Jorge, but I can't even remember walking in here.

Looking around, I see that we're most definitely not alone. The room is large, with many rectangular tables just like ours, and the nervous chatter of dozens of people fills the air around us.

A loud buzzing sound comes from somewhere overhead, and women begin walking in, one by one. When Ma appears, it takes me a second to realize it's her. She looks different, but not necessarily in the ways that I would've expected. I thought she would look tired, or frightened, or underfed, but no. She looks calm, dignified. She walks with her back straight and her face serious. That's what it must be—she looks robotic somehow. There's no light in her eyes, no trace of a smile on her lips.

The second she sees us, all of that changes. Even from far away, I notice how her chest deflates as she lets out her breath. I can tell her legs have started shaking, and that it's taking all of her effort to stop herself from running toward us.

"Mijos," she says, wrapping both Sophie and me in an embrace. I smell her hair, feel the pressure of her hands on my back, and suddenly, everything is okay. My sister and I are exactly where we need to be. But then we hear a guard clearing his throat behind us, and we have to break away from her.

"How are you feeling, Ma?" Sophie asks before we've even taken our seats. Ma and Sophie sit on one side of the table, and Jorge and I take the chairs facing them.

"I'm okay, mi nena," Ma answers. "Just hanging in there."

She has never been the type of mom who wears a lot of makeup or cares much about her appearance, but sitting here with her hair dirty and her skin dry, she looks so different from the person I see in my mind when I think of her.

"What's it like here?" I ask, looking over my shoulder. For a so-called detention facility, this place looks and feels a lot like a prison.

"It's..." Ma begins, but she doesn't finish. "I just hope to be out of here soon."

"What have they told you?" I ask, at the same time that Sophie says, "Are you coming home?"

"I want to hear about you," Ma answers, ignoring our questions, because this is what she always does. She doesn't like to talk about sad or difficult stuff. She likes to focus on the good things.

"How is staying at Uncle Jorge's?" she asks us. From her

tone, you would think that we're staying at our uncle's place for a long weekend. You'd think we're there on vacation.

"It's good," I answer, because I can't really tell her about the sleepless nights or Ellie's crying.

"Amy made fake tacos," Sophie says, and I turn sharply toward her. A part of me wants to laugh, but I'm too aware of the fact that Uncle Jorge is right here.

Ma does let out a small chuckle. "I'm sure they were great," she says, and she throws an apologetic look in Jorge's direction. From the corner of my eye, I see that his mouth is also twisted into a smile.

"We need to talk about your options," he says. "I spoke to the immigration lawyer earlier this week. He said that—"

"Jorge," Ma says under her breath, and she puts a hand on her stomach, where the scar from her surgery is.

"Are you okay?" I ask, leaning over the table. "Ma, does something hurt?"

"No, mijo," she says, shaking her head. "I'm okay. It's just...I don't want to talk about lawyers, and immigration, and all of that." She looks straight into Jorge's eyes. "Can't we talk about that on the phone tomorrow? I just...I want to be with my children right now."

Uncle Jorge gives a small nod. "Of course," he says. "We'll talk about it tomorrow."

Ma turns back toward Sophie and me. The light in her eyes

returns, and all of a sudden she looks a lot more like herself. "How is school going?"

Sophie and I tell her it's going well, even though we both know we've been slacking. With everything that's happened, homework, projects, and exams have been the last things on my mind.

"Good," Ma says. "Maybe when school is out, Uncle Jorge can take you to the beach."

Something deep inside of me hurts when I remember those summers, what feels like so long ago, when we would set up an umbrella on the beach, and Sophie and I would run around in the sand, while Ma soaked her feet in the water, and Pa tried to read the newspaper even though the pages kept blowing in the wind.

"We'll all go," I say to Ma. "When all of this is over, we'll go to the beach together."

For a second, Ma looks sad. She looks down, and I'm scared she might start crying. But then she lifts her gaze, and with a calm expression on her face, she looks at me and says, "So tell me, have you been watching *Pasiones*?"

MONDAY MORNING AT SCHOOL IS THE WORST. I can't stop thinking about Ma, can't stop wishing that we hadn't had to say
goodbye to her, that we could have her near, that we could
see her again soon.

I'm walking quickly to get to English literature, my mind
filled with images from our visit, when all of a sudden, I hear
a voice calling my name.

"Mateo?"

I turn around to find Miss Callahan, my college advisor,
sticking her head out from the doorway of her office. Her hair
looks shorter than it did last time I met with her, and there's
also something different in her eyes—something that tells me
I might be in trouble.

"Do you have a few minutes?" she asks me.

"I, uh—I have to get to class."

"You can go in a few minutes late. Don't worry, I'll write you a note."

I wish I could make up another excuse, but then, when Miss Callahan raises her eyebrows at me, I have no choice but to step into her office.

"Sit down," she says. It's also in her voice—that thing that tells me I'm not here for a good reason. When she takes a seat in front of me, though, her eyes soften, and she stares at me through her thick glasses with the same eagerness as always. Miss Callahan is one of the few people at school who cares. While all the other teachers just show up to talk about math, or science, or English, she shows up because she genuinely wants to help—or at least that's how she's always made me feel.

"It's come to my attention that you haven't been going to SAT prep lately."

My stomach drops. Since Ma and Pa were detained, I haven't even stopped to think about that. During the first week, my top priority was getting myself over to Maria's right after school to pick up Sophie. And now that we've moved in with Jorge, I've been heading straight to the bodega, trying my best to keep the business running.

"I . . . I've just been busy. You know, with homework and stuff."

Miss Callahan leans her head slightly to one side. "Is that true?" she asks. "Because I've also heard that your grades are slipping."

I look down at my hands, not saying anything.

"What's going on, Mateo? Only a few months ago, you were here asking me what SAT scores you needed to get into NYU, and you were so excited about Tisch and about a career in theater."

"I still want those things," I answer slowly. "I just—"

"Then you need to keep your grades up. You have to go to SAT prep. Mateo, you know I helped you get a spot in that course because I believe in you."

I look away from her eyes and stare at the posters on the wall instead. The school offers special help for students who need it, which means that Ma and Pa had to pay close to nothing for my SAT prep course. All I had to do was show up, study hard, stay focused, but now I don't think I can do it anymore.

"I just . . . I think I'm gonna take the SAT in the fall instead."

"You'd said you wanted to take it this spring."

"I changed my mind."

The corner of Miss Callahan's mouth twists downward, but she doesn't argue.

"Can I get that note from you?" I ask. "To get into class late?"

Miss Callahan blinks slowly. Something tells me that she hasn't given up—that before I know it, she'll be calling me back into her office, but at least she seems to think that there's nothing left to say for today. Readjusting her glasses with one hand, she reaches for a blank piece of paper with the other and starts writing.

As soon as I take a seat in the English lit classroom, I start asking myself if I'm being stupid—if I should go back to apologize, to tell Miss Callahan that I still want to get into Tisch and that I'll keep going to SAT prep. The thing is, as much as I want to, I don't think I would mean it—not with everything else that's going on.

At the very least, I tell myself, I'll have to focus on my grades. I may be able to take the SAT later than I had planned, but I won't be able to fix my GPA if I mess it up now. All these years of working hard, of taking such careful notes, of obsessing over my grades could be for nothing if I keep slacking.

And so, when I get back to Uncle Jorge's after my shift at the bodega, I open my chemistry textbook. I have a quiz next week that I need to prepare for, but I've barely started solving practice problems when Jorge walks in with a smile on his face.

"I just talked to your dad," he says, and I jump up from my chair.

"What did he say? Is he coming home?"

"Well . . . no. But we can go see him tomorrow."

Just like that, chemistry and my quiz are the last things on my mind again. I focus all of my energy on getting through the next twenty-four hours, on the idea of seeing Pa, telling myself that after our visit, when we've hugged him and talked to him again, maybe I'll feel a little more motivated to focus on school.

★ ★ ★

The following day, I sneak out of school early, go to pick Sophie up, and head back to the apartment to find Jorge ready and waiting for us to hit the road.

The drive to the jail where Pa is being held is both the same and different from our trip to see Ma. It's the same because there's also heavy silence in the car, because I feel the exact same way as I did before seeing my mom. It's different because it's shorter, despite all the traffic getting into the Holland Tunnel.

In the back of my mind, I'd been expecting the Hudson County jail to look like the detention center in Buffalo, but it's nothing like it. This place is dark, with small windows and narrow hallways that make me feel claustrophobic the second we walk in. The visiting room is also different. This one is long, and there are a couple dozen small booths. A glass wall divides our side and the prisoners' side, and there are phones in each booth.

This is the sort of room where you would visit a murderer or a drug dealer, and as I take small steps toward the booth where Pa is sitting, I feel anger swelling up inside me—anger at the fact that Pa ended up here, when all he ever did was work hard and look after our family.

There are only two chairs in each booth, so Jorge and I sit

down, and Sophie stands in the small gap between us. I pick up the phone first.

"Hola, Pa."

"Hola, mijo." He sounds tired, defeated. "How are you?" he asks, his eyes traveling to Sophie.

"We're good, Pa. And you?"

For a second, he doesn't answer. I'm reminded of the night after the ICE agents showed up at the bodega for the first time and how Pa's silence just felt so wrong. This time, it's much, much worse. His silence means he can't even find the strength to comfort us. It means he's losing hope.

"My master calendar hearing is next week," he says.

"Papi, I want to talk to you, too," Sophie interrupts in that moment, pressing her hand against the glass.

"Wait a second, Sophie," I say, holding the phone tighter against my ear. "Pa, what does that mean?"

"I'm gonna go in front of an immigration judge. I—I decided I'm gonna ask for relief. I'm gonna ask the judge to let me stay in the US. I'm going to trust the system."

"That's good," I say. "Just remind the judge that you've been here all this time. Tell him about Sophie and me. No one in their right mind would ask you to leave the country if they understood who you are."

"*Papi,*" Sophie says.

"Fine, you talk to him now," I say, handing her the phone.

While Sophie and Pa talk, his face changes. He smiles, which makes the wrinkles around his eyes look a little deeper. I wish this window wasn't in the way. I wish he were able to give us a hug, if not for me, then for Sophie's sake.

When they're finally done, it's Uncle Jorge's turn to pick up the receiver. At first, I don't even pay attention to what they're saying. I tune out, thinking about the way the air in our booth has become serious all of a sudden. But then I realize I can hear what's coming through the phone. Even though Uncle Jorge has the receiver pressed against his ear, I can still make out bits of what my dad is saying.

"—barely been sleeping. There are just too many things that I—"

The room gets louder every now and then, with two dozen families having conversations with their loved ones. I lose track of what Pa is saying, but I quickly realize that it helps if I stare at his lips while I listen to the murmur coming from the phone.

"—be able to stay. And I've been going over it in my mind again and again, trying to imagine what might happen if things don't go the way we expect them to."

"What do you mean?" Uncle Jorge asks beside me.

"Mateo and Sophie," Pa answers. "What will they do if me and Adela end up getting deported?"

Uncle Jorge clears his throat. "Amy and I will do everything we can."

"We shouldn't talk about this anymore. Not here."

They must be aware that I can hear everything Pa is saying. And if I can hear, that means Sophie probably can as well. I turn toward her, but she's just standing there waiting, with her face a little too close to the glass.

"Keep my children safe, Jorge," Pa says after a moment of silence. "Please, just keep them safe."

Uncle Jorge looks right into Pa's eyes. "I will," he answers. "Te lo prometo."

Pa nods once, but his expression falls. Seeing him like this, with tears building up in his eyes, I can't help myself—I blurt out all the things I've been trying to hold in.

"If you get out of here, we're gonna go to the beach." It doesn't matter that Jorge is still holding the phone. I know Pa can hear me. "We talked about it with Ma. If both of you come back home, we can all go to Coney Island, and everything will just go back to the way it used to be."

Pa swallows hard, somehow managing to make the tears in his eyes disappear. "Sounds good, mijo."

But for the rest of our visit, the image of Pa with teary eyes is all I can see. And no matter how many times I force myself to blink, I can't make it go away.

13

On the day of Pa's master calendar hearing, I skip my shift at the bodega. Even the guilt I feel about leaving Erika to manage the store on her own isn't heavier than my anxiety to know what happened at the hearing, so I head straight to the apartment after school and sit with Amy and Sophie at the kitchen table while we wait for news.

"Anything?" Jorge asks when he gets home from work, but we all shake our heads. Even though we've been waiting for hours, the phone still hasn't rung.

When Pa's call finally comes, we all give small jumps in our chairs. He tells us that the hearing didn't go as he expected. It lasted less than ten minutes, the judge barely even looked at him, and the only thing that came out of it was that another hearing was scheduled for the Thursday before Memorial Day weekend, which is only three weeks from now.

"It's called an individual merits hearing," he says.

"What does that mean?"

"ICE will list out all the reasons why I should be deported… and my lawyer and I will have to tell the judge all the reasons why I shouldn't."

"So, what—it comes down to your word against ICE's?"

"In a way, yes," he says. "But I've been talking to the lawyer. We're going to put up a fight. It's not over yet, mijo. We can bring witnesses, and…and I was hoping you would come testify."

"Me?" I'm all too aware that he's on speakerphone. Sophie, Jorge, and Amy are all looking at me, and I wish I could hide away. I don't want this responsibility—I don't want my words to be a deciding factor in whether my father will be allowed to stay in the country or not.

"The lawyer thinks Sophie's too young to come to the hearing. So it has to be you, mijo."

"Okay," I say, nodding my head slowly. "I'll come."

All of a sudden, I'm glad to be busy with school. Not wanting to sit around thinking about what's gonna happen at the hearing, I push myself even harder to focus. I start making lists, the way I used to. I spend every free second of my time studying, trying to memorize all the things I didn't bother to learn in the past several weeks.

Even though Kimmie won't stop insisting that I should join her and Darryl for lunch, I almost never do. I keep telling her that I need to go to the study room, that I have work to catch up on, and even though it's true, I'm not sure she believes me.

"There you are," Kimmie says when I run into them in the hallway on a Tuesday. "I feel like I haven't seen you in forever."

"It's only been a few days," I say, sneaking a quick glance at Darryl. He's smiling at me, but I can't help thinking about what he said last time we talked—how Kimmie's been upset because I'm acting weird.

"You could take a break every now and then, you know?" she says, but I don't really listen.

Every night after dinner, I stay up for hours, forcing myself to do more work. Studying at Jorge and Amy's isn't easy, though. It's not like in our old apartment, where I had a desk and a bedroom door that I could close. Here, I have no choice but to study at the kitchen table. And when everyone's gone to sleep and I'm still up, going through endless textbooks and notes, all I can think about is that the door of Amy and Jorge's room won't close because the crib takes up too much space. I wonder if they're lying in bed, wide awake and upset because the light from the kitchen is filtering into their bedroom.

The same worries I've had since day one have not left my mind. I still worry that Sophie and I are bothering them, disrupting their routine. I worry that Jorge and Amy are going to get tired of having us here, and that if my parents' hearings don't go well, Sophie and I will have nowhere else to go.

★ ★ ★

I come back from my shift at the bodega on Thursday to find a weird scene inside the apartment. Sophie and Amy are sitting at the dinner table, while Jorge leans against a wall with his arms crossed. There's an untouched plate of cookies and a full glass of milk in front of my sister, and it looks like she's been crying.

The second I walk in, they all turn to look at me, but no one says anything.

"What's going on here?" I ask, closing the front door softly.

Uncle Jorge walks up to me. "She won't tell us. She came home from school in tears, but she doesn't want to talk about what happened."

I remove my bag from my shoulders and leave it by the door, and then I take a few slow steps toward my sister.

I sit down at the table beside her and reach for her hand. "Sophie?" I say. "Do you want to tell me what happened?"

She shakes her head.

"How about if we go over there?" I nod my head in the direction of the living room. "We can talk, just the two of us. Would that be better?"

Sophie hesitates for a second, but then she nods. I help her out of her chair and lead the way to the far corner of the living room. We sit down on the couch side by side, while Jorge and Amy pretend to be busy in the kitchen.

"Well?" I ask. "What's wrong?"

Sophie takes a deep breath. Her chest shakes a little as she says, "Kelly O'Brien called us *dirty*."

"Us?"

"You, me, Ma, and Pa."

"Wait a second. Start from the beginning. Why did she say that?" I've heard Kelly's name before. Even though I have never met her, I've never really liked the sound of her. She's the girl who tried to convince Sophie and Leslie to pull the fire alarm at school last year. I don't understand why Sophie insists on beings friends with her—or, actually, I do. Sophie just likes to be friends with everyone.

"She asked me what I'm gonna do for Memorial Day weekend, and I said I wasn't sure, because we're going to spend it with our uncle and his wife instead of our parents. And then she asked where Ma and Pa are."

My stomach drops. "What did you tell her?"

Sophie's chest starts shaking again, and a single tear comes rolling down her cheek. "That Ma and Pa were taken away by those ICE people. That they might have to go back to Mexico."

"And what did Kelly say?" I ask, even though I already know the answer.

"She said people like Ma and Pa shouldn't be allowed to

stay in the US because they don't belong here. She said Mexicans are dirty."

"Sophie." I sigh. A part of me wants to ask my sister what made her tell Kelly the truth about Ma and Pa, but deep down, I can't help but feel as though this is my own fault. Maybe I should've had a talk with her sooner. I should've told Sophie that, even though Leslie's family and our parents' friends now know about what happened, it doesn't mean we should tell everyone else. I should've explained to her that there are people out there who might say bad things, mean things, but that she shouldn't listen to them.

I'm trying to think of something to say—something that will make my sister feel better—but I'm having a hard time coming up with anything. There's anger boiling inside my chest—anger at Kelly, and at her parents, who surely say these things at home when no one else is around. Anger at the fact that even with all that's happening, even after our family's been torn apart, there are people who would rather see my parents on a plane back to Mexico than at home with their children.

Suddenly, I realize that Amy is standing in front of us. I look up at her, but she isn't staring at me. She's looking down at Sophie, and there's a deep frown on her face.

"That's not true," Amy says. She kneels in front of the couch and holds both of Sophie's hands in hers. "You do know that, don't you, sweetheart?"

Sophie doesn't say anything at all. She remains motionless, staring back at Amy.

"Sophie," Amy says. "I need you to listen to me very carefully. *What that girl said is not true.*" In that moment, the air in the apartment becomes still. It's as if all of us—Sophie, Jorge, me, and even Ellie—are holding our breath, listening to Amy.

"There will always be people who think someone is worth less than they are because of what they look like or where they're from. But just because there are people who believe these things, it doesn't make any of it true. Do you understand that?"

Slowly, Sophie gives a small nod.

"Your parents are good people, and they don't deserve what's happening to them. And, honey, you can't forget that your worth isn't based on what some silly girl at school says. Your worth is in here." She points a finger at Sophie's heart. "Can you promise you won't forget that?"

Again, Sophie nods.

"Good." Amy gets up from her knees. "Now come. Let's eat those cookies. We can't just leave them out."

Sophie follows Amy back toward the dinner table, and while she starts eating the cookies, I'm left sitting on the couch feeling a little shocked.

I don't know how Amy found the strength to step up when neither Jorge nor I knew what to say. I had no idea she respected my parents so much, that she cared about Sophie this deeply.

I'm not sure if something inside of her has changed, because the Amy we used to know would've never done or said anything like this. Or maybe we'd just never given her a fair chance—maybe Ma and Pa were always a little bitter toward her just because Jorge started spending less time with us once he started seeing Amy. Either way, it doesn't really matter. As I watch her eating cookies with my sister, getting Sophie to smile and laugh even after what happened today, it's as if I'm seeing Amy for the very first time.

★ ★ ★

After spending my lunch hour in the study room for two weeks straight, a part of me is starting to believe that I might just manage to make it through the end of the school year without failing any of my courses.

On a Friday in mid-May, I'm deep in concentration, headphones on and books spread out on the table in front of me, when I start to feel as though someone is watching me. Lifting my gaze, I see a pair of eyes looking through the glass on the door of the study room. A second later, the door swings open, and Kimmie walks in.

She comes up to the table where I'm sitting and puts a brown bag in front of me. "I brought you fries."

I peek inside the bag. It's only half-full, and the fries look kinda cold.

"Fine, they're leftover fries," Kimmie adds quickly. "But still—I thought you might be hungry."

"Thanks," I say. As she pushes a chair back to take a seat in front of me, I notice she's wearing bright pink Nikes. I've never seen her in these shoes before, but they look pretty worn. If I were in a better mood, I would ask her where she got them, and she'd probably tell me about this new thrift shop she found and how we should make plans to go over the weekend, but I don't say anything at all.

"How's the schoolwork coming along?" asks Kimmie, looking at the books spread all over the table.

"It's good." I shut my chemistry textbook, and the loud sound it makes earns me a few annoyed stares from people sitting nearby.

Kimmie nods slowly. "Have you talked to Adam lately?"

"I haven't really seen him since he started rehearsals. I just—"

"I haven't seen him much, either," she says. "But I still think you should reach out to him...you know, whenever you're ready."

When I don't answer, she leans over the table, so that her face is closer to me. "I miss you, Matt," she says. "Everything's just so...*boring* without you."

"I thought you were busy with Darryl, and the band, and everything."

"I mean, yeah," she says, and she can't keep herself from

smiling. "But with you spending lunch hour here and Adam off at rehearsals, I feel…weird. The guys in the band are nice, but it's not the same. There are things I just can't talk about with anyone but you." Kimmie looks over both her shoulders, making sure no one is listening in, and then she whispers, *"We did it."*

"What are you talking about?"

"It. Darryl and I did it."

"Oh." Whenever we get drunk, we always end up asking ourselves the same question: Out of Kimmie, Adam, and me, who's gonna be the first to lose their virginity? I always knew it wasn't gonna be me, even though I hoped it would be. *"Oh. And how was it?"*

"Amaaaazing," she says. "I went over to his place after school yesterday, and his parents weren't home, so…"

"Did you use protection?"

"Of course," she says.

"That's good," I reply. "I'm happy if you're happy."

"I am. *So* happy," she says. "But again—I miss you. And Adam's been stressing so much. Between finals coming up, and the play, and you not talking to him, he's barely been himself lately. He needs you to be there for him."

I wish I could tell her that I am—that no matter what happens, I'll always be here for the two of them. But what I really, truly wish I could say is that I've also barely felt like myself lately. I want to tell Kimmie that I need her and Adam more than they could ever need me, especially now that Pa's hearing is getting closer.

"I'm sorry," I say, and I really mean it. "I'm sorry I've been acting so shitty lately. I'm just so—"

"You don't have to explain. I know you've been focusing on school and everything, but . . . don't forget that we need you."

I bite my lip. "Memorial Day is coming up."

Kimmie's face lights up. We've had a tradition since freshman year—on the Friday of Memorial Day weekend, we pick an area of the city to go out in, and we try to find a bar that won't card us.

"Why don't we go out? You, me, Adam, and Darryl?"

"Let's do it," Kimmie says. She straightens her back, shifting her position in her chair, and suddenly she looks much more relaxed. "We probably shouldn't go back to Chelsea, though." She makes a face, and I can't help but laugh. Last year, we got kicked out of not one, and not two, but three bars for being underage.

"Why don't we go to Hell's Kitchen or something?"

"Done," she says. "I'll let Adam and Darryl know."

She smiles at me. I return the smile, and just for a second, I feel a little more like myself. In the back of my mind, I think about the fact that by Friday, my dad's future will have been decided, and if we're lucky, at least part of this nightmare will be behind us.

★ ★ ★

When I walk into Jorge and Amy's apartment later in the day, Sophie is waiting for me by the door.

"Pa called," she says as soon as she sees me. "You just missed him."

"What did he say?" I ask. I can't help the way my heart starts pounding, preparing for bad news.

Amy turns toward me. She's sitting on the couch, cradling the baby. Lately, she doesn't seem to want to put Ellie down for more than a few minutes at a time, and I think I know why—she's supposed to be going back to work at the art gallery soon. "Just that he's been preparing for his hearing next week," she says. "And the lawyer is coming over tomorrow, so you can also get ready for speaking in front of the judge."

A nasty feeling starts swirling in my stomach, threatening to shoot up my throat. "That's good," I say, trying not to show Sophie how scared I am. "I'll need all the help I can get."

I take my backpack off my shoulders and set some of my books down on the kitchen table. I start doing homework, and after a while, Sophie and Amy join me.

"Hmm, that's not quite right," Amy says softly to my sister. "Come on, let's try counting with our fingers. One, two, three..."

Watching Amy help Sophie with her homework makes me feel all kinds of things. I'm relieved, because not having to do this myself means I get to focus on my own stuff. It also warms my heart a little to hear the way they speak gently to each other, as if they're trying hard to figure out what tone of voice is the most appropriate to use. Mostly, though, it makes me a bit sad, because this is exactly what Ma used to do, and the fact that Amy has had to step into her shoes is just a reminder that she's been taken away.

When the clock on the wall marks four thirty, I know it's time to head to the bodega. I don't want to be late, especially not now that I've been working shorter hours and Nelly and Erika have been doing so much of the work by themselves.

"I'll be back for dinner," I say to Amy and Sophie.

"Have a good shift," Amy says in the same gentle tone she's been using with my sister.

I stop with my hand on the door. I wish I could thank her, or say something about everything she's been doing for my sister lately. I meet Amy's eyes and open my mouth to speak, but in the end I just walk out of the apartment without saying anything.

14

THE IMMIGRATION LAWYER THAT UNCLE JORGE FOUND for Ma and Pa is a skinny man with graying hair. Having never met my own grandfathers, he looks to me like a stereotypical grandpa in the making: round glasses, hunched shoulders, wrinkles around his eyes. He has a low, soothing voice and a warm smile, and when he sits down next to me on the living room couch, the air around us shifts. There is a calm quality about him that I can't really explain.

A part of me is grateful to him for taking my parents' cases. I know he's working pro bono, so he's not making a penny out of this, but I also kinda hoped that he would be a bit more energetic. When I think of who I'd want to defend my parents in court, I like to imagine a lion—someone who's going to fight for them to the death. Whether Mr. Wilkins will fight to the death, well...that's to be determined.

"Your dad is lucky that his hearing was scheduled so soon," he says to me. "Sometimes these things can take months."

Lucky is one way to put it, I think to myself. Potentially getting kicked out of the country sooner rather than later isn't exactly my idea of luck.

"Why is it happening so fast? And why is my mom's process happening so slowly? She hasn't even been in front of a judge yet."

"All cases are different," Mr. Wilkins says. "Your mother must've not mentioned this to you yet, but our request for a bond hearing went through."

I straighten my back in my seat. "When is it?"

"Next Friday."

"You mean the day after my dad's hearing?"

Mr. Wilkins nods.

"So she has a little under a week to prepare."

"There's a different lawyer from my firm who'll be taking the lead on your mom's case. He'll make sure she has everything she needs, but for now, you and I need to focus on your dad's merits hearing."

I nod once. "Let's get to it, then. What do I need to do?"

I'm hoping Mr. Wilkins will hand over all the answers to me. I'm hoping he will tell me exactly what to do, and what to say, and what types of things will sway the judge's opinion so she'll allow my dad to stay in the country. But instead, he asks me a question.

"Why is it important for you to have your dad remain in the United States?"

"Excuse me?"

"Why should he be allowed to stay?"

"Because...he's my *dad*! How can you even expect me to—"

"Now, don't get mad at me," Mr. Wilkins interrupts me calmly. "Because these are precisely the types of questions that you might have to answer in front of the judge. And you need to be ready."

I take slow breaths, trying to think of a good enough answer.

"I guess I...I need my dad to stay because of my sister. She needs him—we both do, and I can't raise her on my own."

I can tell that Mr. Wilkins isn't satisfied. Truth be told, I'm not satisfied with myself, either. Why is it that I'm having such a hard time coming up with something? Deep down, I know the answer to his questions. I can *feel* it—I feel the need to have Pa here, but I just don't know how to put my feelings into words. I have no way of speaking up about all this longing, this anger, this sadness in a way that will make sense to someone else. I have no way to make other people see the hole that my parents left in our lives when they were detained.

Mr. Wilkins asks me a few follow-up questions, tries to get to the bottom of my emotions so I'll be able to express them in front of the judge, but we don't have much success.

The longer we sit here, the more anxious I get. Every time I think about being in a courtroom, I start to feel nauseous. Once or twice, my stomach twists, and I almost get up to run to the bathroom, thinking I'm gonna throw up.

I don't know how I'm going to do this. I don't know how I'm gonna be able to convince the judge that my dad deserves to stay in America when lately, I haven't been feeling American myself, when I've been thinking about everything that separates me from Kimmie and Adam, when I've spent the last six weeks feeling like an outsider.

In the end, there's not much left for me to say but, "Can you promise me something?"

Mr. Wilkins raises his eyebrows, listening intently.

"Will you promise that you will do everything you can to help my parents stay in the country? That you'll fight for them as hard as you can?"

Mr. Wilkins is silent for a second. He remains still, looking down at the floor, but then he turns toward me and stares at me without blinking. It isn't until that moment that I notice how blue his eyes are, how deep they seem. "Mateo," he says, and I feel a chill running down my spine because Ma and Pa always call me that. "I promise that I will do everything in my power to keep your mom and dad in the United States. I'll fight as hard as I can. *As hard as I can.*"

I nod slowly. This has to be enough for me. Even if I'm not one hundred percent sure I believe him, I have to hold on to his promise with all my strength.

★ ★ ★

Over the next couple of days, the air at Uncle Jorge's seems to shift, and the baby starts crying at night again. It's as if she knows that something is wrong—as if she's also anxiously counting down the seconds until Pa's hearing.

Wednesday at school feels weird. I can't shake off a feeling that everything is about to change—summer is right around the corner. We're about to be done with junior year, Adam is going to make his off-Broadway debut in July, and Pa's destiny will be decided within twenty-four hours.

"Is Friday still happening?" Kimmie asks me when I run into her in the hallway.

"Yeah," I say. "Of course it is." No matter what happens at the hearing, I know it's a good idea to have plans for Friday. If the judge decides to let Pa stay in the US, I'll definitely be in the mood to celebrate. And if it turns out that he has to go back to Mexico... well, it'll probably be good to keep busy. God knows I'll need my friends if that happens.

That night, Amy makes burgers for dinner, but she burns the buns when she's trying to heat them up, so in the end we're stuck with having only the patties and a side salad of lettuce and tomatoes.

Uncle Jorge looks serious. He shaved in advance of the hearing, and this is the first time I've seen him without a beard. He barely looks like himself, and the fact that he's frowning so deeply makes him look even less like the man I know. In the back of my mind, I feel like we're sitting next to a complete stranger.

Sophie tells us about her day at school while we eat, and how her teacher asked her class to make a drawing of their favorite moment of the school year. I'm not sure she understands how important tomorrow is. Or maybe she does, and she's only trying to make the air feel a little lighter.

Just as we're about to finish dinner, Ma calls my cell phone. At first, she sounds no different than the last time we spoke to her. I can tell she's worried, exhausted. But then, all of a sudden, she breaks down crying.

"I can't believe your dad's hearing is tomorrow. I wish I could be there," she mumbles. "You all shouldn't have to go through this alone. I want to be there for you."

"Ma . . . we understand. It's okay that you can't be here."

"But I *should* be."

"You can't be hard on yourself right now, Ma. You need to stay as strong as you can. Sé fuerte y sé valiente," I say. A part of me can't believe I'm the one comforting her, when it's always been the other way around. She's always been the shoulder we cry on, the first person Sophie and I run to when we're in trouble. "And we have Uncle Jorge. He's—"

A phone starts ringing somewhere in the apartment, and we all turn to look at each other. Amy takes a look down at her cell phone, but it's not the one that's ringing. Uncle Jorge feels the pockets of his pants, and when he comes up empty-handed, he runs to the living room to look for his phone.

He answers it as he's halfway back to the dinner table. "Hello?" At first, he looks a little confused, but then he lets out a small smile and says, *"Ernesto!"*

"What was that?" Ma asks. I can tell right away that she's stopped crying. "Did I hear your dad's name?"

"Sí, Ma," I say, my heart beating fast. "He's on the line with Uncle Jorge. Hold on, let me put you on speakerphone."

I lay my phone down on the table, and a second later, Jorge places his phone next to mine.

"Adela?" my dad asks.

"Ernesto?"

Suddenly, their voices are all we can hear. They're

speaking quickly, not even bothering to let the other finish their sentences.

"¿Cómo es el lugar a donde te mandaron?"

"Te he extrañado tanto, y—"

"—los niños. Me han dicho que—"

"—mañana. Tienes que tener fe, porque—"

I look down at my phone and Uncle Jorge's. My heart hurts when I think about the fact that this is the first time they've spoken to each other in nearly two months. It hurts a bit more when I remember that Ma is sitting somewhere inside that detention center in Buffalo, and Pa is in a dark jail. Even when it feels as if they've finally reunited, they still can't be together.

"Tengo miedo, Adela," Pa says at some point, and my mom chokes on her own words.

We've never heard Pa admit that he was scared. Even when times were tough—when we were running low on money, or before my mom's surgery—he had never spoken these words. He's always tried to stay strong, to be the rock we need whenever everything seems uncertain, so now that he's said it, none of us knows what to do. Should we comfort him? Should we tell him to be strong? Should we remind him we're here with him, and that he's not alone?

In the end, Ma is the one who speaks up. "Todos tenemos miedo," she tells him, and it's the truest thing she could've spoken. When I look around the kitchen table and meet

Sophie's and Jorge's eyes, I see it more clearly than ever—we're all scared.

"But you're gonna be okay, Papi," Sophie says suddenly. And in the second that follows, a lot of things happen. Pa sighs loudly into the phone. Ma goes awfully quiet. Amy relaxes her shoulders, and Uncle Jorge starts nodding to himself. Meanwhile, I become aware of something awakening deep inside of me. It starts as a small ray of hope, but it becomes bigger and brighter, until it starts to overpower the fear I had inside of me a minute ago.

"Everything's gonna be okay," my sister adds.

And so, during the last few minutes that we're ever going to share together as a family before Pa's future is decided, we all choose to believe that Sophie's instinct is right. We choose to hold on to what little hope we have left, and to the thought that maybe—just maybe—by this time tomorrow we'll be sitting here again, and Pa is going to be sitting right next to us.

★ ★ ★

That night, Sophie and I watch *Pasiones* in the living room with the volume turned down really low. This is the way we've had to watch it lately, because Jorge, Amy, and Ellie usually go to bed early. At times, when something unexpected happens and Sophie and I let out loud gasps, I worry that Uncle Jorge will come out of his bedroom and tell us to keep quiet, but that hasn't happened yet.

After the episode is over, I decide to go straight to bed. I know I should stay up studying for a trig test I have on Friday, but I don't think it would make much of a difference anyway. I'm too distracted to memorize formulas and solve practice problems at this point, so I hope that whatever I studied earlier in the week will be enough.

Only a few minutes after Sophie and I turn off the lights, however, I begin to wonder if trying to sleep was a good idea after all. Now that the ray of hope I felt earlier is all gone, the fear has come back, and it's darker and heavier than before.

I don't know how long I've been lying here—a couple of hours, at least—when I realize I can't do this any longer. I throw the covers off me, and being careful not to wake Sophie, I get up from bed and sneak out of the room.

I tiptoe my way down the hallway, thinking I'll grab a glass of water from the kitchen. I'm nearly there when, all of a sudden, I hear someone moving nearby.

"Is someone there?" I ask into the darkness of the apartment.

"Matt?" Jorge's voice answers. Blinking a few times, I make out the shape of him sitting on a stool at the kitchen counter. "What are you doing up?"

"I couldn't sleep," I say. "You?"

"Me neither."

I pull back the second stool and sit next to him. "What do you think is going to happen at my dad's hearing tomorrow?"

It takes him a few seconds to answer. "I'm not sure," he says. "But I do know Mr. Wilkins is the best lawyer I could find. And you and I will both be there to try and convince the judge to let your dad stay."

"What if it doesn't work?" I ask. "What if the judge orders Pa to go back to Mexico?"

"We're going to do everything we can to—"

"I know," I interrupt him. "But *what if*?"

Jorge sighs. "I don't know."

"What would Sophie and I even do? I mean, if both of our parents were gone, we'd have nowhere to go. We all know she and I can't live with you forever."

Uncle Jorge turns toward me. Even though I can't make out his face in the dark, I imagine he's frowning. "I promised your dad that Amy and I would take care of you no matter what."

I open my mouth to say something, but then I close it again. I just don't think Jorge knew exactly what he was signing up for when he made that promise. I don't think he imagined Ma and Pa would actually get deported, or that he ever pictured Sophie and me living in this tiny apartment permanently. He might've not even thought about the fact that he and Amy would have to raise Sophie themselves if my parents were deported.

"Your dad saved me, you know that?" he says slowly. "If it wasn't for him, I'd probably be in jail by now. Or worse."

I don't say anything. Jorge has never talked to me about his gang years, and I've never felt the need to ask.

"I don't know what your dad saw in me—why he went out of his way to make sure I stayed out of trouble. I don't know why he cared, cause no one else did. But if he hadn't, my life wouldn't have turned out this way. I'd have none of what I have today. In a way, your ma and pa are my parents, too." He turns away from me slightly, so that all I can see is the side of his face silhouetted against the light outside the windows. "I have this instinct deep inside me to go to your dad for help, to ask him what to do, and this time he can't give me the answers."

I catch a gleam in his eye as he turns back toward me. Jorge has never found it easy to talk about his feelings, but all of a sudden I can see all the things he's struggling to say—that he, too, feels lost, that he's not sure he'll be able to keep the promises he made to Ma and Pa, that he's terrified of what will happen if they're not allowed to come home.

I'm not sure how to respond to that. I don't think there's anything I could say that would make Jorge feel any better, so we remain silent for what feels like a long time, breathing quietly in the darkness.

"I never thought this was gonna happen to us," I say. "Even

though we'd always had this fear in the back of our minds, I didn't think it was actually going to come true. Deportation always seemed like something that happened to other people...not us."

"No one ever likes to think that it's gonna happen to them."

Suddenly, I feel weak, powerless, which isn't exactly a new feeling. In the weeks since Ma and Pa were detained, I've thought a lot about the things I wish were different—and the things I wish I'd done differently. I wish I'd never taken my parents for granted, not even for a second. I wish I'd told Ma I loved her before leaving home on the day they were detained, and that I'd said the same thing to my dad before going to bed the previous night.

Even though I've thought about these things to the point that they're all I see in my dreams, there is one question I've tried hard not to think about—a question that I haven't been brave enough to ask out loud until now.

"Do you think we could've prevented this? Is there anything we could've done to keep my parents from being detained?"

"Mateo," Uncle Jorge says. "There's no point obsessing about these things."

I look down at my lap. Even though I can't even see my own hands, I start to fidget with them.

"*Mateo,*" my uncle says again. "We can't do this right now.

What we need to do is focus on tomorrow. We need to make sure we're at our best so we can help your dad."

I almost argue. I want to tell him that I need something to hold on to—an explanation for why this happened to us. But then I look at the time on the microwave and realize it's almost one in the morning.

"You're right," I say. "We should try to get some sleep."

Even though we both go back to bed, I feel less tired than I did before. While I lie next to Sophie, desperately wanting to get some rest, I wonder if Uncle Jorge is still up as well. I wonder if he's also tossing and turning, worrying about what's going to happen when morning comes.

And then I start thinking about Pa. I wonder if somewhere inside that jail, he's also lying awake, dreading the moment when he'll be standing in front of the judge, and thinking about how our entire lives could change in a matter of hours.

I HAD IMAGINED THAT PA'S HEARING WOULD happen in a grand courtroom, with tall ceilings and large windows, but this place is nothing like that. It's just a small room with wood paneling on the walls. There's a large desk, behind which the judge is sitting, and there are two tables facing her. My dad and Mr. Wilkins sit at the table on the right, and the ICE lawyer, a short man with a thick mustache, sits at the one on the left. Uncle Jorge and I are on a bench right behind Pa and Mr. Wilkins. It's lucky that the judge can't get a good enough view of us, because both of our legs are shaking pretty badly.

While the judge puts on her glasses, Pa turns around to look at me. We only stare into each other's eyes for a second before he turns back to face the front, but that second is enough to bring a sharp pain to my heart. All I want is to run to my dad and wrap my arms around him, but I force myself to remain still.

"Good morning to all," the judge says. She clicks on a recording device that is in front of her, and then she starts reading off a piece of paper. "I am Judge Olivia Meyer, sitting in an immigration court in New York, New York. These are removal proceedings in the matter of Ernesto Armando Garcia. The respondent is present in court along with his legal counsel. Mr. Samuel Gordon is appearing on behalf of the government and..."

Even though I try to pay attention to what she's saying, it's hard to keep track. She's speaking too quickly, and I'm not sure I even understand exactly what she's talking about. It isn't until Judge Meyer turns to look directly at Pa that I straighten my back and make sure not to miss a single word.

"Mr. Garcia, I will be asking you some questions now. Your legal counsel has stated that you do not need an interpreter. Is that correct?"

"Y-yes, Your Honor," Pa answers. I never really notice an accent when my parents speak English. To me, the way they speak sounds natural—it's the way they've always sounded. But now that he's in front of the judge, I feel my stomach drop a little. I worry about how heavy Pa's accent actually is.

I worry that it'll make the judge see him as foreign, that it'll make her automatically assume that he doesn't belong here.

"Please state your full name," the judge says.

"Ernesto Armando Garcia, Your Honor."

"What is your country of birth?"

"Mexico, Your Honor."

"How old are you?"

"Forty-one years old, Your Honor."

"How old were you when you first came to the United States?"

"Seventeen years old, Your Honor."

"Have you been here ever since?"

"Yes, Your Honor."

I'm pretty sure he doesn't have to say "Your Honor" every single time he speaks to the judge, but still, he does it. It's just who Pa is. He'd be uncomfortable if he felt as though he was being disrespectful. The questions that follow are pretty standard—the judge asks what his address is, whether he's been working, how many years of education he's completed. And then she asks if he's legally married.

"No, Your Honor," Pa says. It takes me a second to remember the time my parents explained to me that a priest at the Church of Nuestra Señora de Guadalupe unofficially married them, but they never signed legal documents. They were too scared to go to city hall, so they decided to have only a religious ceremony.

The judge then asks if he has children, and Pa starts talking about us. "I have two kids, Your Honor—a son, Mateo, who is here today, and a seven-year-old daughter."

When the judge is done asking Pa about me and Sophie, both Mr. Wilkins and the ICE lawyer take turns asking Pa questions. I notice the way he starts sweating as soon as Mr. Gordon begins to ask for more details about why he overstayed his tourist visa. He does his best to remain composed, and he manages to do it pretty well. He keeps his expression neutral, his tone always measured and polite, and I struggle a bit as I watch Pa turn into this artificial version of himself. I wish I could make them see the real him—the father that carries Sophie on his shoulders, the friend who's always there to give advice, the neighbor that's always willing to help.

It feels as though one second I'm sitting here, watching Pa answer questions about why he deserves to stay in the US, and the next, everyone in the room is looking at me.

I blink, not really sure what's going on. Did they say my name? Am I supposed to go on the stand now? It seems unlikely to me that I would've missed something like that, but judging by the fact that even the lawyers and my dad have turned to face me, I'm guessing that's what's happening.

"Go on," Uncle Jorge whispers in my ear, giving me a small pat on the shoulder. "You can do this."

I get up from my chair and begin to take small steps closer to the judge. My legs feel like jelly. I'm afraid they're going to collapse under my weight any second, but they manage to carry me until I reach the judge's desk, and I take a seat right beside it.

As I lift my gaze to face the room, I start feeling sweaty. The fact that I'm wearing a suit doesn't help. I feel stifled, like I'm being choked. Pa took me to Canal Street a few years ago to buy this suit, just so I had something to wear to baptisms and first communions, but I've grown quite a bit since then, and now it's several sizes too small. I wish more than anything that I could at least loosen up a button, but I keep my hands firmly on my lap, waiting for the first question to come.

"Can you please state your full name for the court?" the judge asks me. I don't know if I'm only imagining it, but I'm pretty sure her voice sounds a bit softer now that she's talking to me and not my dad.

"Mateo Garcia."

"Please stand and raise your right hand."

I do as I'm told.

"Do you swear that the statement you are about to give is the truth, the whole truth, and nothing but the truth?"

"I do."

The judge nods once. "You may be seated." The second my butt touches the chair again, she asks me her first question. "How old are you?"

"I—I'm sixteen years old, Your Honor."

"And what is your relationship to Ernesto Garcia?"

I swallow back the knot that's growing in my throat. "He's my dad."

The first few questions are easy to answer—where was I born, where do I go to school. The judge then asks me where my mother is, and I have to explain to her that Ma has also been detained by ICE.

By the time Mr. Wilkins steps in front of me, I feel a little relieved. I find some comfort in his familiar blue eyes and soothing voice.

"Mateo," he says. "Tell me: Where have you been living since your parents were detained?"

"With a family friend." Mr. Wilkins specifically told me not to refer to Jorge as my uncle, since we're technically not related and all. "He's here today," I add, looking right at him. He's sitting still as a statue, but with every sentence I speak, he gives a small nod, as if encouraging me to go on.

"Can you explain the living situation?"

I look away from Uncle Jorge. I don't want to sound ungrateful that he took us in, but Mr. Wilkins said it was important for the judge to understand how we've been living.

"Jorge lives in a tiny apartment in the West Village. There are only two bedrooms, so Jorge, his wife, and baby have been sleeping in one bedroom, and my sister and I have been sharing the other."

"Five people living in two bedrooms," Mr. Wilkins says slowly, as if the judge couldn't do the math herself. "Would you say it would be possible to live this way in the longer term?"

Again, I make sure to avoid looking into Uncle Jorge's eyes. "No," I answer. "Especially not when the baby gets older."

"Do you have any other family in the United States?"

I clear my throat. "No, I don't."

"So if your parents were gone, and it became impossible to continue living with your family friend, what would you do?"

For the first time, I look directly at the ICE lawyer. I imagine that, to him, the answer to this question is pretty simple. In the back of his mind, he's probably thinking Sophie and I could go into the system. It probably doesn't seem like a big deal to him if Child Protective Services came and took us. But, staring at the ring on his left hand, I wonder if he has any children of his own. I wonder what he would think if his son or daughter were sitting right here where I am. Would he feel as comfortable with the idea of his own children being taken away from their parents?

"I don't know," I say. "We would have nowhere to go."

For a moment, Mr. Wilkins doesn't say anything. He stares at me, then at the judge, and then back at me. A second later, he launches into a million other questions, but there are no surprises, just as he promised. He asks only the things we practiced beforehand—what life at home is like, how loving Pa is with Sophie, the way he's always willing to help out anyone who needs him. Mr. Wilkins then asks whether I think Pa would be okay if he was sent back to Mexico.

"No," I answer. "Of course he wouldn't. He hasn't been there in over twenty years. That isn't his home anymore—New York is. We need him here. He needs to be at home, where he belongs."

"I have no further questions, Your Honor," Mr. Wilkins says, and then he turns around to go sit beside Pa.

"Mr. Gordon?" Judge Meyer says. "Do you wish to cross-examine the witness?"

"Yes, Your Honor."

The ICE lawyer pushes his chair back and stands up. He takes a few steps closer to me, and the sound of his shoes rings loudly against the walls of the courtroom.

"Mr. Garcia," he says to me, "what grade are you currently studying?"

I'm thrown off a little by his first question, but at least it's easier than I'd expected. "I'm a junior in high school. I'll be a senior in September."

"And what are your plans for after graduation?"

Again, I'm a little confused about why he wants to know this, but I answer anyway. "I want to go to college. I wanna get into Tisch Drama."

"So you're hoping to go off to college a year from now, give or take a few months?"

That's what I just said, I think. Instead, I say, "Yes."

"With that in mind, would you argue that your dad's potential deportation would severely alter your life? After all, you're planning to begin your adult life only a year from now."

"Objection, Your Honor," Mr. Wilkins says from his seat, but Judge Meyer lifts her hand up slightly, and then turns toward me to hear my answer.

"I never said I was planning to move away from home. Even if I were in college, I'd still need a place to live. I'd need my parents' help to pay for school."

"Would you say that having your father in the United States is the *only* determining factor in your ability to go to college? Would you argue that there are no affordable housing options in the greater New York City area? Or financial help available to students in your position?"

"This isn't about me," I say, fire rising in my chest. I do my best to keep it under control, but I'm having a hard time. My voice comes out a little louder than it did before. "Or not *only* about me, I should say. It's about my sister, Sophie. She's seven years old—she's so young, and so... *terrified* of what's happening. She cries herself to sleep almost every night, and it hasn't even been two months since our parents left home. How could she spend the rest of her life without them?"

I pause, not because I don't have anything left to say, but because the fire inside of me is burning so hot that I can barely breathe.

I look around the courtroom, trying to find a spot to fix my gaze on. I'm trying to calm myself down so I can keep speaking, and that's when I find Pa's eyes staring right at me.

It's as if the courtroom is completely empty except for the two of us. I stare at him, and he stares back, and we say a thousand things to each other without saying anything at all. He thanks me for being here, for fighting for him, for being strong even though this is one of the hardest things I've ever had to do. I say to him that I'm sorry he has to be here, that I'm trying my best for him, that I desperately hope this will be enough to save him.

"Your sister may not have chosen to be put in this situation," Mr. Gordon says slowly. "But your father did. He *chose* to come to this country illegally."

"I don't like that word, Mr. Gordon," I say, and the whole room goes quiet—quieter than quiet. It's as if everyone has stopped breathing. No one moves, no one blinks, no one says anything. Everyone is just staring at me, and suddenly I feel the need to speak up, to explain exactly what I mean, so that the judge won't think I'm being rude for no reason.

"When you talk about illegal immigrants, you see faceless people in your mind," I say, staring right at Mr. Gordon. "You see people with no hearts, with no voices. You see them as an evil force, which is just here to take something from you. But when I hear people talk about immigrants, I see my mom and dad. I see my neighbors and my parents' friends. I see people with stories, with difficult pasts and fears so big that they keep them up at night. I see people with dreams and hopes for a better life.

"My dad *can't* go back to Mexico. He can't abandon the life he's built over the past twenty years, or leave his family behind. We need him here. My mom, my sister, me—we all need him here. And it's not just us. It's also our community, our neighborhood. I mean...the women who work at the bodega—who else is gonna give them a job that allows them to switch their hours around so they can study for nursing school or take their kid to the doctor? Who else is gonna be there to give people discounts when he knows they're struggling with money? Or to help a teenager who needs someone to believe in him?" I look at Uncle Jorge and notice the way he's stopped blinking. "There are so many people who can't imagine life without him. He's part of this city, of this country. We're here talking about how my dad's deportation would affect Sophie and me...but at the end of the day, it's about so much more than just us. We all lose."

Mr. Gordon frowns. For a second, it looks like he's about to say something. I put a hand on my stomach, preparing for his retaliation, but then he clears his throat.

"No further questions, Your Honor."

Mr. Gordon goes back to his desk, and the judge straightens her glasses. "We are running out of time," she says. "We will reconvene tomorrow at ten AM. Court is adjourned."

She bangs her gavel against her desk, and I turn to look at Mr. Wilkins.

What does this mean? I try to ask him using only my eyes, and he gives me a small shrug in response. I know exactly what it means—that this is not yet over. That we won't find out what's going to happen to Pa today. That our nightmare has just been extended for one more day.

The second question I ask with my eyes is a little more difficult to communicate, but somehow, Mr. Wilkins seems to understand it. *Did I screw up? Did I ruin Pa's chances of staying in the country by going off like that?*

He gives me a small nod, which tells me that I did a good job—that I accomplished what I came here to do. And when his lips twist into the faintest of smiles, I feel a wave of relief spreading through my body, because at least I did everything I could to help Pa come back home.

210

16

WHEN WE TALK TO MA ON THE phone that night, she's freaking out.

"I thought it would be over by now," she says. "I thought we would at least know what's gonna happen to your pa."

"Me too, Ma," I say. "We all did."

"I can't believe Jorge has to go back to court with your dad tomorrow. I was hoping he'd be there with me. I just—"

"It's okay, Ma. You'll be okay."

"I don't know, mijo. I'm not sure how I'm going to do this."

I wish desperately that I could be there—that I could hold her hand during her hearing, or that I could go back to court with Pa, but I know I can't. I need to be at school tomorrow. I have a trigonometry test that I can't miss.

"You won't be alone," Jorge says suddenly. I turn toward him, unsure of how long he's been standing behind me.

"Wh-what do you mean?" Ma asks.

"People have been calling, asking how Ernesto's hearing went. So many of them asked if they could come with you that I had to turn down their offers, but you'll have two people there: your neighbor, Mrs. Solís, and Lola Suárez, your coworker from the hotel. She became a citizen last year, and she really wanted to be there for you."

"Okay," Ma says with a small sigh. "Okay, that's good."

"Everything's gonna be okay," I say to her. "Just call us as soon as you can tomorrow. And who knows—maybe, if we're able to pay the bond, you could even come home."

"Yes," Ma says, but she doesn't sound convinced. "Maybe."

* * *

When I wake up the next day, I know right away that there's something unusual going on. I'm just not sure what it is. Truth be told, I feel good. I feel rested, the muscles in my back are loose, and the light of the rising sun is coming in softly through the curtains.

That's when I realize what it is—I woke up before my alarm went off. Last night must've been the first real sleep I've gotten in weeks. I'd forgotten what this felt like.

I pick up my phone and look at the time. I could easily

fall back asleep for another hour, but I decide not to. I roll out of bed and turn to take a quick look at Sophie, who's still sleeping peacefully under the covers. Sneaking out the door as quietly as I can, I head straight for the bathroom to start getting ready for the day.

Since we first came to stay at Uncle Jorge's, I had never gotten up before him and Amy. They're early risers, but today is Friday and they probably want to take advantage of the fact that Ellie hasn't woken them up yet. The apartment feels calm and silent as I tiptoe my way to the living room to review one last time before my trig test.

I try not to think about Pa's or Ma's hearings, and it's surprisingly easy. It's as if I gained a new clarity in my sleep. In fact, I feel nothing. I'm able to focus on studying and nothing else.

Even when Jorge, Amy, and Sophie wake up, the air in the apartment remains calm. Maybe we're all just tired of stressing. For the first time, it's as if we're all willing to be patient. We're willing to wait until we find out what happens at my parents' hearings before we allow ourselves to be stressed again.

★ ★ ★

A part of me wishes I could hold on to that state of mind for the entire day, but sooner rather than later, I have to admit to myself that it was only temporary.

After I walk out of my test, I start to feel anxiety deep inside my chest, and it continues to grow until I'm a nervous mess. I check my phone every few minutes, hoping to get news from either of my parents, even though I know it's pointless. Pa's hearing will probably go on for at least another couple of hours, and Ma's won't even start until later this afternoon.

By the time the last bell rings, announcing not just the end of the day but the start of the long weekend, I know I should feel relieved, but I don't. The anxiety just keeps growing and growing.

I walk out of school expecting to find Kimmie standing on the front steps. Instead, I find Adam. I'm not sure why it is, but he looks different to me. He's not flashing his perfect white teeth the way he usually does. There's only a small smile on his face, and when he looks right at me, the spark I'm used to seeing in his eyes isn't there.

"Hey," I say to him.

"Hey," he says back.

We stand awkwardly in front of each other while people continue to burst out of school through the doors behind us. Even though I'm pretty sure only a few seconds have passed, this moment seems to stretch on forever, as all the things we're not saying linger in the air around us.

"I'm sorry, Adam," I say finally. "I'm sorry I said what

I said when you told us you'd gotten the role. That was so shitty of me, and I—"

"It's okay."

"No, it's not. We should've celebrated and—"

"I'm sorry, too," he says, and I choke on my own words. "I shouldn't have talked so much about the callback and all that. I didn't mean to rub it in. I was just—"

"You were happy," I say. "And nervous, and excited, and you had a right to be."

Adam opens his mouth to say something else, but then he closes it again. He smiles a little at me, and I smile back, and all of a sudden it's as if a huge weight has been lifted off my shoulders.

"What did your parents say when you told them you'd gotten it?" I ask.

"They, uh…they weren't thrilled," he says. "Well, my mom kinda was, but she couldn't really say it out loud—not when my dad was going off about how I'd gone to the audition behind their backs and all."

"I'm sorry."

"Ah, it's fine. They'll be over it by opening night." He smiles again, but I can see right through him. I know how much he wishes his parents understood that he was born to be on a stage and not to take over the family business.

My stomach falls. I hadn't thought about the fact that the

last few weeks must've been hard for Adam, too. Not only did I rain on his parade right after he got the biggest news in his acting career so far, but he's had to deal with his family's reaction as well. And with the end of the school year coming up, I wonder how he's been balancing rehearsals, and projects, and studying for finals. He hasn't asked if we can study together like we always do, hasn't come to me for help. I want to ask him how he's been doing with trig, whether he needs me to tutor him, but I stop myself as soon as I remember that I wouldn't be much help anyway. I'm trying to catch up, too.

"How are rehearsals going?" I ask him.

The corner of his mouth twists involuntarily into a wider smile, and this time, it seems genuine. "They're going great," he says. "I mean...I've only been to a few so far. I've had to leave school early to make it to the theater on time, but it's been awesome."

"Well, the school year is almost over, and you'll be able to focus on that for the summer."

"Exactly," he says, nodding once. "How about you? Are you thinking of doing that workshop again this summer?"

"No," I say quickly. Last year, I took an acting workshop at the New York Public Library, but I haven't even had time to think about doing something like that this year. "I might just try finding an online course or something. I think—"

"What *I* think," Kimmie says, appearing between us suddenly, "is that we'd be much better off with a drink in our hands."

I turn toward her. "Is Darryl not coming?" I ask. I'm hoping he will. I'm sure he would help break the tension between the three of us a bit, but Kimmie shakes her head.

"He's down in Philadelphia for the weekend," she says. "So . . . should we get going?"

I sneak a quick glance at my phone, only to find that there's still no news from my parents. The last thing I feel like doing is going to a bar, but I'm not brave enough to back out at this point.

Adam answers for the both of us. "Let's do it."

We could probably walk to Hell's Kitchen, but Adam insists on taking the subway. I don't have the energy to argue, so we start walking toward the nearest station, and I do my best to pretend that I'm okay. I just can't stop thinking about Ma and Pa. Even though Kimmie and Adam are next to me, making jokes and laughing, it feels like I'm walking alone with no direction.

The subway ride feels eternal. It doesn't help that the train is moving like crazy, because my legs are shaking so badly that it's hard to stay balanced as it is. I look down at my phone, even though I already know there's never service on the C train. I shouldn't feel disappointed when I realize that, indeed, my phone has zero bars. I shouldn't feel so desperate to go back aboveground, because I know there probably won't be any news from Ma and Pa even then, but I can't help it.

While I shove my phone back in my pocket, I catch a snippet of what Kimmie and Adam are saying.

"—gay bar on Forty-Sixth. It said online that they cater to a 'Broadway crowd.'"

"Broadway crowd? What does that even mean?"

"I dunno."

"I mean, are they talking about actors? Or just Broadway fans?"

"I guess we'll find out when we get there."

"*If* they let us in."

"We'll find another place if they don't."

Soon enough, I start to wish that I could be in on the conversation. I wish more than anything in the world that I could be like them—that my biggest concern right now was figuring out which bar to try first. I wish I could have a normal life, a normal family, a normal home, like I used to before this whole mess started. I wish I wasn't standing here with my heart stuck in my throat, waiting to find out if my parents are going to get deported or not.

"Matt?" Kimmie says suddenly. I turn toward her, and I realize the subway doors are open and she and Adam are halfway out of the train. "Come on, hurry up."

I join them on the platform a second before the recording overhead announces, "Stand clear of the closing doors," and I follow them through the packed station toward the exit.

I pull my cell phone out of my pocket before we're even done climbing the stairs up to the street. I wait for a second as my phone picks up a signal again, and then my heart stops. I have a missed call and a text from Uncle Jorge. *Call me as soon as you can*, the text says.

My legs freeze in that moment, and the woman that was going up the stairs behind me puffs angrily as she steps around me. I don't care, though. It doesn't even matter that Kimmie and Adam are ahead of me and haven't realized I've fallen behind. All I can do right now is focus on steadying my shaking hands long enough to call Jorge's number.

He answers right away. "Mateo?"

"Uncle Jorge?"

Hope swells up inside me. I'm waiting for him to tell me that everything's okay, that the judge is gonna let Pa stay in the US, but he doesn't say anything at all, and his silence tells me everything I need to know.

"*No.*" The word escapes my mouth without me even realizing it.

"I'm sorry, Mateo," Uncle Jorge says. "We tried. We all tried—you, me, Mr. Wilkins, your dad. But it didn't work. The judge said he has to go back to Mexico."

I put a hand on my chest, clutching my shirt so hard that it might just rip. "No, no, no, no, no."

"I'm sorry," Uncle Jorge says again. I've never seen him cry in my life, but suddenly, he's struggling to get the words out. "At least we did everything we could."

"Did we really?" I ask. "Was there nothing we could've done differently?"

"Nothing, Mateo. Nothing at all."

Despite the fact that I feel as though the whole world is spinning, I'm able to formulate a single clear thought inside my mind: *Sophie*. What am I supposed to tell her? How am I going to explain that our dad is getting kicked out of the country, and that it might be a really, really long time before we see him again? How can I tell her that all those nights she spent crying and praying for Pa to be able to come back home were for nothing? That there's no hope left to hold on to?

There is desperation inside of me unlike any I've ever felt before. I can't just stand here in the middle of the stairs. I need to move, or do *something*. I take a few clumsy steps up, and as soon as I reach the street, the light of the afternoon sun hits me right in the eyes, blinding me.

I look around, feeling disoriented. I can hardly remember how I got here, let alone the fact that I'm supposed to be with Kimmie and Adam. I turn on the spot, while people rush past me on their way up and down Eighth Avenue, but I have no idea where to go or what to do.

"Mateo?" Uncle Jorge asks. "Are you still there?"

"Yeah," I answer in a weak voice. "I'm here."

"Where are you?"

"I—I'm in Midtown."

"Can you come to the apartment?"

I nod to myself, but I don't say anything. I suddenly remember that I was with my friends a minute ago, but I see no sign of them.

"Yeah," I answer. "I'll be there as soon as I can."

I hang up and turn toward the subway entrance, thinking I'll text Kimmie and Adam later and explain that I had to leave. I'm about to head back down the steps when I hear my name being called.

"Matt?"

I lift my gaze to see both of my friends walking toward me with worried looks on their faces.

"What happened?" Kimmie asks. "You were right behind us, and all of a sudden you were gone."

I shake my head. "I'm sorry," I say. "It's just...something happened, and I need to go home."

I'm hoping they'll understand and just let me go. I don't have time to waste. I need to get back to Uncle Jorge's apartment. I need to be with Sophie.

Right away, I know they're not going to budge that easily. Their faces shift from surprise, to anger, to pure disappointment.

"You can't leave now," Kimmie says. "We haven't even gone to the first bar."

"It's not like I *want* to leave."

"So don't."

"There's somewhere I need to be. It's important."

"Then tell us," Adam says. "Matt, what's wrong?"

I can't hold it in any longer. Something starts swelling up in my chest, and I know that a bomb is about to go off, but there's nothing I can do to stop it.

"My dad is getting deported!" The words come out as a yell. People walking past us turn to stare at me, but no one lingers for long. They move away quickly, while Kimmie and Adam remain frozen, staring at me with identical blank looks on their faces. They don't blink. They don't say anything. I'm not even sure they're breathing.

Kimmie is the first one to find her voice. "I thought your dad was from Texas."

"Well, he's not," I say, shrugging my shoulders. "He was born in Mexico. And he doesn't have papers to be able to stay in the US."

There's a moment of silence between us. All around, we can hear the sounds of the street—cars driving down

Eighth Avenue, and taxis honking, and people going about their lives.

"How?" Adam asks. "I mean . . . *when* did this happen?"

"My uncle just called to say that my dad's gonna have to leave the country." Now that I've told them what's really happening in my world, my entire body feels loose. I don't have the energy to tell any more lies. I just let the truth leave my mouth without putting up any resistance. "But he and my mom were detained almost two months ago."

Kimmie and Adam speak up at the exact same time.

"So it's not just your dad?" Kimmie asks.

"This has been happening for almost *two months?*" Adam says. "Why didn't you say anything?"

"Because I couldn't."

"Of course you could. You should've—"

"I didn't know what you were going to think!" I interrupt him, and my voice comes out higher than I intended it to. "If I told you that my parents didn't have papers . . . that might've changed the way you saw me."

"But, Matt . . . nothing would've changed," Adam says. "It wouldn't have mattered. We would've been there for you."

"I have to go. I need to get back to my sister," I say, turning away from him, but he wraps a hand around my arm and stops me.

It all happens so quickly. One second, I'm trying to free

myself, pushing toward the subway, and the next, Adam pulls me into his arms and everything disappears. With my face buried in his shoulder, the light of day fades away, and just for an instant, everything feels okay. But then, when Adam doesn't let go of me, I realize something—his lips are pressed against the top of my head, and there's something about it that just feels so wrong.

I step away from him, looking into his eyes. At first, he seems confused. It's as if he's not even sure what he was doing, why he held me the way he did.

"I'm sorry," he says. He looks down, shifting awkwardly on the spot. "Are you okay? I just wanna make sure you're okay. I just...I wanna be there for you."

Everything around us stops. The air becomes still, the sounds of the street fade out. It isn't just what he's saying, but the way he's saying it.

"Adam, I..." I say, shaking my head. "What does that even mean?"

Adam presses his lips together. For a second, he seems to be debating with himself, but then he lets out his breath. And somehow, without even saying anything, he lays it all out in the open. His wall comes down, and in his eyes, I see a million different things—sadness, and fear, and longing.

Suddenly, it all starts making sense—the way his face lights up when he looks at me, the way Kimmie offered to give up her *Hamilton* ticket so he and I could go together, Adam's eagerness to teach me more about theater, to run lines with me, to spend as much time as possible together.

"Why didn't you tell me before?" I ask.

"Because I didn't know if you would feel the same way."

I sneak a quick glance at Kimmie. I'm hoping to find a raised eyebrow, or a smile, or any sign that could suggest that this is all a big joke, but she's looking down with her arms crossed.

"But—but your neighbor. You've been crushing on him forever."

Adam shakes his head slowly. "There's no neighbor," he says, putting his hands in his pockets. "It's always been you. Tell me what I can do to help—whatever you need, I'm here."

I blink a few times, feeling lightheaded all of a sudden. It just seems so unlikely that all of this is happening—that Uncle Jorge called to say Pa is getting deported, that Adam just confessed he has feelings for me.

"I can't deal with this right now," I say. I can't afford to waste any more time—not when Sophie is waiting for me back at Uncle Jorge's. "I'm sorry. I—I have to go."

I meet Adam's eyes one last time, and I see heartbreak in them. I notice the way he sighs, emptying his lungs after holding his breath for too long. My stomach twists, but I can't think about any of this too much. Not now.

I turn around, run down the steps of the subway station, and rush toward the downtown platform, terrified of what I'm going to find when I get to Uncle Jorge's.

★ ★ ★

When I walk in, the first thing I notice is how *quiet* the apartment is. The air feels heavy and grim. Someone may as well have died.

Sophie is sitting on the couch next to Amy. During the subway ride here, I imagined a million different scenarios—my sister weeping, screaming, hiding away in the bedroom, but no. She's sitting with her back straight and her chin up. Her face is streaked with tears, but she looks calm as she holds Amy's hand.

"I'm sorry it took me so long to get here," I say to Uncle Jorge, who is leaning against the kitchen counter, holding a glass of water.

"It's okay. We've just been..." He shrugs. *We've just been sitting here*, I'm sure he was going to say. There's nothing else to do. The battle is already lost. My dad is going back to Mexico, and there's nothing we can do to stop it.

I have a thousand questions on my mind: When is he going back? Where is he going to stay? Is he still in detention, or have they already put him on a plane? I just don't have the strength to ask them. Thinking I'll get answers eventually, I go sit on the couch next to Sophie.

"I'll go check on Ellie," Amy says a second later, and after gently running a hand down Sophie's back, she walks off into the bedroom.

"How are you doing?" I ask my sister softly. She turns toward me, staring at me with vacant eyes, but she doesn't say anything. I put an arm around her shoulders. "We're gonna be okay. I promise, Sophie, we're gonna be okay."

"It's not over yet," she reminds me. "Ma could still be allowed to stay."

I nod, but even as I do, a tear comes rolling down my face. Ma's situation is no different from Pa's. If Judge Meyer decided Pa had no right to stay in the United States, why would another judge say anything different about Ma?

I don't know what it is—if it's the fact that we're talking about her, or divine intervention, or just coincidence—but my phone rings in that moment. And when I look at the screen, I know right away that it's my mom.

I answer on speakerphone, so Sophie can listen in. "Ma?"

"Mateo," she replies.

"They're sending Pa to Mexico, Ma. The judge—"

"I know, mijo," she interrupts me. "Mr. Wilkins called to tell me before I went into my hearing."

I swallow hard. "How did that go?" I'm hoping for a bit of good news. I know it's the only thing that's keeping my sister going at this point—the idea that our mom could still come back home. But Ma stays silent. She doesn't say anything, but then I hear a muffled sob, and I know that she's crying.

"Ma? What happened at your hearing?"

"I—I decided to ask for voluntary departure."

It's as if the walls of the apartment come crashing down on us. The floor beneath the couch seems to crumble, and I can feel myself falling, falling, falling.

"No, Mami!" Sophie screams beside me.

"It's okay, mi princesa. I'll be okay. I need to do this."

"Why?" I try to ask, but the only thing that leaves my mouth is a weird sound. The knot in my throat is too big for me to speak.

"I was scared," Ma says, her voice shaking. "I was scared that the same thing was going to happen to me—that I'd go through the entire process, only to have the judge send me back to Mexico in the end. The lawyer said that the sooner you ask for voluntary departure, the better, so I did it."

"But that's as good as giving up."

"It's not, mijo. It's the right thing," Ma says. "You already know this—you know what voluntary departure means. Your pa can't turn back time, but it's not too late for me. If I leave now, I might be able to come back in a few years. If we're lucky, we both could."

"Years?" Sophie says, at the same time that I say, "But what about us?"

"I'll see you soon. We'll have time to say goodbye before I have to leave for Mexico."

There's a short moment during which none of us says anything, and I just breathe heavily, feeling as though my lungs have collapsed.

"I'm running out of time. I need to go, but I'll call back as soon as I can," Ma says. "I love you."

When she hangs up, all I can hear inside my mind is an alarm. *Both of my parents*, the alarm seems to be screeching. *Both of them are going back to Mexico.*

I thought I was prepared to hear this news, but now that my mom has said it aloud, I feel empty. There's nothing inside of me. No hope, no light, no heartbeat. Nothing. I feel as though life itself has been stolen away from me, and all I can see in front of my eyes is darkness.

I pull my sister closer to me. She leans her head against my shoulder and cries into my shirt. And as I run a hand through her hair, trying my best to calm her down, my biggest concern is that this feeling of emptiness has taken over her as well.

PART

TWO

17

As I walk into our empty apartment, I can't help but feel the city pulsing outside the windows. In the back of my mind, I wonder what is happening out there.

Taking a step deeper into what used to be my home, I wonder if right now, while my chest is heavy and my throat feels like it's about to close, someone else in New York is having the best day of their life. I wonder if, as I say goodbye to the only place that's ever truly felt like home, someone is getting the keys to the place they've always dreamt of. I wonder if somewhere out there, someone is feeling the same type of nostalgia that I'm feeling right now.

"Come on, Sophie," I manage to say. "We don't have much time."

The landlord gave us until noon today to be completely out of the apartment. There isn't even much left to do. Over the last few weeks, we sold all the furniture online. We packed as many of our things as we could fit into two suitcases and threw out the rest. Still, I left behind a few things on purpose, just so we would have an excuse to come back one last time.

It seemed like a good idea then—coming back for a final goodbye—but now I'm not so sure. As I look at the bare walls, all I see in my mind are the pictures that used to hang there. Everything looks so *wrong*. I desperately want to bring back the couch, the TV, the dinner table, the magnets on the fridge. I want to turn this into the home it used to be, but I can't. My ma and pa are really, truly gone. The life we used to have—the laughter, and the tears, and the long conversations we shared in this apartment—are all in the past now, and there's no way to bring any of that back.

I head into what used to be my bedroom and Sophie's. We had to tear down the fake wall that divided the master bedroom in two before we handed over the apartment, so now it looks nothing like it used to. All of my pictures, Playbills, and posters are also gone, stored away until we find a home we can call ours again.

I go straight for the closet and grab the bag I left in there, which has a few things I salvaged from the trash pile at the last minute—Ma's recipe book, and drawings Sophie made when she was younger, and Pa's old toolbox. They're things we have no use for but that I just couldn't throw out.

Sophie grabs the second bag, where she put some of the coloring books she couldn't fit into her suitcases, and then we do a final sweep of the apartment to make sure we aren't leaving anything behind.

"Are you ready?" I ask Sophie as we go back to stand by the front door.

She turns toward the empty living room. Staring at her face from an angle, I see a much older girl. She seems to have aged several years in the weeks since our parents were sent back to Mexico. I think it might just be her eyes—as she stares out at her empty home, there's an experienced look in them that doesn't belong to a seven-year-old.

"Yeah," she says, and there's no hesitation in her voice. "I'm ready."

She leads the way out into the hallway, and with a deep breath that makes me feel as though I've stolen all the air around us, I follow her and close the door of our apartment for the final time.

★ ★ ★

"¿Bueno? ¿*Bueno?* Mateo, ¿me escuchas?"

"Yes, Ma. I can hear you."

"Wait, now I think I can't hear you." She turns away from

the camera. *"Ernesto!* Ernesto, is this thing set up properly? I see Mateo's mouth moving, but I can't hear what he's saying."

Pa comes into the picture and puts the camera a little too close to his face. This happens every other day—either they can't hear us, or we can't hear them, or the image quality is terrible, or there's some other glitch with their Wi-Fi.

"There. The volume was turned all the way down," Pa says. "Mateo, try saying something now."

"Hey."

"Mijo." Ma sighs. She does this all the time—she sighs as though she hasn't spoken to us in years. I try to make it a little less obvious, but I usually let out long breaths as well, allowing all the sadness and longing that have been piling up in my chest to leave my body. Even though not a single day has gone by that we haven't talked since they went back to Mexico, I feel a little farther away from them every time we chat. "Where's Sophie?"

"I'm here, Ma."

"Mija." Ma sighs again. "How are you?"

Sophie's answer isn't very different from yesterday, or the day before. She tells Ma and Pa that she's good, that she misses them. She's been spending a lot of time with her friend Leslie lately, so she tells them about her day and how Leslie's mom took them to the playground in Central Park.

"And you, Mateo? How are you?" Ma asks me after Sophie is done speaking.

"I'm good, Ma." I don't have much to say, either—at least not anything that they didn't hear yesterday. "I've just been spending a lot of time at the bodega. It's busy as ever."

"Have you seen Adam and Kimmie? I feel like you haven't mentioned them lately."

"No," I answer a little too quickly. "I, uh . . . I haven't." The truth is, I've been trying to avoid them as much as I can. I barely even saw them during the last weeks of school. Adam only messaged me once, a few days after my dad got deported. He apologized for making things about himself, for letting it slip that he has feelings for me, but I couldn't find the strength in me to write back to him. Kimmie, on the other hand, has been doing what she always does and texts me constantly. I do my best to reply to her, even if it's one-word answers, but I haven't written back in a while.

"Why not?" Pa asks me.

"They've just been busy this summer," I say. I'm not about to explain the full story to my parents—they have more important things to worry about.

"And Jorge and Amy? How are they?"

"They're good," I say. They're not home right now. They went out to run errands, and they took the baby with them. They've been doing that a lot lately—going out on their own. I think it's Amy's idea. Uncle Jorge tries to include Sophie and me in everything they do, but Amy seems to be okay with leaving us behind, especially now that she's gone back to work at the gallery and her time with Ellie is limited. Maybe she just wants to be reminded of what life was like when it was still only the three of them. "Ellie's growing so fast."

We're all silent for a second. We don't like to say it out loud, but I know we can all hear the same clock ticking in our minds, reminding us that Ellie's going to need her bedroom back sooner rather than later, and Sophie and I will have to find a new place to live.

"Tell us about you," I say to my parents, trying to push those thoughts away. "How's the new place?"

They've only been back in Mexico for a few weeks, and they've already had to move twice. After they were deported, they had nowhere to go, so they made the trip down to Puebla, where Pa is from. They slept at a hostel for a couple of nights while they figured out what to do. After being away for over twenty years, there weren't many people they could turn to. Pa's brothers and all of his childhood friends have moved away, or started their own families, or are in no position to help. In the end, Ma and Pa found a small room to rent, but it wasn't long before their landlady kicked them out, and they had to look for a new place to live.

"It's okay," Pa says. "Smaller than the last one, but at least we have our own bathroom here."

"And you, Ma? Are you still having trouble sleeping?"

"It's getting better now," she answers. For the first couple of weeks, she was unable to get any sleep at all. I think it might've had something to do with the fact that she was thinking about Sophie and me being far away, but she says it was the silence of the streets in Puebla that wouldn't let her sleep. She'd become too used to the sounds of the city outside the window—to all the voices and the cars on Avenue A.

"That's good," I say. No matter how hard I try to stop it, the same sadness comes flooding my stomach every time I talk to Ma and Pa. Sometimes it happens right when I answer the phone. Other times, like tonight, it waits just under the surface until it finally breaks free and spreads to every inch of my body.

I hate this, I think to myself as I try to hold in the tears that are threatening to fall from my eyes. I just wish I could speak up. Maybe telling my family about this deep, dark feeling of sadness would help make it go away, but what's the point of talking about these things, anyway? There's nothing we can do. Ma and Pa can't come back. They have to build new lives in Mexico, and Sophie and I have to rebuild our lives here, and the sooner we get used to that idea, the better.

At least Ma and Pa are together now. They're no longer in detention, and we get to talk to them way more often than before. Every night, I repeat this to myself, trying to find a bit of comfort, and it works most of the time.

The problem is, I don't know how much longer I'll be

able to keep telling myself these things. Maybe they're good enough to calm me down for now, but will they be enough in a week? In a month? In a year? And, most importantly, will they ever be enough for my sister? Will Sophie ever get used to life without Ma and Pa? Will she ever stop asking me if I've figured out a way to bring them back yet?

"What else is new, mijos?" Pa asks suddenly. This happens often, too. We run out of things to talk about. It's hard now to look back on a few months ago, when we would sit around the dinner table and find it impossible to stop interrupting each other because there were too many things to say.

"Not much, Pa," I say. "What's new with you?"

I'm starting to feel as though there's an invisible wall between us. It was Sophie who made me start noticing it. Last night, while we were getting ready for bed after talking to Ma and Pa, she turned to me and said, "That wall that people talk about. Is this what they mean?"

For a moment, I didn't know what to say. I'd never thought about it that way. I'd never realized that, even though an actual barrier hasn't been fully built at the border, there are walls that have been put up all around us, keeping Ma and Pa away from Sophie and me, changing our entire lives.

"No, Sophie," I said. "This wall is much, much worse."

★ ★ ★

The bodega is the only place where I feel like being anymore. It's during my long shifts, when I'm busy carrying heavy boxes and restocking the shelves, that I feel like I'm able to breathe normally again. Sometimes, I even manage to pretend that life is still the way it used to be—that Pa is out running errands, or inside the office, and that Ma is at home making dinner, waiting for me to finish my shift.

Nelly and Erika might also have something to do with it. Right now, they seem to be the only people who manage to make me feel a little less alone.

A few days after Ma had to fly back to Mexico, something happened with Nelly. I was restocking the shelves when, all of a sudden, I broke down crying. My chest started heaving so badly that I could hardly breathe. Everything in front of my eyes became too bright for me to be able to make out any shapes, and as I stumbled around the aisle, trying to find my way to the office in the back, I felt an unfamiliar pair of arms wrapping around me. The flowery smell of Nelly's perfume told me everything I needed to know, and I allowed myself to fall into her. She held me without saying anything, and when my tears stopped falling and I was able to breathe again, we just stared into each other's eyes for a moment. "It's okay," she seemed to be saying to me, even though no words left her mouth. "Just keep breathing. You'll be okay."

Luckily, there were no customers around to witness my

breakdown. I went into the office, fixed myself up a bit, and then went back to work. Nelly and I haven't spoken about it since, but things changed after that. I have started to appreciate her gentle nature, the way silence is always comfortable between us.

Things with Erika have pretty much remained the way they used to be, but I still find comfort in her that no one else—not my parents, not Jorge, and not my friends—is able to give me. She always seems to be there, always willing to work longer shifts, or help with restocking, or take over the register. There's something about her that feels familiar and safe, and lately, not many things feel that way.

It's on a slow Sunday afternoon in late June, when we're standing behind the counter together, that she turns toward me and says, "It'll get better, you know?"

I'm not sure what to say. Coming from anyone else, hearing this would've made me angry. When my parents' friends have shown up at the bodega telling me that I'll be okay, that my parents will be okay, that one day we'll look back and understand why things had to be this way, it has taken all my strength to thank them and hold back my anger long enough for them to leave the bodega. But this time, when Erika says it, I want to believe it.

She looks down. It could just be the light, but I'm pretty sure she's blushing. "My dad got sent back to El Salvador when I was three."

"Erika, I—I had no idea."

She shrugs. "I don't even remember losing him, but my mom does, and that's what she said when I told her about your family—that it'll get better."

I'm not sure how long we stand there in silence. The bell at the front door rings as a customer walks in and heads straight for the back of the bodega, and still, Erika and I remain frozen. I breathe quietly, realizing how selfish I must seem to her. These past few months, all I've done is talk about my family, and I've never even bothered to ask about hers.

"Have you seen your dad since he was deported?" I ask.

Slowly, she shakes her head. "He couldn't stay in El Salvador for long. There were people who had threatened to kill him if he ever went back, so he had to go to Canada instead and ask for asylum. My mom used to tell me that, one day, we were gonna drive up there. We were going to meet him somewhere near the border and hug him again. But then he started calling less and less. For two years, he didn't have the guts to tell us that he had started a new family, until one day he finally admitted it to my mom, and now we barely talk about him anymore."

I stare at her, and she stares back. Suddenly, there are a million other things I want to know about her. I want her to tell me every last detail about her life, but I can't bring myself to ask any questions. I seem to have lost my voice.

The customer reappears from between the shelves and comes up to the counter. While I bag her purchases, I sneak glances at Erika, who's fixing up the canned soda section. She's frowning, probably wondering if she overshared, if she shouldn't have said anything in the first place. But when she looks up from the cans and meets my gaze, her expression softens. In her eyes, I find someone who's capable of understanding what I'm going through, who sees me as I am.

For the rest of our shift, we hardly even say anything. It's as if there's an unspoken understanding between the two of us now. We both know we're no longer just coworkers—we're friends.

Sophie's birthday sneaks up on us this year.

Birthdays have always been a big thing in our family—Ma always buys all the ingredients to make flan, and Pa makes sure we're well stocked on birthday candles, because we need as many candles as the age of whoever's birthday it is. There's always homemade food, and presents, and multiple renditions of "Las Mañanitas," the Mexican version of "Happy Birthday."

This time, there's none of that. It feels as though we blink and all of a sudden we find ourselves in July. Sophie doesn't talk about it, doesn't even keep track of the days left until her birthday on a calendar the way she usually does.

When July second comes, I wake up extra early, get dressed, and head out of the apartment as quietly as possible. I run to the party supplies store on East Tenth Street and pick out the biggest balloons I can find. The first is a big, golden eight. The second is round with pink sparkles, and it looks just like the type of thing my sister would love.

When the gum-chewing girl at the cash register tells me how much the balloons are, I hesitate a little, but then I think of how quiet my sister has been lately. I think about how rough the last few months have been, and I decide that it's worth spending this money. She deserves to have balloons on her birthday.

By the time I make it back to the apartment, I find Uncle Jorge, Amy, and Ellie already awake in the kitchen.

"Morning," I say to them as I close the front door behind me.

"Morning," Amy says. She tries to smile, but the corners of her mouth don't move much. This is the way she's been smiling for the past several weeks.

"Is Sophie still sleeping?" I ask.

"She is," Uncle Jorge answers with a nod. "She's gonna be excited when she sees those," he adds, pointing at the balloons.

"I hope she likes the flan I made for her," Amy says, and I lift my eyebrows.

"You made flan?"

She nods. "I got the recipe from your mom. I'm not sure it turned out how it was supposed to, but . . . I guess we'll find out when we try it."

I stare blankly at her. Since my parents left the country,

Amy has been awfully quiet around me and Sophie—she's stopped asking us if we're okay, if we're hungry, if we need a change of bedsheets or fresh towels. I'm starting to worry that she sees us as a huge inconvenience, but then she'll turn around and do something nice like this. I just wish I understood what's actually going through her mind.

"Oh, there she is!" Uncle Jorge says suddenly. "Happy birthday, princess!"

He lifts Sophie off her feet, spins her around, and puts her back down. Then my sister turns toward me, still giggling a little.

"Happy birthday, Sophie."

Her eyes widen as she stares at the balloons. "Whoa."

"Do you like them?"

"I love them!"

She runs into my arms, and I give her a hug. She lingers a little longer than she needs to, with her arms wrapped tight around me.

"I also got you a present," I say. "Wait here."

I run off into the bedroom and yank open the closet door. I reach into the far corner, where I hid Sophie's present earlier this week, and then I rush back to the kitchen.

"Here," I say.

She takes the pink bag from me and peeks inside. "What's this?" she asks, pulling out a small box.

"A nail polish set," I say. It's not much, but it's what I could do with the money I had left in my savings. And since she was so excited when her friend Leslie got one last spring, I figured she might like to have her own set.

She stares down at it with disbelief, as though it's the most precious thing she's ever seen. For a second, I see a glimpse of the girl she used to be before this whole mess started—the one who found happiness in the smallest of things. And as she takes each nail polish out of the box and starts arranging them in the order in which she wants to try them out, I feel warmth inside my chest that I haven't felt in a while.

"Are you ready to eat breakfast?" Amy asks, and Sophie nods quickly.

We've barely sat down at the kitchen table, however, when my phone starts ringing. I wiggle it out of my pocket, and just as I thought, I see Ma's name on the screen.

"Sophie? Are you there?" she asks as soon as I answer.

"She's here, Ma," I say, passing the phone to my sister.

"Happy birthday, mija!"

The kitchen gets loud as Ma, Pa, and Sophie all talk at the same time. Sophie tries to tell them about the present I got her, while Ma talks about how beautiful and grown she's getting, and Pa asks what we've got planned for the day.

"We're going to the Central Park Zoo," Uncle Jorge says.

Ma lets out a small gasp. "That sounds fun!"

"Are you excited, mi princesa?" Pa asks, but there is no response.

I turn to look at Sophie. The hand she's holding the phone with is shaking, and she's staring down at her pancakes without blinking.

"Hello?" Pa asks. "Are you kids still there?"

"We're here, Pa," I say. "Sophie? Are you excited about going to the zoo?"

"Yeah," Sophie answers slowly. "I just wish Ma and Pa could be here."

"Oh, Sophie," Ma cries out. "Me too, mija. Me too."

"We're still here," Pa adds. "We're here for you always. Don't forget that."

Sophie nods to herself, but her hand doesn't stop shaking. I know exactly what she's thinking. Ma and Pa keep saying that we can still count on them, that even if they're far away they'll always be looking out for us, but it just isn't the same as having them here.

It's not the same, I almost say out loud, but I stop myself in time.

"I just...I wanna be with you," Sophie says, and we all go very quiet. "I wanna go to Mexico."

"Sophie, you..." Ma sighs, unable to finish her sentence.

"You don't belong in Mexico, mija. You're much better off in the United States than you would be here," Pa says. "And you have Mateo."

"I don't care," my sister answers quickly. "I don't care

about being in the United States. I just wanna be where you are. Why can't I just come live with you?"

Again, there's heavy silence. I talked about this with Ma and Pa a few days after they were deported—about the thought of me and Sophie joining them in Mexico, but we realized right away that it wouldn't make sense. We can't leave the only country we've ever called home, or our schools, or the stability that Jorge and Amy have been able to give us, especially not while Ma and Pa are still struggling to find their way in Mexico.

"You have to be strong, mija," Pa says.

"Sé fuerte y sé valiente, Sophie. Just hang on, mi nena."

Sé fuerte y sé valiente. I repeat the phrase in my mind, trying to convince myself to do precisely that—to be strong, to be brave, but suddenly the words feel so hollow. How much stronger and braver can Sophie and I get? What is there left for us to do, when we're already trying to be as strong as we can possibly be?

I manage to turn toward my sister and say, "Things will get better," even though I'm not sure of that myself. "I promise, Sophie."

She nods once, but she doesn't look directly at me. I think of how happy she was only a few minutes ago, and I wish I could bring that back. I wish we could give her the birthday she deserves.

"We can't lose hope," Ma says. "In five years, we might be able to apply for a visa to go back to the US. We're just gonna have to be patient."

Five years. I think of all the things that will have happened by then. If I'm lucky, I'll be graduating from college. Sophie will be a teenager. Ma and Pa will have forgotten what life was like in New York, and we'll all have formed new routines that don't include each other.

I take a deep breath, feeling antsy all of a sudden. For now, we may be able to convince ourselves—and convince Sophie—that everything's gonna be okay, but I just can't imagine a life where any of the empty promises we're making will come true.

I also know my sister. I'm certain that she's going to bring all of this up again sooner rather than later, and it'll be up to me to figure out what to say to her when she does.

★ ★ ★

Sophie goes to sleep early that night. She's probably exhausted from all the walking we did around Central Park, and all the food, and all the tears she cried whenever she remembered Ma and Pa weren't there to celebrate her birthday.

Amy and Jorge also look pretty tired. Ellie wasn't a big fan of the zoo, which meant that they had to take turns carrying her, trying to get her to calm down.

"Thank you," I say to them while they finish washing the dishes after dinner.

Amy looks up at me. "For what?"

"For trying to give Sophie a normal birthday."

She doesn't say anything, but I notice the way her chest deflates, the way the corner of her mouth twists into the smallest of smiles as she dries her hands with a towel.

"Don't stay up too late, okay?" Uncle Jorge says to me as he follows Amy toward the bedroom.

"I won't," I say, but I don't really mean it. I know I won't be able to sleep until I talk to my parents, so when all the lights in the apartment go off, I go sit in the farthest corner of the living room and press my knees tight against my chest. With a shaking hand, I lift up my phone and start a FaceTime call with Ma.

It rings for a long time, which makes me wonder if she'll even pick up. The last place they stayed had terrible Wi-Fi, so sometimes my calls wouldn't go through.

"Mateo?" Ma says when she finally answers. "Is everything okay?"

"Yeah," I say. I've never called them this late, but tonight there are too many things I have to get off my chest. "I just..."

Pa's voice interrupts me. "Who is that?" he asks from somewhere in the background.

Ma looks over her shoulder at him. "It's Mateo."

"Mateo?" Pa's face comes into the picture. "How are you, mijo? How was the zoo?"

"It was...weird," I say, trying to keep my voice as low

as possible. I don't want to wake anyone up. "One second, Sophie was running around, looking at the animals, and the next she was crying because she missed you too much."

I look away from the screen, not wanting to see the hurt in Ma's and Pa's eyes as they hear this.

"Did you try to comfort her?" Ma asks. "Did you tell her that—"

"I tried everything," I say. "It didn't work. She kept crying, and all I could think about was what she said this morning— how she wants to go live in Mexico with you."

There's a moment of silence. I almost think FaceTime has frozen, but no. Ma and Pa are just standing too still, holding their breath.

I clear my throat. "Don't you think—"

"No."

"But what if we—"

"Mateo," Pa says firmly. "We can't bring her here. There are some things she can't understand right now because she's too young, but one day she'll see it—she'll see why staying in New York was the right thing."

"Is it, though?" I ask, my voice barely there. "Is it the right thing?"

I know we've talked about this before, but all of a sudden it's hard to remember the reasons we thought it made sense for me and Sophie to be here. And if Ma and Pa had seen my sister today—if they'd had to witness all the times she broke down crying, or if they'd had to be the ones trying to convince her that everything's going to be okay—I'm pretty sure they'd forget about those reasons as well.

"It is," Pa says. "You know it is, Mateo. We don't have a way to look after the two of you right now. There's barely enough space for me and your ma here, and we don't even know how long it'll be before we have to pack up our things again and move to a new place."

"It's true, Mateo," Ma says slowly. "You're safer at Jorge's. He and Amy can give you things that we can't."

"But staying at Jorge's can't be a forever thing," I say. "We all know it's only a matter of time before Ellie needs her room back, and what will we do then? Where will we even go?"

Pa's face crumples up. I can tell he's trying hard to find the right words to say. "For now, you have to stay focused. You need to take care of your sister and keep the bodega running, because the money you and Jorge have been sending our way is the only thing keeping us on our feet right now."

"I just wish we—"

"I also wish for a lot of things, mijo," he interrupts me. "But leaving everything you know is harder than you can imagine. Giving up your education in the US would mean a lot more than just saying goodbye to your friends. You might not see it now, but you'd also be leaving behind a lot of opportunities that you won't have here, and then everything your ma and I did—all the things that *we* gave up so you and Sophie could have a good life—would be for nothing."

Even though Ma nods, there's doubt in her eyes. I can tell how badly she wishes things were different, that the four of us could be together.

"Just hang in there, mijo," she says. "One day, you will look back and realize how strong you've become, and Sophie will, too. She'll get used to life without us. We just have to give her time."

I sigh, trying to figure out the balance between speaking a little louder and still being quiet enough so that my voice won't reach the bedrooms. "It's just . . . I'm worried about—"

"Mateo," Ma says softly. "You feel too much, mijo. But right now, you need to clear your mind. Get some rest."

A part of me wants to argue, but in the end, I choose to listen to her. "All right. Talk to you tomorrow."

"Mateo?" Pa adds right before we hang up. "I know things have been hard, mijo. But don't forget that you and Sophie are all we care about. As long as you're safe, and as long as you have a chance at a better life than us, then it was all worth it."

I try to say something, but the words won't come out. My throat feels like it's about to close, so in the end I just nod quietly, hoping that they already know all the things I can't say out loud—that I love them, that I'm grateful for everything they've done for my sister and me, and that no matter what they say, and no matter how strong Sophie and I may become, I can't imagine there'll ever be a day when we'll stop missing them.

* * *

The next day, I head to the bodega right after breakfast. Summer is our busiest season, so with Ma and Pa gone, we wouldn't be able to manage without me working extra hours. Between our usual customers, and the construction workers who appear all over the city when it's warm, and the tourists who somehow find themselves in the area, there are days when we can barely keep up with the number of people coming in and out the door.

"I'm gonna go restock the chips aisle," I say to Erika once the lunch-hour rush is over and we finally have a second to breathe after being at the cash register for what felt like forever.

Restocking isn't as bad today. I'm almost glad to be able to hide between the shelves and have a few moments of privacy for the first time since my shift started. I'm nearly done with the first box of chips and about to move on to the second when, all of a sudden, I hear a familiar voice nearby.

"Heya."

I look over my shoulder. I must be imagining things, because there's no one there. The aisle is completely empty except for me and the pile of boxes that I stacked next to the shelf.

"Matt?"

My heart starts beating faster. I'm *definitely* imagining things. Maybe the sleepless nights are taking their toll on me. I must be going mad.

I turn back around to keep working, and that's when I catch a glimpse of something fluorescent in a gap between the bags of chips. Kimmie is peering at me from the other side of the shelf.

"Kimmie." I sigh, dropping the bags I was holding in my arms.

She comes around the aisle and stands in front of me. She's wearing that old neon-green jacket that makes her look like an airport employee, and her hair is in a messy bun.

"What are you doing here?" I ask her.

"You haven't been answering my texts."

I open my mouth to say something, but I choke on my own words.

"Can we talk?" she asks me.

I'm suddenly too aware of the weird way my arms are hanging limply by my sides, and I feel the need to do something with them, so I put my hands in my pockets.

"What do you wanna talk about?"

"You know...Broadway shows and stuff," Kimmie answers, and I let out a small laugh, realizing it was a stupid question. Of course I know what she's here to talk about.

"Okay," I say. "I was gonna take a fifteen-minute break soon anyway."

We head toward the front of the store, and I let Erika know that I'm gonna go on my break.

"So," I say as we walk out the door.

"So?"

"How's Darryl?"

Kimmie smiles as we start making our way up Avenue A toward Fourteenth Street. "He's good."

"Still hanging out?"

"Every single day."

"And the band?"

Kimmie presses her lips together. "I'm no longer in it."

"*What?* Why?"

"Boys are so difficult." She throws a sideways glance at me, rolling her eyes. "So I decided to leave and start my own band. I already have two people."

"Who?"

"Vicky and Shareen from school. We played for the first time at a party last weekend. I, uh...I asked if you wanted to come, but you didn't reply to my text."

"Oh." I can't even remember the last time I checked the string of unread texts from Kimmie. "I'm sorry."

"It's okay. It wasn't a big deal or anything, but it was fun to be on a stage."

"What did Darryl say? About you leaving his band and all?"

"He didn't mind. If anything, things have been better since I started doing my own thing. I even met his parents."

"You did?" I say, raising my eyebrows. "How was that?"

She purses her lips for a second. "Just as awkward as I thought it would be."

"Has he met your parents yet?"

"Oh, no," Kimmie says. "I have no idea what they're gonna say when they find out I have a boyfriend, so I've been trying to push that off as much as possible."

I smile a little to myself. Mr. and Mrs. Reid are the nicest people I know, but with Kimmie being an only child, they've always been a little overprotective of her.

"Haven't they asked where you've been all summer?"

"Well, yeah. I've just told them I've been hanging out with you and Adam, which makes me kinda sad, cause, you know . . . I barely see either of you anymore."

We stop at a red light on the corner of Fourteenth and First Avenue. It's one of those hot, muggy summer days, and my shirt is already starting to feel sticky. Just standing here, I can feel the heat radiating from the pavement, but as soon as the little man turns white, we keep walking.

"Have you talked to Adam at all?"

"A little," Kimmie says. "He mostly just asks me if I've heard from you. He's worried you're never gonna talk to him again."

"And what have you said to him?"

Kimmie shrugs. "To give you time." She looks straight ahead, not meeting my eyes. "I just don't know how much time we're supposed to give you."

"Kimmie, I—"

"Matt, I get it," she interrupts me. "You might think that I don't, but I *do*. I get why you didn't want to tell us about your parents, and that being away from them has been hell. I also get that you were shocked to find out that Adam has feelings for you, and that it was the last thing you needed to hear on the day he broke the news to you. What I don't get is why you've pushed me away."

"I'm sorry." I look down at my feet. "I just...I haven't felt like myself. I guess it feels weird to be around you, because I'm no longer the Matt you're used to."

"Well...I'm here for the new Matt just as much as I was there for the old one."

"It's not that simple," I say under my breath. "I feel like we've been living in different worlds all along. I didn't see it for the longest time, but when my parents were taken away, I started thinking about it—all the ways I'm not like you and Adam."

"That doesn't matter. The fact that your parents didn't have a piece of paper doesn't change anything."

"It kinda does," I say. "I mean, there's this whole part of my life you guys knew nothing about. And it's not just me. It's Adam, too—I mean, he's had feelings for me this whole time, and he's only just telling me about it? We both had these hidden sides to us, and now that we've shown them... I don't know how the three of us fit together anymore."

I can't think of the last time Kimmie was left speechless. I can't remember a situation where she simply had nothing to say, but this time it happens. She walks beside me in complete silence.

"Did you always know?" I ask her. "That Adam was into me?"

"I mean, not *always*," she says. "It took me a few months to figure it out. But yeah... I knew."

"So the time I overheard you two talking about that guy Adam had a crush on—the one he found it hard to be around..."

"We were talking about you. Adam had to make something up on the spot, so he just told you he had a crush on his neighbor."

"Why didn't you say anything before?"

"Hey, it wasn't my secret to tell," Kimmie says, raising an eyebrow. "And Adam was scared. I mean...can you blame him? He didn't want to risk losing you as a friend. And since you were not showing any signs of being into him, well...he just chose to keep it a secret."

"I just...I wonder what would've happened if he had told me before."

Kimmie turns sharply to look at me, and she almost crashes into a woman who's walking in the opposite direction. "Would you have been able to see him that way?"

"I don't know."

"Do you think you'll *ever* be able to see him that way?"

Maybe it's just the heat, but all of a sudden I'm sweating a lot more. "I don't know," I say again. "I need more time to think."

Kimmie nods. As we start to see Union Square ahead, we slow down a little. We both know my break will be over soon, and I'll need to head back to the bodega.

"He got us both tickets to the opening night of his show," she says as we turn around to walk in the direction we came from. "Will you at least come?"

"I..." A part of me wants to say yes right away, but there's anxiety rising up my throat. I don't know if I'm ready to watch Adam playing the role I also auditioned for but didn't get. I don't know if I'm ready to face him after what happened the last time I saw him. "I'll think about it."

The rest of the walk back to the bodega is mostly quiet. There doesn't seem to be anything left to say, so neither of us tries to speak up. We just walk comfortably in silence, the way that only real friends can. That's another thing Abuela used to say: *La más importante señal de una verdadera amistad no es tener conversaciones interminables, sino la habilidad de compartir el silencio. The greatest sign of true friendship isn't having endless conversation, but the ability to share silence.*

When we finally reach the bodega, she turns to face me and looks into my eyes. "I miss you, Matt," she says. "*So* much."

"I miss you, too. I'm just—"

"I know," she interrupts me. "I know."

I walk into the store and try to get back to work, but I can't focus. I can't stop thinking about the way she looked at me before we said goodbye. The truth is, I don't think I deserve Kimmie's patience, or her willingness to pick things up right where we left off.

It takes me a surprisingly long time to finish restocking the chips. As I pick up the empty boxes to take them to the back, it occurs to me that even if that's true—even if I don't deserve a friend like Kimmie—I can't forget that I need her, now more than ever.

OVER THE NEXT COUPLE OF DAYS, I try my hardest to stick to what has become my new routine. I show up at the bodega early in the morning and stay until closing time. I push myself to reply to Kimmie's texts, apologizing again and again for taking so long to respond, promising her that I'll try to do better. At night, I watch *Pasiones* next to my sister, noticing the way she curls up close to me, not moving, not talking, not doing anything except stare blankly at the screen.

On a Monday evening, I give Maria a call, thinking that going on a playdate would be good for Sophie. Right after we agree that I'll drop my sister off at her apartment at noon tomorrow, Maria gives a long sigh into the phone.

"I'm worried about her," she says.

"Why?" Even as the word leaves my mouth, I realize I already know the answer. Staring at Sophie from the corner of my eye, I feel pain in my chest. She's slumped in the farthest corner of the couch, staring down at Jorge's phone. Even though there's a movie playing on the TV, all she cares about is hitting the call button again and again, because that's what she does—if Ma and Pa don't answer on the first try, she's incapable of giving up. Last week, she kept calling back for forty-five minutes before they finally picked up.

"She's been quiet," Maria tells me. "Too quiet."

"I—I know. I think she just needs to—"

"Mateo," she says sharply. "She keeps saying she wants to go live with your parents in Mexico."

I pull a chair back and slowly sit at the table. "What else has she said?"

"That's about it. It's the only thing she talked about last time she came over."

My heart breaks. I want to put the phone down, run to my sister, and give her a hug, but I can't move my legs.

"Mateo, I—"

"Thank you, Maria," I say. "For telling me this."

She goes silent, and for a couple of minutes, we just breathe quietly through the phone. "So you'll drop Sophie off at noon, right?"

"Yes," I say. "I'll see you tomorrow."

* * *

The feeling of heartbreak stays with me until dinnertime. It's only made worse by the fact that Jorge came home from work looking a little flustered. He had a whispered conversation with Amy in the kitchen while they were making dinner, and now he's looking more serious than I've seen him in a while.

"How was work today?" I ask him, because that's what I assume is bothering him—something must've happened at the office.

He shakes his head a little. "It was a crazy day."

Amy sighs loudly, but she doesn't say anything. I watch her closely while we eat. She holds her fork and knife delicately, eating small pieces of chicken. After every few bites, she lets out another loud sigh.

I turn to look at my sister instead, who has put her fork down and is staring at her plate with a blank look on her face. Even though I want to say something—bring up the things Maria said to me on the phone, or ask my sister how she's feeling—I can't bring myself to speak all through dinner.

"You can talk to me, Sophie," I say to her later that night while we settle on the couch to watch *Pasiones de tu Corazón*. "You know you can tell me anything, don't you?"

"Yeah," she replies without even looking at me.

A part of me wants to dig deeper into what's going through her mind, but I'm also afraid—afraid of what she might say, of having to explain to her once more why we can't go be with Ma and Pa.

The opening credits of *Pasiones* start playing before I can say anything else. Even though my eyes are fixed on the screen, I just can't focus on tonight's episode. I can't stop thinking about Sophie's silence, or beating myself up for not being brave enough to start the conversations we should be having.

★ ★ ★

Later in the week, we wake up to a loud *bang* that makes the windows in the apartment rattle.

I shoot up from bed, my heart pounding against my chest. The first thing I realize is that Sophie is beside me, and she's also sitting up. I give a small sigh of relief, because at least she's safe. Then I look around the bedroom. The curtains are still drawn, but there's warm sunlight coming in through a small gap, which tells me it must be seven or eight in the morning.

For a second, everything is quiet, as it should be. If it wasn't because of the fear I see reflected in Sophie's eyes, I would think that I probably just imagined the bang.

"Wait here," I whisper to her as I get out from under the covers. Stepping softly over the wooden floors, I move closer to the bedroom door. My hand is about to touch the doorknob when I hear something that makes me stop—hushed voices somewhere in the apartment, speaking quickly.

"I'm sorry. It's just that—"

"I know."

"—these things keep happening, and I—"

"I know."

"—getting frustrated, with Ellie not sleeping well again, and—"

"You don't have to explain. You've had a lot on your plate."

There's a short pause, only long enough for me to let out my breath.

"Can you talk to them?" Amy says. I'm trying to figure out where she and Jorge are. Their voices seem to be coming from down the hallway, close to where the bathroom is.

"Of course. I'll ask them to clean up the bathroom."

My stomach drops. I know exactly what they're talking about. I guess after sharing a single bathroom with another three people my entire life, I just don't notice these things anymore, but I can understand why Amy wouldn't like to see puddles of water on the bathroom floor after we come out of the shower, or toothpaste smeared on the sink from when Sophie brushes her teeth.

"It's not just the bathroom," Amy says. I'm not sure why, but her voice comes out a bit muffled. "It's the crumbs, and the dirty dishes, and—"

Uncle Jorge makes a shushing sound. "It's okay. I'll talk to them. You don't have to worry," he says, speaking more softly than before. I can picture him hugging Amy out there, maybe kissing the top of her head.

I go back to bed. I know Uncle Jorge is gonna bring this up sooner rather than later, but for now, I wanna pretend I never even overheard that conversation.

"What was it?" Sophie asks me.

"Nothing," I say quickly. "Everything's fine. We can go back to sleep."

Even though I manage to fall asleep for another full hour, all I see in my dreams is Amy's angry face. I've never actually seen her looking upset, but I imagine this is what she would look like: red cheeks, nostrils flaring. I can even imagine what her voice would sound like if she were screaming. In my dream, I hear her saying a single sentence, over and over again: *"Get out of my home!"*

★　★　★

"Yes, Uncle Jorge," we say for what feels like the thousandth time.

"We just want to make sure we're all helping out so the apartment is always clean."

"Yes, Uncle Jorge."

This conversation feels like it's been going on for ages. Jorge chooses to have the talk with Sophie and me that night while

269

Amy is in the bedroom, putting Ellie to sleep. From the moment he started talking, I wanted to ask him to stop—I wanted to tell him that we understood, that we were gonna be more careful from now on. I just wasn't brave enough to interrupt him, so in the end I had to let him say all the things he had planned.

"Thanks, guys," he says finally, and I feel my chest deflating. At least this is over.

Later, after we turn off the lights and we're about to go to sleep, Sophie turns toward me.

"Is it because of me?" she asks.

"You heard what Uncle Jorge said—it's not just you," I tell her. "But we can help each other out. We'll make sure we're always cleaning up after ourselves."

Even as I tell my sister not to worry, I feel a wave of anxiety sweeping through my body. Earlier, I noticed that the doorframe in the bathroom looked a little crooked. Amy must've banged the door shut in frustration, which is what caused the loud bang that woke us up.

For the rest of the week, the air in the apartment feels a little more tense than usual. Even though Amy pretends that everything's okay, I see right through the act she's trying to put on. I'm reminded of the reasons Ma used to say that Amy made her think of a robot—her slow, calculated movements, her way of speaking in a monotone, the way her eyes don't light up even when she smiles.

And so I do everything I can to keep her happy. At night, Sophie takes a shower before me. She does a pretty good job at drying the floor with the mat, but I still do another sweep of the bathroom after I'm done showering. I look in every last corner, making sure there are no puddles, that the entire place is spotless.

It doesn't end there—I try my hardest to make sure that our bedroom is clean, that I wash both Sophie's and my dishes right after we're done eating, that we never leave a single thing out of place. Still, none of that seems to be making a difference. Amy seems as unhappy as ever.

To make matters worse, I quickly start to realize that Jorge doesn't seem like his normal self either, and I'm pretty sure I know why. His biggest goal in life is to make Amy happy . . . and right now, he seems to be failing miserably.

When Ma and Pa ask me how things are going, I tell them everything's okay. I don't want to worry them, because there's nothing they can do anyway.

"We're all still adapting," I say, which is my way of telling them that life just feels like an uncertain mess right now. "How are you?"

"Good. We're just . . . good," Pa replies, which is his way of saying that life for them feels the exact same way.

"How's the job search going?" I try not to ask them about these things in front of Sophie, but right now she's in the shower, and Jorge and Amy are out. They went to dinner at their friends' place and took Ellie with them, so my parents and I are free to talk about anything we want.

"I spoke to Julieta, an old friend, yesterday. She said her brother might have something for me on his ranch, so we'll see." It's been a long time since I've heard Pa get excited about a job opportunity. All the other ones have led nowhere, so I can't blame him for feeling a little apathetic at this point.

"How about you, Ma?"

"I'm also still looking, mijo," she says. She's been going around town every day, asking at every single store, restaurant, and hotel if they're hiring, but she also hasn't had any luck.

"And the new place?"

"It's okay," Pa answers. "We had a bit of an issue with the kitchen sink yesterday—broken pipe, won't bore you with the details. It's fixed now."

"Don't worry about us, Mateo," Ma adds quickly. "You don't need to carry that extra weight."

There are so many things I wish I could say right now. I want to tell Ma that it's not like I can just choose to put this weight down, that the responsibility of keeping the bodega running and taking care of Sophie is becoming too much for me, and I don't know how much longer I can keep doing those things. Mostly, though, I want to tell her about what things have been like at Jorge and Amy's lately, but I can't get any of the words out.

The shower stops, and I know Sophie will be coming out of the bathroom any minute.

"I have to go," I say to my parents. I notice the way they look directly at the camera and open their mouths, but I end the call before they have a chance to say anything else.

★ ★ ★

During breakfast on Sunday, I watch as Sophie plays around with her bowl of cereal for thirty minutes, barely eating anything.

"Come on, Sophie. Just eat a little more. You don't have to finish it."

"I'm not hungry," she says with bitterness in her voice that has never been there before.

I turn toward Jorge and Amy. I'm hoping they'll help me, that they'll know what to do, but neither of them speaks up. When I remember that Sophie also barely ate during dinner last night, however, I know I need to do something—anything.

"Wanna come with me to the bodega today?" I ask her.

She stares at me thoughtfully for a moment, and then she nods. She might be thinking the same thing as I am—that a change of scenery wouldn't be the worst thing.

When we get to the bodega later in the day, Erika lets out a happy squeal the second she sees Sophie. I've been telling her about my sister—how she's barely been eating, how I'm running out of ways to make her feel better.

At first, Sophie runs around the store. She sneaks in and out from between the shelves, and comes to join me behind the counter every now and then just to see what I'm doing. After a while, Erika asks if she can see some of Sophie's sticker books, and they go into the office so Sophie can show her.

While I work at the register, I keep hearing small giggles coming from the office, which brings lightness to my chest. But then, when everything goes really quiet, I start to wonder if something is wrong. I finish bagging a customer's stuff in a rush and then step out from behind the counter, moving slowly toward the door of the office.

Straining my ears, I hear soft whispers coming from inside.

"It's pretty far, Sophie," Erika says.

"How far?"

"Several hours by plane, I think."

There's a moment of silence.

"Are plane tickets really expensive?" Sophie asks.

"Why do you want to know?"

"Cause my friend Leslie's mom told me that they are."

The bell rings suddenly, and a customer walks into the bodega. Letting out my breath through my mouth, I go back behind the counter, but I keep sneaking glances at the office door, praying that Erika will know what to say, that she'll be able to figure out a way to comfort Sophie that I haven't thought of yet.

I WAKE UP THE FOLLOWING DAY TO the sound of my phone buzzing. At first, it feels distant, as my mind struggles to cross from sleep to wakefulness. I stretch out an arm, feeling around for my phone. When I find it, I press it against my ear and mumble, "Hello?"

It keeps buzzing. I pull it away to stare at the screen, and I realize that I'm not getting a call at all. There's a string of unread messages from Kimmie, and she keeps sending more, so my phone is buzzing nonstop.

I swipe right on the screen to read the first message: *Matt, are you up?*

Slowly, I scroll down. Even though she only sent the first text a couple of minutes ago, she's quickly becoming desperate.

I really need to talk to you.

MATT.

I need you.

It's really important.

Please just call me when you see this.

PLEASE.

I throw off the covers and sneak out of bed. Looking down at the time on my phone, I see that it's really early. Jorge and Amy aren't even up yet, so I step out of the apartment and call Kimmie from the hallway, just to make sure I won't wake anyone.

She answers right away. "Matt. *Thank God.*"

"Kimmie, what's wrong?"

"I need to explain in person. Can I see you?"

I almost say no. I'm half asleep, and she won't even tell me what's going on. But then an instinct kicks in deep inside of me. She sounds so scared. I have to get to her.

"Of course," I say, feeling wide awake all of a sudden. "Where?"

"Central Park? I'm by the West Ninetieth Street entrance."

"Okay. I'll be there as soon as I can."

"Thank you," she says quickly. "*Thank you*, Matt. I really—"

"Kimmie," I interrupt her, because she's starting to scare me. I've never heard her sound this upset. "Are you okay?"

"I—" She chokes. "I'll be better when you get here."

"Just hang on."

As soon as we hang up, I rush back into the apartment. I

change into the first clothes I can find, and I write a quick note on a pad that's in the kitchen drawer.

> I had to go somewhere. Text me if you need me. —Mateo

I leave it on the table for Jorge, Amy, and Sophie to find when they wake up, and then I run out the door.

★ ★ ★

I find Kimmie pacing around a bench. I figure she might have been sitting earlier, but she must've gotten impatient and started walking around in circles.

"Matt!" Even though her face lights up when she sees me, something about her seems off.

"Kimmie," I say as she wraps her arms around my waist. I return the hug, patting her softly on the back. "What's going on?"

She pulls away from me and stares deeply into my eyes. "Matt, I—I think I might be pregnant."

"Oh." On my way here, I thought about a thousand things that Kimmie might want to say to me, but this was not one of them. I'm speechless for the longest time, as different images flash before my eyes—Kimmie with a big, round belly. Kimmie holding a baby. Darryl standing next to her, looking scared.

"You—you *might* be?" is the first thing that comes out of my mouth. "So you're not sure yet?"

Kimmie shakes her head. "I went to the drugstore and all, but I ended up leaving without buying a pregnancy test. I couldn't do it. That's when I asked you to come."

I nod to myself. There's an alarm going off in my head, but I know I can't freak out right now. I need to be calm enough for the both of us.

"We can go together," I say. "We can get the pregnancy test, and then we'll—"

"Can we hold on for a minute?" Kimmie asks, panting a little. "I'm not ready yet."

"Of course."

She sits down on the bench and wraps her arms around herself. I join her after a second.

"So..." I begin, just because I feel like I need to fill the silence. "What are the chances that you're actually pregnant?"

Kimmie's face crumples up into a grimace. "Pretty high, I guess?" she says. "My period is four days late. *Four days, Matt!*"

"Okay," I say. "H-has this ever happened before?"

"I mean... once or twice, but it's usually right on time," Kimmie says. "This can't be a coincidence. I just—"

"I thought you and Darryl were using protection."

"We are. Every single time. But these things can happen.

I was just googling it, and condoms are not one hundred percent effective. Did you know that? I mean, what if—"

"You need to take a pregnancy test first," I say to her. "You have to be sure this isn't a false alarm, and then we can worry about everything else."

She nods a little to herself. "Okay," she says. "Let's do it. There's a Duane Reade on Ninetieth and Columbus."

She shoots up from the bench, and I do the same. We walk quickly, decisively, Kimmie always one step ahead of me. When we get to the drugstore, though, she stops suddenly.

"I'm here for you," I whisper. "You got this."

Kimmie reaches for my arm and grips it with all her strength. Even as we walk into the store, toward the Family Planning section, and try to find the least expensive pregnancy test, she doesn't let go.

After Kimmie pays, we rush to the back of the store, and she walks into the small bathroom. But before closing the door, she peeks out to look at me. "What are you doing?" she asks.

"I'm . . . waiting for you outside?"

"No, you're not. Get in here."

I think about it for a bit, but then I squeeze into the bathroom with her, and she locks the door.

"Okay," she says, gripping the box with both hands. She's shaking so much that she must barely be able to read the instructions. "How do I do this?"

"I think you just gotta pee on the stick."

"Pee on the stick," she repeats to herself. "All right. That's simple enough."

I turn to face the wall as she squats over the toilet, and after a few minutes, I finally begin to hear a stream hitting the water.

"What now?" Kimmie asks, and I reach for the empty box, which she left next to the sink.

"Now we wait," I say, reading the instructions.

"For how long?"

"Five minutes."

"*Five minutes.* Wow. Okay." She lays the test down on the sink and turns away from it. "What am I gonna do, Matt?" she says. "What if I *am* pregnant?"

"Don't get ahead of yourself."

"But I already know what it's gonna say. Oh my God, this is bad. I don't know what my parents will do if they find out about this. I mean, they're gonna kill me. They would—"

"Not even need to find out," I finish her sentence. "Even if you *are* pregnant, you get to decide what you want to do. Don't forget that."

Slowly, Kimmie begins to nod. She stares straight ahead, not meeting my eyes, but I can tell she's deep in thought.

"I'm here for you," I remind her.

"I know." She leans against the bathroom wall. With a long sigh, she slides down until she's sitting.

I hesitate for a moment. A part of me doesn't want to sit on the dirty bathroom floor, but then I swallow my pride and join her.

"Why did you call me?" I ask her softly. "Why not Darryl or Adam?"

She gives a small shrug. "You were the first person I thought of."

"I'm sorry I've been such a shitty friend lately."

"It's okay," she says, hugging her knees. "I get what you said on the day I went to the bodega. I understand why you've been questioning our friendship and—"

"It's not just that," I say. "I've been questioning *everything*."

Kimmie turns toward me, but she doesn't say anything.

"I barely know who I am anymore. It used to be so simple. I was a born-and-raised New Yorker, and an American. I was my sister's brother, and my parents' son, and your and Adam's friend. Now it's just all mixed up. I don't feel American, but I don't feel Mexican, either. I'm my sister's caretaker, my parents' distant relative, and the breadwinner in my family. I don't even know how to explain what I am to Adam," I say. "There's one thing I'm sure of, though. I'm your friend. Always have been, always will be. No matter what that pregnancy test says, and no matter what happens after."

Kimmie blinks a few times. I know how much she hates crying in front of people. "I love you."

I reach for her hand and squeeze it tight. "I love you, too."

"Has it been five minutes already?"

I look down at the time on my phone. "Nope. Two minutes left."

Kimmie hits the wall with the back of her head. "You know . . . sometimes I'm not sure who I am, either."

"What do you mean?"

"Well, I feel like people are always trying to tell me who to be. They're always dumping their expectations on me about how I should behave, or how I should think, just because I'm Asian." She scoffs. "I've spent so much time trying to figure out who *I* want to be—what clothes I wanna wear, and deciding how *I* see the world. But now I feel like I've become someone completely new, and this girl scares me a bit—the one who likes to drink, and play in a band, and have sex with her boyfriend. The one who's sitting on the bathroom floor at Duane Reade, waiting to find out if she's pregnant."

"You'd never told me any of this," I say slowly.

"I know," Kimmie answers. "I guess . . . you and Adam weren't the only ones who had hidden sides."

I sit next to her in silence, watching as she takes slow breaths through her mouth, trying to hold back tears.

"I kinda want to go back, you know?" she says. "To when I could hang out with the two of you during the week, and sing at church on Sundays, and everything was so simple. And don't get me wrong—I'm not saying I don't want to play music, or that I would give up what I have with Darryl. It's just that...lately, I don't feel like the old Kimmie. And I kinda miss her."

"You're still that Kimmie," I say. "You can be both."

"Maybe," she says, turning away from me. "But...if I can do that, maybe you could, too. Maybe we could figure it out together."

I reach out to squeeze her hand again. She squeezes back, and we stay like that for a few seconds, until I think to look down at my phone and realize that the full five minutes have passed.

"It's time."

"Oh my God." Kimmie gets up from the floor. "You look at it first. Or no—*I* have to look at it first."

I get up slowly, watching as she takes a few steps toward the sink. She picks up the stick, holding her breath, and lifts it up to her face.

"It's positive," she says.

"What?"

"Oh my God. I'm pregnant."

"It's probably not completely accurate. You could still—"

"It's right here, Matt! One line—*pregnant*."

"Wait, one line?" I ask, picking up the box again. "Kimmie, that means *not* pregnant."

"*What?*"

"Here," I say, stretching out the box toward her. "Two lines means pregnant. One line, not pregnant."

"Oh my God," she says. A second later, she lets out a shriek. "*Oh my God!* I'm not pregnant!"

She wraps her arms around my neck.

"Everything's okay," I whisper into her ear. "It's all good."

"Thank you, Matt," she whispers back. "I don't know what I would've done if you hadn't been here."

"Anytime," I reply. "Now come on. Let's get out of here."

I open the bathroom door and walk out quickly, with Kimmie right behind me.

"Can we get a snack or something?" she asks me. "I kinda need it."

That's when I realize I'm hungry, too. I didn't eat anything for breakfast. "Let's do it."

We end up getting ice cream sandwiches, and we carry them back to the park. I'm not sure if the weather changed in the twenty minutes we spent inside the drugstore, but everything seems a bit brighter now. The air feels warmer, and the sky looks bluer than before.

"I can't believe I thought I was pregnant," she says, taking a big bite out of her ice cream sandwich.

"You just gotta keep being careful. You know, with Darryl."

"You bet I will be."

"What's it like, Kimmie?" I ask after a short moment of silence. "Having a boyfriend?" Before any of this happened— back when Ma and Pa were still here and my life hadn't yet been turned upside down—I used to think about this a lot. It was the kind of thing I would daydream about when I was bored in class, or imagine right before I fell asleep.

"It's like having a best friend, only... different. Better, almost," she answers. "With Darryl, things have always been easy. When I'm with him, I don't have to wonder who I am. He gets me."

I take a bite out of my own sandwich, not saying anything.

"Have you thought some more about Adam?" she asks me.

"Not really," I answer. "I mean, deep down, I..."

"You what?"

"I wonder what we would be like together." During my long shifts at the bodega, when Nelly or Erika are busy at the register and I'm fixing up the shelves, I've wondered what would've happened if Adam had told me how he felt about me at a different time—if he had told me sooner. Once or twice, I've asked myself if, in a different world, Adam and I could've ended up together.

"And?"

"And... who knows? Maybe we would make sense," I say slowly. "We were best friends, and we have so much in common. I'm not used to thinking about him that way, but maybe it's because I didn't think we *could* ever be anything more than friends."

Kimmie takes a deep breath. "Just come to the opening night of his show. No matter how you feel about him, you *have* to come. He would be so sad if you didn't."

All of a sudden, everything just seems a lot less complicated than I'd made it out to be. So what if I do go to his show? I don't need to make a decision about how I feel before then. I could just go, and support him, and figure everything out later.

"I need a little more time to think," I say in the end.

"Well... not to add any pressure or anything, but the show's this Saturday," she says, wrapping her arm around mine. "Darryl's coming, too, you know?"

"He is?"

"Yeah, and..." She looks away from me. "Let's maybe not tell him about what happened today?"

"Of course," I say. "I won't tell anyone."

From the corner of my eye, I see that she's smiling. "If you're still wondering... that's the reason why I called you and not anyone else," she says. "You're the person I trust the most."

I pull her arm a little closer to me, smiling as well. Suddenly, I feel happier than I've been in a while. As I walk through Central Park arm in arm with Kimmie, everything feels normal. Everything feels okay. Everything feels exactly how it should be.

As the week goes by and we get closer to Adam's big night, I start to imagine a million different scenarios in my mind—what would happen if I go to the play? What would happen if I don't? What's it gonna be like to see Adam again after everything that's happened?

At night, I have trouble sleeping. The AC in Jorge's apartment isn't that great, so even when it's cranked up as high as it can go, the air still feels hot and muggy. Ellie cries for a few hours each night, probably because she's too hot to sleep, and while I lie awake staring at the ceiling, I can't help but wonder if Sophie is also awake.

I'm starting to think that, between worrying about my sister, trying to decide whether to go to Adam's opening night, and Ellie's crying, I'll never be able to get a good night's sleep again in my life. And that wouldn't be such a problem if the exhaustion wasn't starting to affect my ability to get my work done at the bodega.

On the Thursday before Adam's debut, after I almost hand a few customers the wrong change, Erika has to offer to take over for me at the cash register.

"Are you okay, Matt?" she asks.

"Yeah," I say, stifling a yawn. "Just tired."

"You could go home, you know? I can handle the bodega on my own."

At first, I turn down her offer. In the back of my mind, I hear Pa's voice telling me to look after the business, to keep the bodega running, because the family depends on it. After a couple of hours, though, when things slow down and Erika and I are just standing around waiting for the bell at the front door to ring, I finally find the strength to tell her that I'm heading home early.

"Don't worry," she says to me. It's almost as if she can sense the guilt I feel about leaving her alone. "Try to take it easy tonight, maybe go to bed early. You look like you need it."

"Thanks, Erika," I say as I push the front door of the bodega open.

I'm walking across Avenue A with my thoughts firmly set on taking a shower and a nap as soon as I get to Uncle Jorge's, when my phone buzzes inside my pocket.

It's a text from Adam. *Hey*, it says. *What are you up to?*

I don't know what to say. I almost shove my phone back inside my pocket, but I choose to ignore my instinct and begin to type. *Hey. Just leaving the bodega. Heading home now.*

My hands feel sweaty as I start making my way down Eleventh Street. Ironically, all of my exhaustion has vanished. Now that Adam's text has brought adrenaline rushing through my veins, a part of me wonders if I should just head right back to the bodega and finish my shift.

Before I can make up my mind, my phone buzzes again. *I'm on my way downtown*, Adam writes back. *Can I see you for a bit?*

My fingers hover over my phone for a second. Trying not to overthink it, I write, *Okay.*

Where should I meet you?

You could come to my uncle's place. I send him the address, and then I speed up a little, wanting to make it to Jorge's before Adam gets there.

When I walk into the apartment, I find Sophie sitting on the couch next to Amy. They both stare at me with a surprised look on their faces, which makes me feel as though I just interrupted them doing something important.

"What are you guys doing?"

"We're reading books," Amy says.

I smile at them, but then I notice the way Sophie is slumping on the couch, staring blankly at the book she has open in front of her, and the same old helplessness washes over me.

I'm about to go sit down next to her, but then my phone buzzes again. *I'm here.*

"I have to go meet someone," I say to Amy. "I'll be back."

I run out of the apartment and down the stairs. When I push the building door open, Adam is standing right there on the steps, with one hand in his pocket and another holding a small bag.

"Hey," I say as the door swings shut behind me.

"Hi."

We look into each other's eyes for a minute, neither of us sure how to break the silence. But then we both try to speak at the same time.

"I'm sorry for—"

"I just wanted to say that—"

Adam and I both smile a little. He lifts his eyebrows at me, as if waiting for me to say what I had to say, but I keep my mouth shut, wanting him to speak first.

"I'm sorry about everything, Matt," he says. "Starting with the day we went to the audition—I should've spoken up. I should've said something to that guy, but instead I just froze. And on the day you told us about your parents—it was so stupid of me to tell you how I felt. That wasn't the right time." He frowns a little. "I know there are so many things I don't get about everything you've been through these past few months, but I want to. I *want* to get it, and if you let me, I'll—"

"Adam, I—"

"I just . . . I want to make things right between us."

When I stare into his brown eyes, something lights up inside of me. It's been such a long time since I've thought about this, but suddenly, it comes back to me: the day I first met Adam back in freshman year, when he sat in front of me in math. I think about the chill that came running down my arms and legs on that day, and the way I had to ask him to repeat himself because I was so nervous around him that I could hardly pay attention to what he was saying.

Over the years, I somehow forgot about that. It became hard to see Adam as anything other than one of my best friends, but now I'm starting to feel it again—the tingling shooting up and down my legs, which makes me feel as though I'm gonna crumple on the spot.

"I, uh . . . brought something," he says, lifting up the small bag he's holding. "It's not for you, though. It's for your sister."

"Oh."

"I've been talking to Kimmie, and she told me something about Sophie that I couldn't stop thinking about—how she keeps asking to borrow your phone so she can talk to your parents, so I thought she might need a cell phone of her own."

I must've mentioned this to Kimmie several weeks ago,

back when she was texting me nonstop and I had to explain to her why I didn't have my phone with me at all times. Swallowing hard, I think about how big of a difference this would make to Sophie, how much better it would be for her to feel as though she can reach out to Ma and Pa whenever she wants.

"Adam, I don't think we can take it. It's too much, I—"

"Yes, you can. It's not even a new phone, but I got my first paycheck for the play last week, and I just . . . wanted to do this."

I notice the way he's holding his breath, praying that I'll reach out and take the bag from him.

"Sophie's upstairs," I say, nodding toward the door. "Why don't you come up and give it to her yourself?"

He shakes his head. "You should tell her it's from you. It'll mean more that way. I—"

"Come on," I say, and without another word, I pull the door open and lead the way up the stairs.

Sophie and Amy are still sitting on the couch. Their eyes widen when they see Adam walking into the apartment behind me.

"Sophie, do you remember Adam?" I say.

"Yeah," she answers in a small voice. I only ever invited Kimmie and Adam over for dinner a couple of times. A part of me was a bit embarrassed to let them into our home—to have them see how cramped life was inside our old apartment.

Now, I feel a bit stupid, not just because Kimmie and Adam never commented on any of that, but because I miss that apartment more than anything. If I could go back, I would invite them over more often. I would let my friends into my home, into my family, and not think twice about it.

"He brought something for you."

Sophie's eyes travel down to the bag in Adam's hand. Frowning a little, she gets up from the couch and comes toward us.

"Here you go," Adam says softly as he hands her the bag.

"What's this?" Sophie asks, peeking inside.

"A cell phone," I say.

She stares up at me with wide eyes, and then she pulls the phone out, her mouth hanging open as she holds it up in front of her. "But Ma and Pa said I couldn't have one."

"That was last year. You actually need it now."

She nods, clutching the phone against her chest. Staring at Amy, who's remained very still on the couch, I see that she's pressing her lips together. I could be wrong, but I'm pretty sure she's holding back tears.

"Why don't you try calling Ma and Pa?" I say to Sophie after we've connected to Jorge's Wi-Fi. "See if it works?"

She tries FaceTiming Ma's phone, and someone picks up right away.

"¿Bueno?"

"Ma, it's me!"

"Sophie, I—where are you calling me from?"

As Sophie explains that she got a phone from Adam, she sounds exactly like she used to—loud, happy. And as she skips around the apartment, holding up the phone in front of her face while Ma and Pa laugh along with her, I feel warmth inside me that I haven't felt in a while.

For the first time in months, I feel a little closer to my parents. The invisible wall that has come up between us fades a little, and I'm reminded of what things used to feel like before everything changed.

Amy asks Adam if he wants to stay for dinner. After much back and forth of him saying that he has to get back home, and Sophie telling him that he has to stay, he finally agrees, and we sit down at the table.

"My nonna's gonna kill me," he whispers to me. "She was making gnocchi tonight."

I keep sneaking glances at him all through dinner. Sitting so close to him, his dimples look deeper, his smile bigger. When Jorge asks him about the play, his eyes light up brighter than ever. I lean closer to him, not wanting to miss a single word he says, realizing just how much I've missed him.

At the end of the night, I walk with him down the stairs. We step out onto the street, and he turns toward me.

"I, uh...I had fun tonight," he says.

"Me too. Thanks for coming."

He nods once, putting his hands in his pockets. "So . . . will I see you on Saturday?"

"Yes." The answer slips out of my mouth easily. There's no more doubt left in my mind, no more need for second-guessing. "I'll be there."

All of a sudden, it looks almost as though he's leaning closer toward me. Maybe he's just getting ready to leave, but for a second, my heart stops as I look down at his lips and ask myself if he's about to kiss me.

"Good night," he says, and I let out my breath.

"Get home safe."

Even as he turns around and starts walking down the street, my heartbeat doesn't go back to normal. It seems to be going crazy, skipping beats every time I think about Adam's lips.

★ ★ ★

On Saturday evening, I meet Kimmie and Darryl in front of the theater. The second I see them, I feel a little underdressed in my button-down shirt and white sneakers. Darryl is wearing a dark blue jacket and a tie, and Kimmie is in a short red dress.

"Heya," Kimmie says to me, smiling as far as her lips will go.

"Hey," I say. "How's it going, Darryl?" I add, throwing a nod in his direction.

"It's going all right," he answers, flashing his bright smile at me. "Ready to go in?"

As Kimmie and I follow Darryl into the theater, she gives me a knowing look. Even though her pregnancy scare already feels like a million years ago to me, it must still be fresh in her mind. I give her a small smile just to remind her that her secret is safe with me.

The theater is not nearly as glamorous as I thought it would be. To be honest, it's a bit run-down, but I'm still a little awestruck. The lights are bright and the people well dressed, and there are posters on the walls with Adam's name on them: WITHIN WALKING DISTANCE—A PLAY STARRING LINDSAY COLLINS AND ADAM CARUSO.

As we make our way toward our seats, I wonder how Adam's feeling right now. Is he nervous? Is he excited? Is he ready? It isn't until the lights go out and he comes onstage that I get the answers to my questions.

Focused. That's the only word that comes to my mind when I try to decide how he's feeling. He's in the zone, and everything about his performance—his voice, his dancing, his expressions—is just perfect. The same can't really be said for the rest of the cast, but it doesn't seem to matter. Whenever

Adam is onstage, the spotlight seems to be shining on him and only him.

About halfway into the first act, we get to the scene that I had to practice for the audition. As Adam speaks the words I memorized, the ones I stammered in front of the casting director, I have no doubt in my mind that he was the right actor for the part. No one else could deliver that dialogue as passionately as Adam does.

"But how could I do that?" he says, and his voice quivers in a way that brings a knot to my throat. "I'd never be able to forgive myself."

I can't help but wonder what would've happened if that guy hadn't been standing in line in front of us on the day of the audition, if he hadn't said what he said. Would I have gotten a callback, like Adam did? Maybe not. What surprises me is that, for the first time ever, that thought doesn't bother me. Maybe this was never meant for me. Maybe, despite all the days and nights I spent rehearsing, this was Adam's dream all along, and not mine. It *can't* be mine. I used to think that it was—that all of Ma and Pa's hard work had been for this, so that I could run off and make it big on Broadway, but now I finally see things clearly.

I feel stupid for getting blinded by those crazy dreams, when it's so obvious where I belong: at the bodega. I've known this for a while, but as I sit in the dark theater, it starts to feel more real—the fact that working at the store is no longer something I do to help out my parents. It's something I do because I *need* to. And if I manage to keep the business running, who knows? Maybe Sophie will actually have a chance. Maybe she'll be able to go to college and do all the things that it's too late for me to do now.

As much as the realization brings deep sadness to my chest, it also brings a feeling of relief. I no longer have to worry about SAT scores, and my GPA, and college applications. I'll get to focus on the only thing that truly matters—looking after my family.

And so, when the play ends and the cast takes a final bow, I get up from my seat. I join Kimmie and Darryl in their standing ovation, telling myself that I'll be happy for Adam, because he deserves this, and because if it was me up on that stage instead of him, he would be cheering me on, clapping for me until his hands turned red.

★ ★ ★

"You were *amazing*."

"Really good job, man. Seriously."

Adam's eyes seem to sparkle. "Did you really think so?"

Kimmie and Darryl nod quickly. "Definitely."

"No one could've done it better than you," I say. Even though we've been bathing him in compliments for the last few minutes, he blushes a little when I say that.

"And the play itself?" Adam asks.

There's an awkward pause. I swear, for the briefest moment, Kimmie looks directly into my eyes and makes a face, but then she turns toward Adam and smiles.

"*So* good."

"I already want to see it again," I add quickly.

"That goodbye scene at the end?" Darryl lets out a low whistle.

"Back onstage in ten minutes for a surprise, everybody!" yells out a girl who's wearing a headset. All around us, people turn to look at her. Everyone is chatting, and smiling, and moving from one group to another to say hi to people.

Darryl lifts his eyebrows. "A surprise?"

"It's just cake." Adam chuckles. "I gotta get out of this costume first, though." He's been saying that to people for almost half an hour, but between us, his parents, his brothers, and all the other people coming up to him to congratulate him, he hasn't had a chance to step away from the spotlight even for a second. "Do you guys wanna come with me? I can show you my dressing room."

Kimmie and Darryl turn to look at each other.

"We, uh..."

"I should probably..."

"We're gonna run to the bathroom," Kimmie says, grabbing Darryl's wrist. "We'll see you in a bit."

Before Adam or I can say anything, they turn around and disappear into the crowd.

"The bathroom's the other way!" Adam yells after them, but they don't look back.

My hands start sweating. I debate making up an excuse as well and running off, but then Adam turns toward me.

"Wanna come with me?" he asks. The second I look into his eyes, something inside me melts, and I nod without thinking.

"Come on," he says. "This way."

We make our way through the crowd with a bit of difficulty. Anyone who lays their eyes on Adam wants to talk to him, but he manages to shake them off, saying he'll be back soon.

When we finally step out of the busy room and start walking down a long hallway, I don't say anything at all. I just follow Adam, wondering if his heart is also pounding inside his chest.

"This is it," he says, pointing at a door that has his name on it. He unlocks it, and we both step into the tiny dressing room.

"Not as fancy as you would think, huh?" he says to me as I look around. There's nothing but a tall cabinet, a table, a chair, and a mirror.

"Still, you get your own dressing room. That's pretty cool."

The sound of a hundred voices is ringing in my ears. Even though it's mostly silent in here, I feel as though I'm still back in that other room, surrounded by all those people, all those faces, all that movement.

"I don't think I got a chance to say thank you," I say slowly. "For the cell phone."

"You're very welcome."

For a while, we stand there in silence, listening to the far-off murmur of the crowd outside the door.

"I want everything to go back to the way it used to be," Adam says. "Can we try to be friends again? I—"

I shake my head. "Adam, you—"

"—promise I can get over it. We don't have to be anything more. I just—"

I take a step forward, closing the distance between us, and he goes quiet. I can feel my face turning red, but when he smiles a little, I smile back.

I'm not sure exactly how this happens, but suddenly our noses are almost touching. Looking into his eyes, I realize there's a bit of green in them. Not a lot—just speckles here and there, which I had never noticed in the three years I've known him. He stares back into my eyes, and my head starts spinning. *This is it*, I think to myself. Something is about to happen.

Slowly, he leans forward to press his lips against mine, and fireworks explode inside of me. He puts his hands on my back, and I grab the back of his neck, feeling longing I've never felt before. He holds me as though he never wants to let go, kisses me as though the world is about to end.

Whenever I imagined my first kiss, it was always a big musical moment: the swell of an orchestra in the background and the soft glow of the stage lights. It was powerful, dramatic—stage-worthy. But this is nothing like that. This moment feels intimate, like the curtain has been drawn, and Adam and I are the only two people left on the stage, the only two people left in the world. All that really, truly matters is the feeling of his lips on mine, and the pulse in my veins, and the sparks of the fireworks that are still booming in my chest, filling every corner of my body with light.

When we finally separate, the fireworks die out instantly. I swallow hard, remembering where we are, how we got here, what's happening outside of the walls of this dressing room.

"How are you feeling?" he asks me. He must've sensed the way my body went still.

"I'm great," I say. "It's just that . . . there's so much going on with my parents, and my sister, and—"

"Matt," Adam says. "It's okay."

"No, it isn't. Everything is just up in the air, and I don't know if now's the right time to—"

"You don't have to do it alone," he says, looking into my

eyes. "We can take things as slow as you want, but I wanna be there for you."

I forget what I was going to say. Suddenly, I can't think of any good reasons why we shouldn't give this a try. As quickly as they appeared, all of my doubts go away.

"Come on," he says to me, slipping his hand into mine. "They're probably waiting for us to cut the cake."

"But I thought you wanted to change out of your costume."

"Ah, it's okay."

He tightens his grip on my hand and leads the way out of the dressing room. As we walk back toward the voices, toward the action, fireworks start exploding inside of me again.

We step out onto the stage, and people start cheering as soon as they see Adam. While flash lights go off and loud voices fill my ears, I have to remind myself that this is real. I'm here, and so is he. We really kissed. He's really holding my hand. And even though everyone's eyes are on us, he doesn't let go of me, not even for a second.

Among all the noise, I hear Kimmie calling my name somewhere nearby. "Matt! Adam!"

Turning around, I see her and Darryl pushing their way toward us. They both give Adam and me an up-and-down stare at the same time, and when they realize we're holding hands, they throw me subtle smiles.

"You can thank us later for leaving you two alone," Kimmie whispers into my ear, and all I can do is roll my eyes at her.

The rest of the night is a bit of a blur, with all the photos, and the speeches, and the fireworks still going off in my chest. But at some point, when Adam, Kimmie, Darryl, and I are in a corner of the stage eating cake, I remind myself of something—that feeling too much isn't always bad, that I'm also capable of feeling too much of the good things. And right now, there is a glow inside me, and it's shining brighter than the lights above the stage.

2.2.

WHEN I WAKE UP ON THE MORNING after Adam's debut, all I hear is silence. It buzzes in my ears, tingles on my skin, seeps into me through my breath.

I'm not talking about *real* silence. The apartment is usually pretty noisy in the mornings, with the sounds of the street outside the window and Amy and Jorge getting ready, and today is no different. This silence isn't something I can hear as much as feel. For the first time in a really long while, I'm not flooded by a million thoughts the second I open my eyes. I'm not forced to relive nightmares involving my parents, and Sophie, and ICE agents walking into the bodega. I'm not immediately hit by the realization that our lives have become a mess.

I try to hold on to this peace for as long as possible. It's surprisingly hard to do—it means I have to ignore Amy's huffing and puffing and Jorge's sweatiness. I'm not sure exactly what's going on this morning, but I'm guessing they're mad at each other. Even though they never argue in front of Sophie and me, it's never hard to tell when they've been fighting, because this is all they seem to be able to do afterward—breathe loudly and sweat.

Sophie, on the other hand, sits next to me at the table without moving. The cell phone Adam got for her is leaning against her glass of orange juice, and she's staring at the screen, waiting for it to beep with a new text message. I'm starting to realize that the excitement over the phone isn't gonna last long. She's been doing this since yesterday morning—texting Ma nonstop, spending half her time just waiting for her to write back. I keep wishing I could do something, that I could bring back her excitement, but it's as if a light inside her has been dimmed, and it's shining a little less bright every day.

The good thing is that she has a playdate with Leslie scheduled for today, which I'm hoping will help. After breakfast, I wash both of our dishes while Amy feeds the baby, and soon enough we're on our way to Maria's.

"How's Leslie doing?" I ask as soon as we get off the bus at Tenth Street and Avenue D.

"She's okay."

"Do you know what you guys are gonna do today?"

Sophie shakes her head without looking directly at me, and I decide not to press any further. While we walk silently, I think about the girl who couldn't keep her mouth shut for longer than a minute, who couldn't wait to tell us every last detail of what had happened at school each day, and I miss her more than ever.

When we get to Maria's, she opens the door to her apartment with a gentle smile on her face.

"Mateo, Sophie. How are you?" She speaks in a kind, soft tone, the way you would when visiting someone who's very old or very sick. There is pity in her eyes as she stares at me and my sister, and I can't help but wonder what Sophie has been telling her lately—if she's spoken about how tense things have gotten at Uncle Jorge's, or if she's still talking nonstop about the idea of going to be with Ma and Pa in Mexico.

"We're doing okay," I reply. For some reason I can't explain, my own voice also sounds different around her. It comes out muffled, almost as if I were holding back tears, even when I'm not.

"Sophie!" a girl's voice comes from the background before Maria can say anything else. Leslie appears behind her mom and gestures for Sophie to come inside the apartment.

"I'll see you tonight," I call after Sophie as she and Leslie disappear into one of the bedrooms, but she doesn't reply. She doesn't even look at me.

With a deep breath, I turn toward Maria. "I'll pick her up after my shift," I say, and she smiles kindly again before closing the door of the apartment.

★ ★ ★

By the time I get to the bodega, my mind is loud and busy. It isn't until about thirty minutes into my shift that my phone buzzes inside my pocket, and I take it out to find a welcome distraction: a text from Adam.

Morning!

Heya, I write back. *What's up?*

Just getting ready for the matinee show, he says. *Are you free later?*

I feel a wave of anxiety in my stomach. I remind myself that we're supposed to be taking things slow, that it's okay to say I can't hang out today. It's okay to be honest.

Not today, I write back. *Gotta work at the bodega until late.*

Aaaah gotcha, he says. For a few seconds, my phone remains still, and I think hard about what to say next. Before I can come up with something, it buzzes again. *And everything we talked about last night . . . do you still want to give it a shot?*

Yeah, I write back. I don't even need to think about it. This is one of the few things in my life I'm certain of. *Let's hang out this week.*

Sounds good. Can't wait to see you.

Me neither, I write. *Break a leg at the show today!*

He sends me a dancing boy emoji. *Talk to you later.*

Text me when you're done.

I return to work with a smile on my face. The rest of my shift feels a little easier, as I think about Adam—Adam and the way he kissed me yesterday. Adam and the fact that we're hanging out again this week. Adam and the shape of his lips, and his dimples, and the green in his eyes.

When the time finally comes to close the bodega for the day, I thank Erika for all her help and run straight to Maria's. Deep down, I feel longing to pick up Sophie, to see her, to spend time with her after a busy day at work, but there is pain in my chest as I think about this morning and the way she turned away from me without even saying goodbye.

"How was your day?" I ask her as soon as we walk out of Maria's building.

"Fine," she says, putting her hands in the pockets of her jeans.

"What did you guys do?"

"Ate hotdogs."

I'm about to ask where exactly they went for hotdogs, when I instinctively stop, noticing the way Sophie is turning toward Third Street.

"It's this way," I say gently, pointing toward Avenue D. "We gotta take the bus at Tenth to get back to Jorge's."

"Can we just walk?"

I don't have the energy in me to argue. With a small nod, I put a hand on my sister's shoulder and follow her down Third Street.

I'm not sure if something's happened. I wish I could read Sophie's face, but she stays one step ahead of me, walking with her sight set firmly on the street ahead of us. She turns right on Avenue B, and I don't even know if she's fully aware of where she's leading us. A part of me suspects she's following her instinct, and that it is leading her closer to the bodega, closer to our old apartment, to a place that feels familiar and safe. As long as we keep moving in the general direction of Uncle Jorge's, I choose not to say anything.

Just as we reach Tompkins Square Park, thunder rumbles overhead. Looking up at the sky, I see dark clouds closing in, and I speed up a little to match Sophie's pace. The air is starting to feel heavy, the way it always does before a storm.

"We should probably just head straight up to Fourteenth and get on the subway, Sophie," I say. "I think it's gonna start raining soon."

If she heard me, she doesn't show it. She keeps walking, still not looking directly at me.

"Sophie, don't you think—"

"Why can't I go to Mexico?" she asks me, and we both freeze on the spot. Looking into her eyes, I see all the anger she's been holding back since this morning.

I can't find it in me to move my legs, so I just stand there, staring blankly at her. "Sophie, you... you know how hard it's been for Ma and Pa to return to Mexico, don't you?" I say, trying to choose my words carefully. "You know they've had to move from one place to another, and they haven't even been able to find jobs yet."

"So what? That doesn't mean I can't—"

"It does, Sophie. It means that, as much as they wish they could, they can't take care of you right now. They can't take care of either of us."

"But they're gonna find jobs—Pa told me the other day that it's gonna happen soon."

Letting my breath out through my mouth, I think back on the last few times we've talked to Ma and Pa, and their desperate attempts to reassure Sophie, to promise us that life will get better one day. While I try to find the right way to explain to Sophie that things aren't as simple as that, I sneak a glance up at the dark clouds above.

All around us, people are starting to scatter. Some guys that were playing in the basketball court are walking away. Babysitters are putting babies back in their strollers, and passersby are speeding up. Meanwhile, Sophie and I remain still, standing in the middle of the park.

"We just have to wait," I say to her. "We have to wait and see what happens with Ma and Pa... but, Sophie, it might be a long time before life feels normal for them in Mexico. And even then, it might still not be the best thing for us to go live with them."

"So we're just gonna keep living at Jorge's?" she asks, her voice breaking.

"We have no other choice, Sophie."

"Things are just gonna keep getting worse if we stay there."

I don't even know what to say. I don't know how to convince her otherwise, because I know she's right, and when things do blow up at Jorge and Amy's, we'll have nowhere to go.

Thunder rumbles again, louder than last time. The air seems to be getting heavier. It's gonna start raining any minute, but neither of us moves. My heart beats fast and my legs shake as I try hard not to break down crying in front of my sister.

"Sophie, we also have to think about our futures," I say when I finally find my voice, and I hate how much I'm starting to sound like Pa. "I know how badly you wanna be with Ma and Pa. But in the long run, being here is gonna be better. One day, we're gonna look back and know it was worth it."

"I don't care," she says, big tears sliding down her face. She wipes them away, but more come, even as her tiny chest starts trembling so bad that she's having trouble breathing. "I—*don't*—care."

A few drops start falling from the sky, and I reach for Sophie, trying to bring her into my arms, but she steps away from me.

"I don't wanna do this anymore. I don't wanna hear the baby crying all night, or worry about what Jorge and Amy are gonna say or do," she says. She draws in a deep breath, her chest shaking more than before. "I...am...tired. I just... want...Ma and Pa."

No matter how hard I try, I can't use my voice again. Sophie turns around and starts walking away, leaving me frozen with nothing but the sound of thunder still ringing in my ears.

★ ★ ★

"Oh my God," Amy says as soon as we walk into the apartment. "Hold on—let me get towels."

She runs off down the hallway while Sophie and I remain still by the entrance, dripping water onto the hardwood floors. It started pouring the minute we left the park, but we didn't even care. We didn't bother to run or to seek shelter until the rain slowed down a bit. We kept walking in the direction of Jorge's apartment, putting one foot in front of the other, while our conversation replayed in my mind.

Amy returns holding two pink towels. "Here," she says, handing me one and wrapping the other around Sophie. As I take a few clumsy steps to go sit at the table, Amy looks down at the trail of water I'm leaving behind, but she doesn't say anything about it.

"Come on," she says to Sophie. "Let's get you out of these wet clothes."

They disappear into one of the bedrooms. I know I should also go change, but I remain frozen in my chair.

"Forgot to bring an umbrella, did you?" Jorge says from the living room.

I try to laugh, try to say something, but no words come out.

"Matt?" he asks, leaning forward on the couch. "Are you okay?"

"Yeah," I say, shivering a little. "I just, uh...I need to talk to my parents."

I reach into my pocket and pull out my phone. I try to start a FaceTime call with Pa, but he doesn't answer. I try again, and this time he appears on the screen of my phone.

"Mijo," he says. "I'm sorry, can we call you back? We were just about to—"

"Can we talk now?" I interrupt him.

"Wha—why? What's wrong?"

From the moment Sophie turned away from me, the same questions have been spinning around in my head. I've been trying to figure out if she's right. I've been trying to decide whether going to Mexico would really be much worse than letting things go on the way they have been lately, but I haven't figured out any of the answers.

"She needs more," I mumble. "We both need more than this."

"Mateo, I don't know what you're talking about."

"Sophie's not doing okay, Pa." I let out a sigh, trying to get my breathing under control. "She just told me everything— how desperate she is to go be with you, and I just ... don't know what to say to her anymore."

"Ernesto?" Ma's voice comes from the background. I hadn't even realized she was in the same room as Pa. "What's happening?"

He doesn't answer. He doesn't even look directly at the camera. The rain pounds against the windows in the living room, filling the silence that has fallen between us.

"It's Sophie," he says finally.

"Ay, Dios mío," Ma whispers. Even though I can't see her, I can picture her face. I can imagine her putting a hand on her stomach, the way she always does when she's worried. "Is she okay? Mateo, tell us. What's going on?"

"I picked her up from Maria's a while ago, and ... she kinda lost it," I say slowly, very aware of the fact that Jorge is staring at me. I almost wish he would give me and my parents some privacy. I wish I could explain to Ma and Pa the things Sophie said about what life has been like in the apartment, but I can't talk about that while he's listening. "I think it's time to decide what we're gonna do. We can't go on living like this."

There's a moment of silence. Ma frowns deeply, and Pa presses his lips together.

"I—I think maybe Sophie should go be with you in Mexico."

"No," both of them say at the same time.

"She can't," Pa says.

"Mateo, that's just not possible," Ma adds, but there's hesitation in her voice that's never been there before. Staring at her face on my phone screen, I can tell she's having a debate with herself—between what she wishes she could do and what she knows is our only option.

"You have no idea what things have been like," I say. "She's not talking, she's barely eating. And today, it finally hit me. She's not gonna take no for an answer—not anymore."

"Ernesto," Ma says slowly. "Don't you think—"

"No," Pa replies with a firm shake of his head.

"But how could we leave her alone when she's like this?" Ma says. "Didn't you hear what Mateo just said? If she was here, we could at least—"

"Where would she even sleep?" Pa says. "We don't have a way to pay for a bigger place right now, no way to provide for Mateo and Sophie." He turns to look back at the camera, directly at me, as if he's hoping I'll jump in and take his side. "Mateo, you know it's your job to keep her safe."

"I *know*," I say, my voice coming out louder and angrier than I intended it to. "But I—I don't think I can do it much longer."

"Mateo," Pa says, his voice rising as well. "You have to be strong. Now more than ever, mijo."

"I just don't think Sophie should be here anymore." Sighing, I admit the truth—what I've been scared to admit even to myself. "*I* don't even want to be here anymore. I think we should start figuring things out so Sophie can go join you in Mexico, and . . . and maybe I could go as well."

"*Mateo.*" I can't remember the last time I heard Pa sounding angry, the last time he yelled at me. Looking at him, with his jaw clenched and his nostrils flaring, I barely recognize him. "This is *our* decision to make."

"*Your* decision?" I snap back, getting up from the chair. "How can it be your decision, when you're not even here to make it?"

"You can't just make up your mind about these things without asking us."

"I *can't*?"

There's anger burning inside of me. I don't even know if I'm angry at my parents, or at the situation we're in, or at the fact that we even need to have this conversation, but I've never felt anything like this. I don't know what to do with these flames rising in my chest, except yell out all the things that I'm holding in.

"I was the one who had to explain to Sophie that you'd been taken, and who's had to listen to her cry every night. I've had to schedule her playdates, and tell her to finish her food, and try to convince her that everything's gonna be okay. I'm the one who's gonna have to give up everything so Sophie—"

"Mateo, what are you talking about?"

"College, Pa!" I yell back. "How can I even go now? How could I dream of studying acting when Sophie's gonna need food, and clothes, and money when it's time for her to go to college?"

"That's the opposite of what you should be thinking about. You need to stay focused on school, on college applications. That's the whole point of you being in the United States—so you can have opportunities that you wouldn't have here."

I shake my head, tears burning my eyes. "I'm stuck, Pa," I mumble. "I'm stuck at the bodega. You've said it yourself—if I don't keep the business running, no one will. What's even the point of thinking about college, when I know where I'm gonna end up anyway?"

"We're here for you, mijo," Pa says. "Even though we're far away, we're still here to help you, and—"

"You don't get to say that anymore. You keep saying you're

still there for us, but you're not. *You are not here*, so don't tell me I don't get to make these decisions."

Ma and Pa remain silent for the longest time. When I look down at my phone, both of their eyes are wide. Their mouths are hanging slightly open, and they seem to be taking slow breaths.

"Mateo, please," Pa says when he finally finds his voice. "Please just—"

I hang up. I don't want to hear him say that I'm wrong, that I don't know what is best for me and Sophie. A second later, Pa tries calling me back, and I feel the urge to throw my phone against the wall. I put it on silent and throw it onto the table instead, trying to make sense of this anger that's taken over me.

I don't know how long I remain frozen on the spot, but even as the clouds outside the window shift and the light becomes a little softer, I'm still standing in the middle of the apartment, still taking deep breaths, still trying to put out the flames that are burning inside me.

"Wow."

I don't say anything.

"*Wow.* Matt, I had no idea any of this was going on."

I lift my shoulders a little. "I know it's crazy. But...that's my family."

"It's not crazy," Adam says. "But what are you gonna do? I mean, aren't you gonna need your parents' help if you want to send Sophie to Mexico?"

"I am," I say. That's exactly what kept me up last night, while me and my sister tossed and turned endlessly in bed. "I think my mom will come around. It's been hard for her to get used to the idea of not being able to raise Sophie herself."

"So what's the problem, exactly?" Adam says.

"My dad," I answer. "He's never gonna give in. He's stubborn—always has been. I guess it's what helped him succeed with the bodega and everything, but now . . . I just feel like he's not seeing things. He can't see that Sophie needs them, and all the promises in the world aren't gonna make a difference unless she's able to go live in Mexico with them."

I turn to look at the water. When I called Adam this morning and asked if we could hang out, it was he who suggested having a picnic at Hudson River Park. He brought everything—the blanket, the sandwiches, the snacks. He even brought a few wine coolers, which are probably responsible for loosening up my tongue. And now that I've started telling him all this, I can't seem to stop.

"Have you talked to your parents since yesterday?"

"No," I say, taking a swig from the bottle I'm holding in my hand. "I've barely even talked to Sophie. She went to bed early last night, and she pretty much ignored me all morning. I feel like she's said what she'd been holding back for weeks, and now . . . she's sort of just waiting for me to *do* something."

Adam remains silent for a long time. But then, clutching his own bottle tight in his hand, he turns to me and asks, "What about you?"

"Huh?"

"Do you also want to go to Mexico?"

I'm scared to tell him the truth. I don't want to disappoint him, especially not now that we've barely started hanging out as more than friends.

"A part of me does," I say, not looking into his eyes. "I get what my dad is saying—that in the long run, our lives would be so much better if we stayed here, and that starting over in a new country is a lot harder than we think it is. But I also don't want to live at my uncle's anymore. And if Sophie left, well... I'd want to be where my family is. I wouldn't want to be here all alone, you know?"

"You wouldn't be alone," Adam says. "You'd have me."

I nod, still not looking at him. "It's not like I can leave anyway," I say. "There's the bodega. I can't just walk away from it."

I turn to stare at a sailing boat cruising along the river. Again, I'm not sure if it's the coolers, but I feel lighter all of a sudden.

Blinking in the bright sunlight, I can't help but think about all the ways I tried to hide the truth about my family from Adam and Kimmie. I think of all the secrets I kept from them, all the shame I've been carrying around for years, and how much it was weighing me down. Now that there's nothing else to hide from Adam, I can feel all that shame leaving my body through my breath, making space for something new.

I reach for Adam's hand and squeeze it tight. I wish I could go back in time and let him see this side of me much sooner. I wish I'd been able to lean on him back when my parents were first detained, and during their hearings, and all throughout this whole mess.

"How are things with your family?" I ask after we've sat in silence for too long.

"Better," he says. As far as I could tell, Adam's parents were all smiles at the opening night of his show, but I didn't get to talk to them much. "We haven't really talked about my future. I think my dad is just hoping that this play will be enough for me—that it'll help me get my fix on the whole theater thing so I can finally start focusing on what I'm supposed to be doing."

As I listen to him talk, I pay attention to all the small things I'd never thought about much before—how his right dimple is deeper than his left, how there are lines around his mouth from smiling all the time. Mostly, though, I pay attention to the sound of his voice, which is so deep and measured. I could listen to him talk about his life all day.

"They're gonna have to see it eventually," I say. "This play is just the beginning for you. You're gonna keep going to auditions, and getting roles, and one day they're gonna realize you don't belong anywhere else."

"I hope they do," he says. He holds my hand a little tighter, and I realize something. For the first time ever, he didn't try to make a joke, didn't try to hide behind his smile. As I look into his eyes, he lets me see everything—how happy he is now that he's been spending time on a stage, how terrified he feels of not being able to go after what he's dreamt of his entire life . . . and how relieved he is to be able to let down his walls and show me the things he'd also tried to hide. "But that doesn't matter right now. We gotta figure out how to help your sister. I mean, there has to be a way to sit your parents down and make them see that you're running out of options here. They have to understand."

"Yeah," I say. Maybe it's just hearing Adam say these things out loud, but without warning, the reality of what's happening with my family hits me like a train at full speed. One moment I'm sitting on the blanket next to him, and the next, everything in front of my eyes starts becoming so bright that I can't make out any shapes.

"Matt," Adam says, but his voice sounds like it's coming from far away.

Feeling like I'm losing control over my own body, I struggle to get on my feet. My chest is heaving, and I'm starting to have trouble breathing. Suddenly, I feel his hand on my back, which is the only thing that tells me I'm still here, that I'm still at the park, that he's still right next to me.

"Matt, it's okay. I'm here. I'm here for you."

Big, hot tears come rolling down my face. I try to turn away from Adam, not wanting him to see me like this, but then his hands find mine, and he pulls me toward him.

While he hugs me, trying his best to hold all my broken pieces in his arms, I realize I love him. I always have—as a friend, of course—but now I feel something completely different for him. I just don't have a way to show it to him right now. I have no way to say the words out loud, but I hope he can somehow feel it. I hope he knows how much it means to me that he's here with me, that he's willing to fight for me and my sister, that he's supporting my weight even while I feel as though the ground is crumbling beneath my feet.

★ ★ ★

When I get back to Jorge's that evening, the apartment is eerily quiet.

Amy is sitting at the kitchen table, holding Ellie tight against her chest. Jorge is leaning against the counter with his arms crossed, and Sophie is in the living room, staring out the window. None of them seem to have noticed me walking in, but when I close the door and the lock clicks softly into place, they all turn toward me with blank looks on their faces.

"What's going on?" I ask. I almost don't want to hear the answer to that question. I'm still feeling weak from the breakdown I had at the park.

"We just talked to your parents," Jorge says, uncrossing his arms.

The way Sophie turns back toward the window tells me

everything I need to know. It's not hard to imagine the things Pa must've said during the call.

"Are you okay, Sophie?" I ask, but she doesn't even look at me.

The apartment remains silent for the next couple of hours. The only one who doesn't seem to know something is wrong is Ellie, who just cries like nobody's business. The second Amy gets her to calm down, though, we go back to it—to the silence, to the tension, to the fear that we've been breathing since I walked into the apartment.

In the end, Sophie announces that she's going to bed early, and none of us tries to stop her. I'm left to have dinner alone with Jorge and Amy, which is the last thing I feel like doing right now.

While we sit around the table, I look at their faces carefully, trying to figure out what they're thinking. Amy is cutting her food into even smaller pieces than usual, but her expression doesn't give anything away. I wonder if she secretly agrees that Sophie and I should go to Mexico. I could see her getting behind that decision, especially if it meant that she and Jorge could go back to raising Ellie in peace. As for Jorge, I have no idea what's going through his mind, but I have a feeling he'll take my dad's side no matter what, and the possibility that he might stops me from asking for their advice.

★ ★ ★

Later that night, when I'm getting into bed, I notice the way my sister is curled up near the corner of the mattress, hogging all the blankets.

"Sophie?" I ask gently as I lie down next to her. "Are you awake?"

I think she might not be. A car honks on the street below, and the sound echoes in the silence of the room. But then she speaks up. "Yeah."

I search inside of me for whatever scraps of strength I may still have, but I can't find any. I think back on those first nights without Ma and Pa, and how I somehow managed to be there for Sophie—how I was able to at least offer her a few words of comfort. Tonight feels different. There's nothing I can give her. My hands, my heart, and my chest are all empty.

"Everything's gonna be okay," I say after a long moment of silence.

"No, it's not."

"I'm gonna talk to Ma and Pa tomorrow. I'm gonna make them see that you belong in Mexico."

While I was watching *Pasiones* in the living room earlier, I figured that's the only thing I can do. I can't send Sophie to Mexico on my own. I can't submit her passport application without our parents' signatures, or buy her a plane ticket, or make arrangements for when she does get to Puebla. But if I manage to get Ma on my side, I can't imagine Pa being able to put up much resistance. If we all sit down without letting our own frustrations get to our heads, then maybe we'll be able to have a real conversation about where me and my sister should be.

"What did Ma and Pa say when you spoke on the phone?" I ask.

"Nothing new," Sophie answers. "That I have to try my best to get used to the way things are. That I have you."

"You do, Sophie" I say. "You'll always have me, no matter what."

She's silent for a long time—so long that I wonder if she's fallen asleep. After a while, I start wishing my parents and I could have a conversation just like this—in hushed voices, in the dark. It would be so much easier than what I know is coming.

"Do you think it'll work?" Sophie asks in a whisper.

"Of course," I answer. "They have to see the truth, Sophie." Deep down, though, I know it won't be as simple. "Now try to get some sleep. We need to be ready for tomorrow."

As much as I wish I could fall asleep, I can't. While I lie in bed staring at the ceiling, I start hoping that morning will never come—that the night will stretch on endlessly so that I can at least get a bit of rest. Inevitably, though, morning does come. Slowly at first, the daylight breaks through the darkness of the night. It remains soft and dim for the longest time, but then it starts to get brighter. The sun appears outside the window shamelessly, unapologetically. It's as if it's trying to prove to me that no matter what I attempt to do, or how tight I close my eyes, there is nothing I can do to stop it.

No one says anything at breakfast. We hardly even look at each other. Sophie eats quickly, and I can't help but wonder if it's because Amy added some strawberries to her cereal in an attempt to get her to eat something, or if the anticipation of talking to Ma and Pa is what has given her a much-needed boost.

"Are you ready to call them now?" she asks me the instant I finish washing our dishes.

"I am, Sophie," I answer. "But it's probably better if I talk to them on my own."

I'm expecting her to protest, but she doesn't. She nods once, and her eyes follow me as I make my way into the smaller bedroom. As soon as I close the door, though, I hear Sophie's soft footsteps approaching it, and I can just picture her standing outside, trying to listen in on what Ma, Pa, and I are about to say.

Sitting down on the air mattress, I try to prepare myself for what's coming. I'm about to lift my phone up to my ear when, suddenly, it starts buzzing in my hand, and my mom's name appears on the screen.

"Hi, Ma," I answer. "I was just about to call you."

"Mateo," she replies. There's something in her voice that makes me think something terrible has happened. She sounds weak, just as she did when she would call us from the detention center in Buffalo. "Mateo, he's gone."

I choke on my own words. "Gone?" is the first thing I'm able to say. "Ma, who are you talking about?"

"Your dad," she answers. "He...he left to go to Mexico City."

"Ma, that doesn't make sense," I say, my heart pounding. "What happened, exactly?"

Ma takes a deep breath, and I hear the way her chest shakes as she lets the air out. "I woke up this morning and found a note on his side of the bed."

"What did it say?"

"I had to go to the city. I'll call as soon as I can, Ernesto."

"Why?" I ask, my voice rising. I don't even think about the fact that my sister is standing right outside the door. I don't care that she can hear everything I'm saying. "Why would he even do that?"

Through the phone, I hear my mom struggle. A sound leaves her, but she doesn't say anything. It's almost as though she's choking, trying but failing to get the words out.

"Tell me," I say. "Why did he leave?"

"We fought last night," Ma says. Even though the video is turned off, I can tell she's crying. "After we spoke to Sophie, things got heated. I realized that you and Sophie are right, Mateo. You need to come be with us. It was hopeless to think that you two would be able to take care of yourselves, or that Sophie wouldn't need us."

"And what did he say?"

"He wouldn't listen to me at first," Ma answers. "But then . . . it finally got to him. He started to realize things can't go on like this. He said that going to Mexico City was the only choice we have left. We'd talked about it a couple of times—how it might be easier to find jobs there—but we'd decided we didn't want to go. The city is too big, and more expensive, and neither of us knows it well." She pauses briefly. "Last night, I told him that it didn't make sense to move yet again. I thought it would be better for us to stay where we are, to try and build a home so you and Sophie can come be with us, but your dad was set on the idea that we needed to leave Puebla. He's just . . . desperate, and confused, and trying to do the best he can."

All of the things I'd been planning to say have faded to the back of my mind. I stumble around the room aimlessly, trying to make sense of what Ma is saying—of what this means for us.

"I've been trying to call his cell, but I can't reach him," Ma says. "I don't know if he's just not answering, or—"

"What do we do, Ma?" I ask, my voice breaking. *"What do we do?"*

"We'll wait," she says firmly. "We'll wait for him to get in touch with us."

"Okay," I whisper, trying to convince myself that Pa knows what he's doing, that we should trust him.

"We'll get through this, Mateo," Ma says, her voice shaking. "Your dad will figure something out, and we'll all be together again."

I nod to myself, but I don't say anything. We both remain there, together but alone, until we have to admit to ourselves that we can't stay on the line any longer, that we each have to go on with our days, even if our whole world seems to be falling to pieces.

★ ★ ★

For the rest of the day, Sophie and I call Ma a lot. And I really do mean *a lot*. After I break the news to Sophie about what's happened, she asks if we can call Ma back, and the three of us cry on the phone together, wondering where Pa is right now, if he's made it to the city.

"Why hasn't he called?" I ask through gritted teeth. There's anger deep down in my stomach. The more I've thought about it, the harder I find it to believe that Pa would do something like this—that he would leave without telling us exactly what his plan is.

"He will," Ma says softly. "I know he will." She lets out a long breath, and I do the same, telling myself that there's no use holding on to that anger—that maybe Pa will reach out before we know it, and then we'll be able to start figuring everything out so Sophie and I can go to Mexico.

Before dinner, Ma calls again to let us know that she still hasn't been able to get in touch with him, and she stays on the line much longer than she needs to, probably just feeling lonely.

334

This time, it's me who tries to comfort her. "He must be busy—he's probably just trying to find his way around the city."

At ten—nine in Ma's time zone—she calls once again, and we watch *Pasiones de tu Corazón* together. After all the stress of today, none of us wants to talk about Pa anymore. We don't have the energy to keep asking ourselves the same questions, and so we somehow manage to make it feel almost like old times. If I pretend hard enough, it feels as though Ma is sitting right next to me.

"I never imagined my life would turn out this way," she says when we're right in the middle of the episode. "I remember when I first got to the US—the pain I felt leaving my family behind. I remember crying at night because I missed my mother so much, but I always told myself that it would be worth it. And then I met your dad, and had you, and later on Sophie . . . and there was a point where I thought to myself, *This is it. This is the reason why I put myself through all that. Now I have my own family, and all of it was worth it.* I never thought I'd feel this type of longing again—that I'd feel this desperation to have my family near."

Amara, the female lead on *Pasiones*, screams loudly in that moment as she walks into a room to find that her sister has been shot, but we don't gasp in surprise. We don't say anything. I just continue crying silently, holding the phone tight in my hand, wanting desperately to feel closer to my mom.

* * *

When Ma calls the next morning, my heart stops.

"Have you heard from him?" I ask as soon as I pick up.

I'm prepared to hear that there still hasn't been any news from Pa, that nothing has changed. But then she sighs. "I have."

"And?" I say, clutching my chest. "Ma, what happened? What did he say?"

"Not much, mijo," she says. "He told me he made it to the city, but he didn't even say where he's staying. I tried to ask him to come back, to be reasonable, to stop whatever he's trying to do, but he hung up before I could say much. I'm sorry, Mateo. I wish I could tell you more. I just—"

"It's okay, Ma."

"Maybe he'll call again later," she replies, but she doesn't sound convinced.

After breakfast, I call Maria to ask if she can keep Sophie distracted for the day. She agrees right away, and she even offers to pick up my sister and take her and Leslie to the movies.

"Thank you, Maria," I say to her. "Thank you *so much*."

She reminds me once again that it's not a problem, that Leslie loves having Sophie around, and that she'll bring her over later tonight. Feeling as though at least some of the weight in my stomach has gone away, I head to the bodega.

"What's wrong?" Erika asks me when I walk in.

"It's just..." I almost blurt out everything, but I stop myself in time. At least for a while, I want to be able to get lost among the shelves and not think about anything but work.

"Nothing," I say finally. "Everything's okay."

But during our entire shift, Erika keeps staring at me. It's almost as if she knows exactly what has happened, as if the answers to all her questions were written on my face.

★ ★ ★

"No."

"But—"

"That's not what I meant, and you know it."

When I got home from the bodega, Jorge and Amy were having a fight inside their room. At first, I did my best to respect their privacy. I went into the second bedroom and put on my headphones, but after half an hour, when they were still yelling, I just couldn't help it anymore. I paused my music and moved closer to the door, trying to understand what they're fighting about.

"He's not to blame for any of this," Jorge says, and my stomach turns. *He?* I wonder. They couldn't be talking about me, could they? "He's already lost so much."

My heart breaks. So they *are* talking about me. It's one thing to know it—to look around and realize that many of the things that matter most to me in the world have been taken away. It's another thing to hear someone else say it. It makes it feel more...*real*. It makes my throat close and my legs feel weak.

"I know," Amy replies. "I never said he was. But——"

"But *what*?"

"Before any of this happened, we never fought like this, Jorge."

"We just need to find other ways to——"

"To *what*? To vent about what a mess our lives have become?" Amy yells back. "I'm barely learning how to be a mom to Ellie. How am I supposed to be a mom to a teenage boy or to a little girl who's too depressed to even eat? I mean, what is it gonna take for Ernesto and Adela to finally understand that we can't be responsible for their children, no matter how much everyone wishes we could be?"

Jorge's voice comes out muffled, so I can't make out exactly what he's saying.

"Even if that's true, he can't just expect the rest of us to stand by while he runs off to a different city," Amy replies.

"We're all trying our best," Jorge says. "Even him. I know Ernesto's methods aren't always conventional, but——"

"Conventional? *None of this* has ever been conventional— starting with the fact that you and I had to become parents to two more kids almost overnight."

Jorge doesn't say anything—or if he does, he speaks too quietly for me to hear.

"I want our lives back," Amy says.

"I know. And I do, too... but we can't just go back and pretend that nothing's happened."

"Then we need some time to reset—at least while we figure out what the hell Ernesto is trying to do." She pauses for a second. "Maybe Ellie and I could go stay with my parents for a little bit. She needs her own space. *I* need her to have her own space. I need her to not be screaming in our ears all night long."

"How could you two leave?" Jorge says. Even through two closed doors, I can hear his heavy sigh. I can imagine him shaking his head, throwing his hands up in the air. "I—I mean, how long would you even stay with your parents?"

Deciding that I've heard enough, I turn away from the door. I stumble around the room a little, trying to find my balance. When I bump into the bed, I just let myself fall over it.

I can't let this happen. I can't stand by and watch as Jorge and Amy's marriage crumbles. Maybe Amy is right—maybe the time has come for Ellie to have her own space, but if she takes her bedroom back, where will Sophie and I even go?

We have nowhere to go, I tell myself. Nowhere except for Mexico, but we can't do that—not yet. We're gonna need to make travel arrangements, and figure out where in Mexico we're gonna live and what to do with the bodega, and we can't do any of that without our parents.

The answer comes to me suddenly. There is a place where we can go—at least for a few nights. We can make things easier for Jorge and Amy. They shouldn't have to make a tough decision—I can make it for them. They've already done enough.

I take my phone out of my pocket. In the back of my mind, I can hear our old neighbor's words: *I've never regretted asking for help when I needed it.* I scroll through my contacts quickly, and when I find the right number, I press the phone hard against my ear.

"Heya," she answers. "Good to know you still remember who I am."

"Kimmie," I say. "I'm sorry. I'm sorry I haven't texted you back these past few days. I've—"

"You've been busy," Kimmie says. "You don't have to explain."

Even though I've never felt more terrified in my life, a small light comes on inside of me—a light that only Kimmie can turn on.

"Matt, what's going on?" she asks.

"I'm just..." For a second, I can't find the right words. But then I swallow hard and say, "Kimmie, I need your help."

I've only met Kimmie's parents a few times, but they welcome me and Sophie into their home as if we were their long-lost children.

Mr. Reid, a tall man with square glasses and a tucked-in shirt that never seems to move an inch out of place, apologizes to us the second we walk into the apartment for not being able to offer us anything better than their pullout couch. While I wave him away, saying that a couch to sleep on is more than enough, Mrs. Reid helps Sophie take her backpack off.

"You kids must be tired," she says. She has a low, gentle voice, and the kindest smile I've come across in I don't know how long. "Do you want to take a nap before dinner, or do you want to eat now?"

"Let's eat now," Kimmie says from behind me. "I'm starving."

Even though Kimmie has already spoken, Mrs. Reid still waits to hear my response. "Sophie and I are okay with eating now if you are."

We sit down at the dinner table, and Mr. Reid says grace before we eat. Their Harlem apartment is small—even smaller than my family's old place—but it's beautifully decorated. There isn't a single thing that looks out of place—from the plates on the table, to the thin curtains at the window, to the beautiful paintings on the wall, I can tell everything was carefully selected, unlike my parents' apartment, where a million different types of furniture and decorations were forced to coexist.

"This smells amazing, Mrs. Reid," I say. Looking at all the dishes at the center of the table, I wonder if this is a standard night or if she made a big meal just for me and my sister.

"Mom makes the best food in the world," Kimmie says. "The sides are always my favorite part. Those noodles are called japchae, and this right here is kimchi. You *have* to try it."

I just can't stop thanking them—Mr. Reid when he pours glasses of water for Sophie and me, Mrs. Reid when she offers second helpings, Kimmie when she picks up our empty plates and takes them to the sink. Kimmie actually rolls her eyes at me, and I know exactly what she's trying to say—she's telling me that it's no big deal, that Sophie and I can stay here for as long as we need, that I don't need to keep thanking them. But still, I want them to know just how grateful I am that they've given me and Sophie a home when we needed it the most.

★ ★ ★

My phone rings shortly after dinner. I pull it out of my pocket quickly, hoping there'll be news from Pa, but when I see Jorge's name on the screen, I just let it keep ringing. I already know what he's gonna say.

It isn't until his third attempt that I finally choose to answer.

"Hello?" I say as I step out of the kitchen, where I was helping Kimmie's parents do the dishes.

"Mateo," he says. "I'm sorry. You should come back. I never meant for you to—"

"It's okay," I say. When he and Amy finally emerged from their room after fighting for nearly two hours, I told them that Sophie and I were gonna go stay with a friend of mine. I said I'd already packed our bags, and that we were leaving as soon as Maria brought Sophie back from her playdate. Amy was quiet, still as a statue. Jorge was in tears. He apologized over and over again, begged us to stay, but I knew that we couldn't. "We're fine here. Don't worry about us."

"How could I not?" he says. "Mateo, please—"

"Listen, I have to go. I'll talk to you later."

I hang up, turn around, and realize that everyone in the

apartment is looking at me. Sophie has gotten up from the couch. Kimmie, who was wiping the dinner table, has frozen mid-movement, and Mr. and Mrs. Reid have stepped out of the kitchen, still wearing rubber gloves.

"Is everything okay?" Kimmie asks me. I explained everything to her on the phone earlier—the reasons why we needed to leave my uncle's apartment, the fact that we're waiting to hear from my dad. Even though Mr. and Mrs. Reid asked no questions during dinner, I'm sure Kimmie has told them the entire story, and they're all hoping for some good news.

"Yeah," I say. "Everything's fine."

Looking a little embarrassed for listening in on my call, Mr. and Mrs. Reid head back into the kitchen, and Kimmie follows them a minute later. Meanwhile, Sophie remains frozen on the spot, staring fixedly at me. Even though she doesn't say anything, there are questions in her eyes. She's wondering who it was, and what they said, and why I ended the call as suddenly as I did.

"It was just Jorge," I say to her. "He wanted to know if we're doing okay here."

She nods slowly. I try to speak up, but there isn't much more I can say to her. I don't have the strength to tell her that I thought we would've heard from Pa again by now, that I wish we'd never had to leave Jorge's in the first place, or that I desperately want us to find a way to be with Ma and Pa soon.

* * *

Kimmie's parents and my sister go to bed early, but Kimmie and I stay up late watching a movie in her bedroom. Even though I'm staring at the screen, my mind is elsewhere. I can't shake off images of Sophie's face when I told her we were moving out of Jorge's. I can't stop looking back on the moment when I had to call Ma and explain to her that this was our only option. I can't stop thinking about how Sophie cried silently in the cab on the way here.

"I, uh ... I introduced Darryl to my parents," Kimmie says suddenly.

I turn toward her, blinking a few times, trying to remember where I am. I'm not sure I'll even be able to use my voice right now, but still, I clear my throat.

"And?" I manage to ask. "How did it go?"

"Great," she says, letting out the smallest of smiles. "I mean, all the things I feared most happened. My mom made a big dinner, and brought out the fancy plates, and then she and my dad asked Darryl about *a million* questions while we ate, but he survived all of it."

I try to let out a laugh, but I just can't.

"Have you talked to Adam?" she asks me.

"I texted him earlier."

"What did he say?"

"He reminded me again that Sophie and I could come stay at his house instead."

"And what did you say?"

"That we're okay here." I thought about it briefly—asking Adam if we could stay at his place instead of imposing on Kimmie's family, but his apartment is already crowded enough as it is. "Thanks again, Kimmie. I—"

"Stop," she says, holding up a hand. "I would do anything for you. My parents would, too. They know how much you mean to me."

My heart softens in that moment. I almost feel like crying, but then I swallow hard, and the urge goes away. My insides harden again, because no matter what, I know we can't stay here very long. I'll need to figure out what to do soon—about Sophie, about our future. I feel like somewhere in the background, a clock is ticking, and it won't stop pulsing in my ears.

★ ★ ★

"What's gonna happen now?" Sophie asks me in the morning.

It must be six or seven. The first rays of sunlight are coming into the living room through a small gap in the curtains, and we're both lying awake, with the springs of the couch pressing uncomfortably into our backs just as they did all night long.

"We're gonna have to wait a little while longer, Sophie," I

say. "Pa will help us figure out what to do. We just have to be patient."

Almost at the same time, Sophie and I both let out long breaths, filling the air around us with all the fear, all the pain that we're feeling inside.

"I still don't get why he left," Sophie says softly.

"He's trying to fix things. He's trying to see if there's a way that we could all be in Mexico City."

"But why didn't he ask Ma to come with him?"

I hear a sound coming from somewhere down the hallway. I'm not sure if Mr. and Mrs. Reid are awake yet, but I try to lower my voice as much as possible just in case they aren't.

"You know how Ma and Pa have always seemed so perfect for each other? How we've always said that they're like—"

"Pan con mermelada," Sophie says. *Bread and jam*—or Abuela's way of saying that they were inseparable, a perfect match.

"Exactly." I press my lips together. "It... it's just that, sometimes, things don't always work that way. Sometimes things get hard. That's what's happening with Ma and Pa right now, but they're still doing everything they can for us—for you and me."

"So are we gonna be able to go be with them soon?"

Turning sideways to face her, I see hope in her eyes. I don't want to steal it away from her. I don't want her to withdraw into herself again, the way she has during the past few weeks, but I also can't lie.

"I'm not sure, Sophie," I say.

"Why not?"

"Because we have nowhere to go right now. Ma is all by herself in Puebla, and Pa is somewhere in Mexico City."

"But we could go be with Ma. We could live with her while Pa figures out a plan."

There are so many things I don't have the energy to explain to her right now—the fact that we'll need both of our parents' signatures for our passport applications, that I have no idea how long it'll take for Pa to find a job in Mexico City, that just packing our bags and moving to Puebla isn't as easy as it seems.

"It's not that simple, Sophie," I say in the end. "But we have to be hopeful."

As Sophie takes another deep breath, I see frustration in her eyes. I know she's tired of hearing this, tired of empty promises, tired of not having the answers she needs. She turns away from me to stare at the ceiling, and while she blinks slowly in the soft morning light, her expression becomes blank. For the briefest moment, I worry that she's lost whatever strength she had left—that all hope has left her.

★ ★ ★

Over the next couple of days, I learn a few things about Kimmie's family. I quickly realize that helping others is part of their everyday life, and not just something they're doing for me and my sister. Mr. Reid is on the board of directors of a homeless shelter network, and even after going to work, he manages to find time to volunteer at his church a couple of times a week. I learn that Mrs. Reid likes to paint, and she sits by the window in the living room each morning, filling canvases with beautiful images of lakes and mountains and forests, which she later sells. I learn that they like eating dinner early, there is always a pot of hot tea waiting on the stove, and they keep their home incredibly clean at all times. Mostly, however, I learn that Mr. and Mrs. Reid are genuinely kind, and I can see so much of them in Kimmie.

"Do you and Sophie wanna go out for dinner with us tonight?" she asks me on the third morning we've spent here, while we're sitting on the couch and Mrs. Reid is painting. "We usually go to the Red Lobster for my parents' anniversary."

My first instinct is to say no. I barely slept last night—not just because of how uncomfortable the couch is, but because Ma called before Sophie and I went to bed. She said that she's been debating whether to go to Mexico City herself and look for Pa. I tried to convince her not to—to stay where she is, because she'll never be able to find him anyway.

"I don't wanna impose," I answer. "The three of you should go."

"Matt," Kimmie says, rolling her eyes. "Don't be silly."

"Well, Sophie has a playdate, so I'll have to pick her up

tonight," I say. I figured that seeing Leslie would be good for her, especially now, so I called Maria to schedule something for today.

"You could still come and pick up Sophie a bit later," Kimmie says. "We're gonna eat early anyway. And Darryl's coming, too."

"I'll make the reservation for five people," Mrs. Reid says without even turning away from her canvas.

I try to let out a small smile, but my face feels a little stiff. I haven't been smiling much lately. "All right."

The clock on the wall only marks nine thirty, but I know Sophie and I will have to start getting ready soon so I can drop her off at Maria's before heading to the bodega. Now that we're all the way uptown, the long commute is one of the things that makes me miss living at Jorge's the most.

I keep track of the time during my entire shift. I try to put off leaving for dinner with Kimmie and her parents as much as possible, until I finally have to accept that if I don't head out soon, I'm gonna be late. I thank Erika a million times for covering for me, but she doesn't seem to mind.

I've never been to the Red Lobster before, so I'm not really sure what to expect. When we walk in, the first thing I notice is a tank full of live lobsters near the entrance, and I tell myself that I will not, under any circumstances, eat lobster tonight—not that I would've gotten something as expensive as that anyway.

The hostess takes us to our booth. There's a little plaque that reads RESERVED on our table, but it's not like we needed it anyway. All the booths around us are empty.

Mr. and Mrs. Reid take one side of the booth, while Darryl, Kimmie, and I squeeze into the other.

"You kids can order anything you want," Mr. Reid says as he picks up his menu, which brings a little relief to my chest. I wasn't entirely sure that Mr. and Mrs. Reid would offer to pay for my food, so before leaving the apartment earlier, I put a twenty in my pocket and told myself that I would just order an appetizer and say I wasn't too hungry.

"My parents *love* the Red Lobster," Kimmie says to me and Darryl.

"Who wouldn't?" Mrs. Reid says, her face hidden behind her own menu.

I flip through the pages, trying to make up my mind quickly. Ma never really made seafood, so I'm not even sure I know what shrimp tastes like. While I try to decide between fish, or shrimp, or something that's called a surf and turf, Mrs. Reid looks up and folds her hands over the table.

"So, Darryl," she says. "How have you been?"

"I've been great, Mrs. Reid," Darryl answers. "Or, actually...maybe a little nervous. I'm starting orientation at NYU in a few weeks."

Mrs. Reid's eyes seem to sparkle in that moment. "Well,

it's perfectly normal to be nervous," she says. "I'm sure it'll be great, though."

"Have you taken the SAT already, Mateo?" Mr. Reid asks, turning toward me.

He may as well have punched me in the stomach. All the air leaves my body, and I sit there in front of him for a few seconds, trying to remember how to breathe. I know Mr. Reid means well. I know that, under any other circumstances, this question would've been expected, fair to ask.

"Uh . . . no. I was planning to take it this fall." They don't need any more explanation than that. They don't need to know that I'm probably not gonna take the SAT anymore, that all the prep I did was for nothing. I don't need to ruin dinner by explaining that I'm not even sure how or if I'm gonna get through my last year of high school.

Kimmie says something, but I don't hear what it is, because suddenly my phone starts ringing in my pocket. I reach for it, expecting to see Ma's or Jorge's name on the screen. Instead, I see Maria's.

"Sorry," I say, sliding out of the booth. "I'll be back in a sec."

Again, Kimmie says something, but my heart is beating too fast for me to care.

"Hey, Maria," I answer as I sprint across the restaurant, in the direction of the bathrooms. "I'm at dinner, but I can come pick up Sophie in a—"

"Mateo." The way she whispers my name, the way she breathes loudly into the phone makes my stomach drop. Something is wrong.

"I—I can't find her!" Maria says frantically. "She...was right here...and the bathroom was around the corner...but I looked, and...not there. I just don't know where she—"

"Wait a second," I say. "Slow down. Maria, you're not making any sense. What happened?"

She pants into the phone. I'm not sure if she's been running or if she's just so agitated that she can't even breathe, but slowly, she starts to get the words out. "I brought the kids to Central Park. Sophie and Leslie were running around the playground, and then...then Sophie said she was going to the bathroom, and she was taking a long time, so I...went to check on her, and she wasn't there."

"Are you sure?" I ask, my heart pounding in my chest. "Maria, are you sure she's not somewhere around there? Maybe she—"

"I've looked everywhere. All over the north end of the park, and I just can't find her. Mateo, I'm so sorry. I don't know what to—"

"Where are you?"

"At the East 110th Street playground."

"Stay there," I say firmly. "I'll be there as soon as I can."

I shove my phone back into my pocket and start walking

decisively. I've only taken a few steps, however, when I start to feel dizzy. The world around me is spinning, but still, I force myself to put one foot in front of the other until I've reached the table where Darryl, Kimmie, and her parents are sitting.

From somewhere far away, I hear someone saying my name.

"Matt." No—it sounds more like a question: *"Matt?"*

Kimmie's face comes into focus. She and Darryl are staring at me with deep frowns, their eyes moving quickly as they try to read my expression.

"What's wrong?" Darryl asks.

"It's my sister," I manage to say. "She's gone missing."

I'm prepared to tell them that I don't have time to go into detail. I'm expecting everyone to start asking me a million questions, but instead Kimmie says, "What can we do to find her?"

By the time we get to Central Park, the sun is already shining lower in the sky. There's something dreamlike about this whole thing—the yellowish light, the near-empty paths, the fact that I'm walking right next to Kimmie and Darryl on our way to look for my sister.

In the back of my mind, I feel bad for ruining Mr. and Mrs. Reid's anniversary. Kimmie's parents jumped up from the table right away, saying they were going back to their apartment in case Sophie shows up there. Even though I've been hoping that Kimmie's phone will ring and they'll tell us she came back safe and sound, there has been no news since we stepped out of the restaurant.

We find Maria standing anxiously by the playground entrance next to Leslie. When she sees me, she lets out a gasp.

I don't think. I just close the distance between Maria and me and wrap my arms around her. Her arms are very still for a second, but then she hugs me back, and even though she says something, I can't even make out her words. All I can hear is my own sobbing as I cry into her shirt.

"Mateo." She sighs into my ear. From the way her chest is moving, I can tell she's crying, too. "I'm sorry. I don't know what happened."

"We'll find her," I say as I step away from her. "We have to."

"How long has it been since you last saw her?" Darryl asks. Even though I assured him a million times that he didn't have to, he insisted on coming along to help.

"I'm not sure," Maria says, dabbing at her eyes with the sleeve of her shirt. "We've spent at least forty-five minutes looking for her."

"Leslie, did she say anything to you?" I ask.

She shakes her head, making her ponytail swing behind her head. "We were just playing."

I grip my phone tightly in my hand. On our way here, I tried calling Sophie's cell phone, but she's not picking up. I don't know if she was even carrying it. She could've left it back at Kimmie's place, or the battery might've died.

Kimmie clears her throat beside me. "Could she have gotten lost in the park?"

"That's what I thought at first," Maria says. "But we've looked for her everywhere, and—"

"Maybe she went somewhere else," I interrupt her, thinking quickly. "If she got lost and didn't know how to get back to the playground, she could be out there, trying to find me."

"Where could she be?" Kimmie says.

"I dunno...the bodega?" I say. "Maybe she thinks I'm there."

Kimmie's eyes move quickly. "Why don't you head down there? We'll stay here and look for Sophie."

There isn't much time to think. All I can do is nod.

"Call me if anything happens," I say to Maria, Kimmie, and Darryl. After taking one last look at their frightened faces, I run toward the exit of the park.

★ ★ ★

As I look anxiously out the window of the cab, I hold my phone hard against my ear. I've been trying to call Jorge from the moment I left Central Park, but he's not picking up.

"Hello?" he answers on the third try.

"Jorge, has Sophie come by your apartment?"

"Mateo? No, she hasn't. Why? Is everything—"

"We can't find her," I say as the taxi comes to a stop at a red light. I try to explain what has happened as best as I can, even though I keep stumbling over my own words.

"What's wrong?" I hear Amy's voice in the background just as the light turns green and the taxi driver hits the pedal.

"It's Sophie," Jorge says.

My ears ring with the sound of their voices as Jorge repeats everything I just said to Amy.

"Mateo, where are you?" he asks me.

"I'm on my way to the bodega. I think Sophie might've gone there."

"Okay, I'll meet you there. I'm on my—"

"No! Stay where you are. Sophie could also show up at the apartment."

"Amy can stay here," he says. "I'll come meet you."

"Okay," I whisper. "I'll see you at the bodega."

"But are you sure she's not still in Central Park?"

"I don't know. Maria and two of my friends are looking for her there, so we have to cover all our bases."

While the taxi speeds down Fifth Avenue, I start to feel nauseous. Maybe it's just the movement of the car, but soon enough I'm worrying that I'm gonna throw up.

Before I can do anything—crack open the window, or ask the driver to turn up the AC—Jorge clears his throat.

"Call me if you hear something," he says.

"I will," I say, and then, with a heavy heart, I hang up, silently praying that Sophie's okay, that we'll find her, that wherever she went, she'll make her way back to us.

★ ★ ★

When the taxi finally pulls over, I jump out, run across the sidewalk, and storm into the bodega. The bell overhead rings violently, echoing against the silence.

Erika turns toward me immediately. "Mateo? What are you doing here?"

"Has my sister come by the bodega?"

"N-no. It's been quiet around here," she says. "Mateo, what's wrong?"

"She's gone missing." No matter how many times I've said it, it still doesn't feel real. And this time, it only makes the nausea from earlier get worse, as a million images flash through my mind—Sophie lost in the middle of the city, Sophie crying, Sophie watching as the sky gets darker, not knowing where to go, how to find me.

"Oh my God," Erika says. "How did this happen?"

I'm in the middle of explaining everything to her when the bell at the door rings loudly again and Jorge stumbles into the store.

"Mateo," he says when he sees me. "Have you heard anything?"

"No," I say, feeling desperation in the deepest part of my stomach. "Jorge, what do we do? How do we—"

My phone starts ringing in that moment, and I don't even look at the name on the screen before hitting the answer button.

"Hello?"

"Mijo." I can't believe it. It's him. *Him*. Pa.

I have no idea what to say. I don't know how to make sense of the anger I feel when I hear his voice. All I can do is lower my phone with a shaking hand and put him on speakerphone.

"I got Jorge's voicemail," he says.

I turn to look at my uncle, who nods once. "After you and I got off the phone, I tried calling your parents. I figured they needed to know about what's going on."

"Where is she?" Pa asks, his voice loud and desperate. "What happened to Sophie? How could she be gone?"

"I don't know, Pa."

Somewhere deep down, I feel something that doesn't make sense, that doesn't belong at a moment like this. Even though my sister is gone, and I'm furious at my dad for leaving us with no answers, I also feel a glimmer of hope, because at least he's here. Even if we can only talk through a phone, he's with me, and he's gonna help us figure out this mess.

"Why did you leave?" I ask, my voice breaking. "Why haven't you called?"

"I've been trying to find work in the city. I was tired of fighting, of not having answers for all of you. I needed to come here and . . . and *do* something so you and Sophie could come live with us. I'm still trying to find a job, but—but I'll figure something out. I'm sorry I didn't see it before. You were right—Sophie needs to be with us."

We remain frozen on the line for a moment, allowing all the things we can't say to float in the silence between us—the longing we've felt for months, how sorry we both are for what happened the last time we talked, and the hope we're starting to feel for a future where we'll all be together again.

"I need you to think, Mateo. When was the last time you spoke to your sister? Has she said anything to you?"

Looking back on the last couple of days, I can't think of anything that has seemed different about Sophie. She's been quiet, as she has been for weeks. But then I remember the conversation we had on the first morning we woke up at Kimmie's place. I think of the disappointment in her eyes when I told her that we were gonna have to wait a bit longer to know whether we could go to Mexico or not.

"The other day, she asked me if we could go live with Ma. She wanted to go be with her in Puebla while we figured everything else out, but I tried to explain to her that—"

"This is my fault," Jorge interrupts me, running a hand

across his forehead. "You kids should've never left our apartment. If we hadn't—"

"Jorge, don't—"

"—never meant for things to get so out of hand. Amy just—"

"There's no point in beating yourself up."

"—needed some time, and we've been talking about how to—"

"Jorge," I say firmly. "Now's not the time for this. We have to find Sophie."

A weird sound comes out of Jorge's throat. It's as though he's choking—or as though he's having a fight with himself, trying to make up his mind between saying what he's feeling and accepting that what I'm saying is true.

"I—I can think of somewhere to start," Erika says, and Jorge and I turn to look at her at the same time. "Mateo, that day you brought her to the bodega a few weeks ago—she asked me questions about Mexico. She wanted to know how far it was and how to get there."

I swallow hard, thinking back on that day. I remember hoping that Erika would find the right things to say to Sophie, that she'd be able to comfort her, but I never asked her what happened after I stopped listening in.

"What did you say to her?"

"I told her it's far. I said you would need to fly there, and then she wanted to know where 'Nework' was, so I asked if she meant Newark. I said it was in New Jersey, on the other side of the river, but that's about it."

"She's been there before," Pa says in a whisper. "Last year, when we picked up Jorge from the airport—he flew into Newark."

Was that really last year? It feels like forever ago, but it's true—Jorge was returning from Puerto Rico, and he asked Pa if he could come meet him at the airport because he had brought back heavy suitcases. It was Ma's idea that we should all go and wait for him in the arrivals section, just to surprise him, and so we took the train from Penn Station to get to the airport.

"You don't think she would try to go there, do you?" I ask Pa. He's silent for a long time, and I wonder if he's thinking the same thing as I am—that if Sophie was desperate enough, she may have run away. After all the times we told her she couldn't go to Mexico, she might've wanted to take matters into her own hands to try to go be with Ma.

"If she did, she wouldn't have gotten very far," Jorge says.

"That doesn't mean she wouldn't try."

Jorge stares at me with fear in his eyes, and my legs start shaking as I think of all the things that could happen—all the things that could go wrong for Sophie if she actually is trying to get on a train to the airport.

"We need to go to Penn Station," I say, instinctively moving toward the door.

"I'll go to the airport," Jorge says. "She could've made it there by now."

"Pa, I'm gonna have to call you back," I say. Before he can protest, I shove my phone back inside my pocket.

"What can I do?" Erika asks. "I want to—"

"Stay here," I say to her. "Stay here in case she comes by."

Erika nods once. I nod back at her, and then, without another word, Jorge and I walk out of the bodega.

★ ★ ★

I don't think I've ever run faster in my life. I've never been in such a rush to get anywhere. The taxi ride to Penn Station was taking forever, so I had no choice but to hop out of the cab and run the rest of the way.

By the time I finally get to the corner of Thirty-Third and Seventh Avenue, my shirt is sticky with sweat, my stomach hurting and my breathing heavy. In the back of my mind, I can't help but feel as though this is pointless. Sophie may not even be at Penn Station. And even if she did come here, she may have already tried and failed to get on a train to the airport. Or—even worse—she might've figured out how to get a ticket, and find the right platform, and be halfway to New Jersey by now.

I rush down the escalator and slow down only long enough to get a good look at the signs pointing toward the New Jersey Transit corridor.

The place is crowded, filled with commuters trying to make their way back home, which makes it almost impossible to move. As I push my way past groups of people, all I can think about is Sophie's black hair. I look for it everywhere—in the long lines at ticket machines, in the throng of people walking up and down the stairs, and among the crowds that move quickly throughout the station. A couple of times, my heart skips a beat, thinking I've finally spotted her, but when I look twice, I realize it wasn't my sister. And the longer I spend doing this, the lower my stomach sinks. Maybe we were stupid to assume that she would come here. Maybe we're just wasting valuable time that we should've spent searching somewhere else.

Still, I keep moving, keep searching for Sophie's hair. I reach for my phone, pull it out of my pocket, and clutch it tightly against my chest. A part of me is hoping it'll ring. I'm praying that someone else has found her—that Maria, Kimmie, or Darryl have spotted her walking around Central Park, or that she's come knocking on Jorge and Amy's door. But even as I reach the other side of the corridor, my phone remains silent, and all of a sudden, I'm finding it hard to breathe.

I bend over, hands on my knees. Even as desperation spreads to my arms and legs, I tell myself that I need to keep searching for her. She could still be here. Maybe I was walking too quickly, or maybe I wasn't paying enough attention.

I turn around and start running back the way I came. It's getting harder to put one foot in front of the other, and I'm not exactly sure why it is—if I needed a little more time to catch my breath, or if the station is getting more crowded, or if it's just my fear of not finding Sophie here.

I'm slowing down, taking deep breaths, when all of a sudden, I see it—a flash of black hair.

I stop, nearly crashing into a man. My heart is stuck in my throat as I blink, trying to make sure that my eyes aren't playing a trick on me.

She's facing away from me, staring up at the train schedule screens. Something tells me she's been standing there for a while—her shoulders are slumped, and she's fidgeting with her hands.

"Sophie!" I yell across the corridor. It takes her a moment to turn around, and when she does, her face goes pale.

Our eyes meet for only a second, but that's enough for all the weight inside of me to melt away. I feel longing that I've never felt before in my life as I start moving my heavy legs forward, wanting to reach my sister, to wrap my arms around her, but before I can get too close, she turns away from me and starts running.

"Sophie!"

She looks over her shoulder at me, and I don't understand how this happened—how I went from being so close to her, to having to chase her through the crowded station.

"Sophie, please! Just stop."

I try my hardest to keep up, but I can't stop bumping into people, unable to sneak into the small gaps she keeps disappearing through.

"Sophie!"

I can feel a hundred judgmental gazes on me, but no one tries to help. No one tries to stop her—no one does anything.

I push past a group of businessmen, and when I come out on the other side, I see her. She's slowing down a little, probably getting tired, but I keep running as fast as I can. I stretch out a hand, and as soon as I touch her shoulder, she stops and turns around to face me with tears in her eyes.

I wrap her in my arms, sinking my face into her hair. The world around me disappears, and all I know is that her entire body is shaking—or maybe it's both of us. We're both trembling.

"Why are you running? Why are you—" I can't even finish my sentence. Hot tears start falling down my face, and I sink to my knees in front of Sophie, pulling her closer to me.

"I don't wanna be here anymore," she whispers into my ear, her chest heaving uncontrollably. "I want to go to Mexico. I just wanna be with Ma and Pa."

"You can, Sophie," I say. "You can go be with them."

"That's not what you've said. You all keep saying that I—"

"It's different now."

"How is it different?"

"I just spoke to Pa. He—he called me, and he said yes. He said we can go live with him and Ma."

"I don't believe you."

"I'm telling the truth, Sophie."

She pulls away and looks at me. In her eyes, I see all the pain from the last few months. I know she's trying to believe me, to be hopeful, but she can't. With tears falling from her eyes, she silently begs me to tell her the truth, to not make any more promises that I can't keep.

But then, as suddenly as she stepped away from me, she falls into my arms again.

"I'm here, Sophie," I whisper into her hair. "I'm here."

I feel weak, exhausted. All I want is to collapse on the spot, yet somehow, I manage to keep my arms around my sister, feeling the way her chest shakes as she cries into my shoulder.

"We're okay," I say. "We're gonna be okay."

I have no idea how long we remain there in the middle of the station. People keep moving around us, and voices overhead make announcements about safety, and platform changes, and train delays, but none of that matters. The only thing I care about is right here in my arms.

At some point, Sophie speaks up. "Can we get out of here?"

I nod, looking into her eyes. For the first time in a while, they're a little less sad.

She leads the way toward the exit. Holding her with one hand and wiping my tears with the other, we step into the warm night air.

IT FEELS AS THOUGH LATELY, DAYS HAVE been going by quickly, but nights are painfully slow. Waking hours are a blur, but my dreams seem to go on forever.

It is while I'm sleeping that I see it all again. I relive everything that's happened in the past few months. I see myself at the bodega, looking into the eyes of the ICE agents who came asking for my dad. I see myself standing in front of Erika as she explained to me that Ma and Pa had been taken, and the realization that our lives would change forever hits me all over again. I see myself testifying during Pa's hearing, and walking out of the apartment where I grew up for the very last time, and running through Penn Station, trying to find Sophie.

When I wake up, I always feel a little disoriented. My dreams seem more real than the bed underneath me or the walls around me. It always takes me a few moments to remember that all those things are over, that they're in the past, that now we have to focus on the future.

On a Saturday morning in mid-August, I wake up from a dream that involved me chasing after Sophie down a long, dark street. Even though my heart is beating fast and my breathing is sped up, as though I've actually been running, the room greets me with nothing but peace and quiet.

Slowly, I get up from bed. Sophie must've already woken up, because she's not here. I tiptoe toward the door and step out into the hallway.

We've been back at Jorge's for the past couple of weeks, but now that we know this is only temporary, we've all been a little more relaxed. Jorge has been joining us at night to watch *Pasiones de tu Corazón*, even though it's pretty hopeless to think that he'll be able to catch up with the story at this point. Amy's always asking if we're hungry, always making sure we have everything we need. Even Ellie has been sleeping better.

"And we'll never be apart again. I promise," I hear Pa's voice coming from the living room.

I find Sophie sitting on the couch, holding her phone in front of her nose, with Pa and Ma on FaceTime. I sit down on the couch next to her, knowing exactly what's going on. She must've had a nightmare again.

"Never?" she asks, barely noticing that I'm there.

"Never," Pa says.

I've heard him explain this to her a thousand times, but she always seems to want to hear it just one more time. She wants to hear that she will in fact go live with Ma and Pa, that despite everything that's happened, she doesn't have to be afraid anymore.

It was Ma who ended up getting a job offer—she's been helping out in the kitchen of a restaurant in Puebla, and even though it's not a lot of money, it helped them move out of the tiny room they were living in and into an apartment that's a bit closer to downtown. Pa is still searching, but now that Ma has proven that it's possible, he seems to be more hopeful.

"How much longer until I can come to Mexico?" she asks.

"Soon, mija. Very soon."

"Mateo," Ma says when she sees me next to Sophie. "¿Han sabido algo?"

"Not yet," I answer. She's asking about our passports—Sophie's and mine. We submitted our applications a couple of days after coming back to Uncle Jorge's, but they still haven't come in the mail.

"We'll all be together soon," Pa says firmly. "Just hang in there."

We haven't even bought our plane tickets yet. We don't want to risk having a booked flight and not getting our passports in time, so Pa is waiting until we receive them to look into flight options for Sophie and me.

"I can't wait to have you here, mijos," Ma says. "The apartment is starting to look better. We even bought some decorations at the market the other day. I think you'll like it."

This is what I'm talking about when I say that real life feels like a blur. It's at moments like these that I zone out, that I feel as though none of this is even happening. Hearing Ma and Pa talk about our lives in Mexico makes my world spin a little. It forces me to imagine a life that I never even thought was possible—a life that had never been part of our plans.

★   ★   ★

Our passports come a couple of days later. It's Jorge who finds the package in the mailroom downstairs. He bursts into the apartment while Sophie, Amy, and I are watching a movie, holding up a big envelope as if it were a trophy.

"They're here!" he says.

We all sit around the kitchen table and watch as Jorge opens the envelope. Sure enough, when he tips it over, two passports fall out onto the table. They're shiny and dark blue, and they smell like newly printed paper.

"Does this mean we can go to Mexico now?" Sophie asks, staring down at her own photograph in one of the passports.

"It does, Sophie."

That night, when Jorge and Amy head off into their bedroom and Sophie's in the shower, Pa and I talk on FaceTime. We both go through all the travel websites we can think of, trying to find the cheapest plane tickets to Mexico.

"Any luck, Pa?"

He lets out a long sigh in response. "I think that late August flight you found is still our best bet," he says. "But it's more expensive than I'd hoped." He looks directly at the camera, blinking repeatedly. I'm sure his eyes are hurting from staring at the screen for too long. "Have you found anything else?"

It's my turn to let out a long sigh. "I haven't," I answer. "And, Pa, there's something I wanna talk about. I... I've been thinking."

"About what?"

"Mexico. And what my life would be like if I moved there with you."

Pa turns away from me, rubbing his eyes.

"All these months, I've been so focused on Sophie—making sure she's okay, that she has what she needs, keeping her safe. But now that I know she can go live with you and Ma... I've started to think about the things *I* want."

"And what are they, Mateo?"

374

"I want to be wherever you, Ma, and Sophie are," I say. "But I also want to be here. In New York. I want to be with Adam and Kimmie, and graduate high school, and go to college. I mean, you've said it all along—getting into a good college is hard as it is . . . and if I start senior year at a different school, in a different country, well . . ." I take a deep breath. "There's also the bodega. You've worked so hard to build it up. It doesn't feel right for me to just leave it behind."

Pa doesn't say anything for a long time. There's some sort of resistance on his face. It's as if he's struggling with himself, trying to decide whether he should say any of this or not, but then he nods slowly. "I had a call yesterday."

"A call?"

"From people who want to buy the bodega from us."

Suddenly, my throat feels like it's about to close. "Pa," I say. "You can't do this. You can't sell the bodega."

"I don't think we have a choice, mijo."

Taking small breaths through my mouth, I try to imagine a world where Pa's bodega isn't at the corner of Eleventh Street and Avenue A—a world where I no longer see Nelly and Erika every day, where people in the neighborhood no longer have a place to buy stuff at reasonable prices, where the business my parents worked so tirelessly to build no longer exists.

"When were you gonna tell me this?"

"Soon," he says. "I, uh . . . I'm talking to these people again tomorrow. I think I'm gonna accept their offer." Pa lifts his gaze to look at me, and there are tears in his eyes. "The bodega was what allowed us to give you and Sophie a good life all these years. And now, if we sell it, it can help us keep doing that. We can use that money to send Sophie to a good school here in Mexico, and...if that's where you want to be, it can also help pay for your education."

A spark lights up in Pa's eyes. I know how much pain he's in, just imagining the idea of letting go of the business it took him so long to build, but I can tell he's also imagining something else—a future where Sophie will have healed, where I will have graduated high school and gotten into a good college, a future where everything that's happened in the last few months will seem like a distant memory.

"There's something else—something you don't know," Pa adds. "They haven't said anything because they haven't signed the contract yet, but...Jorge and Amy found a house in New Jersey."

"They're moving?"

"That's the plan. The apartment is getting too small for them, especially if they want to have more kids. And...they also said the house they picked has a finished basement. They threw it out there themselves—the idea that if you wanted to go live with them, you could. You'd have your own part of the house."

Is this real life? I have to shake my head a little, close my eyes and open them again, just to make sure I'm really here, that Pa is really saying these things.

"I—I don't know if . . ."

"You don't have to decide right now. Think about what's best for you. And I'm here for you, whatever you choose. You know that, don't you, mijo?"

I press my lips together, swallowing a lump in my throat. "I know it, Pa."

★　★　★

"New Jersey? But you're a born-and-raised New Yorker."

"So?"

"So . . . you should live in New York. Not New Jersey."

"I know, Kimmie. But it's a better option than going to Mexico."

"Well, duh."

"It would only be across the river. It's not like I would have to transfer schools."

"You wouldn't?" Kimmie asks, lifting an eyebrow.

I feel myself blushing. "We asked our old neighbor, Mrs. Solís, if we could use her address for registration."

"I guess I could live with that," Kimmie says, smiling a little. "I wouldn't want you going off to a different school, making new friends in Jersey."

A seagull flies close to the water, and I turn my neck slowly, following it along its path. We're sitting on the grass at Hudson River Park. It's the middle of the day, and the sun and the humidity are as strong as ever.

"Are you really gonna do it?" she asks me. "Are you gonna move to New Jersey?"

"I dunno," I say. "I keep asking myself the same questions, over and over again: *How could I do this? How could I stay?*"

"Matt," she says, staring deep into my eyes. "How could you go? This is where you need to be. If you want to do everything you said you would—get into Tisch and make it to Broadway, you *have* to stay."

I look down, start playing with the grass. I haven't told Kimmie that I'm not sure I want those things anymore—that what matters most now isn't Tisch or Broadway, but figuring out what my new dreams will be. I need something different—something stable, something that would allow me to send money to my parents back in Mexico.

"There's also Adam," I say. "I feel like it would be such a waste to end things with him when they've barely even started. Is that stupid? Is it stupid that he's part of the reason why I don't want to go?"

Kimmie shakes her head. "It's not. You deserve to see where things go with him. Besides, I'd like to think that it's not just him. I'm also part of the reason why you don't wanna go, right?"

I look up to see that she's smiling. Letting out a small laugh, I say, "Yes, Kimmie. Of course you are."

"Where are they, anyway? He and Darryl said they'd be here twenty minutes ago."

I look down at my phone. I have a new text from Adam. "The subway was delayed," I say, reading out loud. "He says they'll be here soon."

"Heya," we hear Adam's voice behind us suddenly.

I turn around to find that the two of them are walking toward us. Kimmie lets out a small sigh when she sees Darryl, but I only have eyes for Adam. His hair looks blond in the summer sun. His eyes are bright, and his smile is bigger than ever. He sits down next to me on the grass and gives me a quick kiss on the lips, and just like that, everything feels right again.

We end up going to SoHo, and we do the same thing as always—we look for a place that doesn't have security at the door, which isn't hard to find in the middle of the day. Then Kimmie and I go wait in a corner while Adam and Darryl, who are the tallest and oldest-looking of the group, try to order at the bar.

Kimmie and I hold our breath as we watch. This is always

the moment when the bartender either nods once and starts pouring the drinks, or narrows his eyes and asks to see an ID. For a moment, the guy who's working at the bar seems undecided. He looks from Adam to Darryl for a second, but then he reaches for a glass.

"They did it," I whisper to Kimmie. And sure enough, a minute later Adam and Darryl turn toward us, each holding two beers.

"Cheers," Kimmie says once they've reached our corner of the bar.

Our glasses make a loud sound as we clink them against one another, and then we each take our first sips.

"So," Kimmie says, her upper lip covered in foam from the beer.

"So?"

"What are you guys doing Labor Day weekend?"

Darryl bites his lip, and I know right away that something's going on.

"I'm not sure," Adam answers slowly. "Why?"

"The girls and I are playing again," Kimmie says, and our corner of the bar gets loud all of a sudden as Adam and I ask her when, and how, and at what time.

While she answers our questions, I see it so clearly—I need to stay. I need to be at Kimmie's next show. I need to be here to watch Darryl's band take off. I need to be at the opening night of whatever play Adam is cast in next and have him by my side as I figure out my future.

"I can't believe summer's almost over," Adam says, putting an arm around my shoulder.

Kimmie nods once. "Senior year, baby."

"Gonna be the best one," I say.

Darryl cringes a little. "Uh, maybe try not to get your hopes up too high."

We all burst out laughing, and as I stare into my friends' eyes, the glow from the night of Adam's debut comes back, shining even brighter than before.

★ ★ ★

"Are you sure about this?"

"I am." The answer comes easily, even though deep down, I feel as though someone is clenching my heart in their first, squeezing it hard.

I'm sitting at the kitchen table in Jorge's apartment with Pa on the line. He's about to buy Sophie's plane ticket to Mexico.

"If you change your mind, we can still buy you a ticket later on."

"I know," I say, swallowing hard. "But I don't think I'll change my mind."

Earlier today, Jorge and Amy drove Sophie and me to New

Jersey to see their new house. I wasn't sure what to expect, but when we got there, it seemed to me like something straight out of a movie—the front lawn, the big kitchen, the backyard. It may be small by suburban standards, but having lived in Manhattan my whole life, it seemed to me like more space than anyone could ever need.

"This is where you'll live," Jorge said to me when we went down to the basement, and I could see it right away—I could picture myself waking up there every day, and having Kimmie and Adam over on weekends, and pacing around my big room while I study for the SAT.

"All right," Pa says, bringing me back to the present. "I bought your sister's ticket."

Just like that, the clock starts ticking. Ten days—that's all the time we have left together before Sophie flies to Mexico to join Ma and Pa.

I try my best to enjoy it, all too aware that it might be a while before I see my sister again. I help Jorge and Erika clean out the bodega, and I try to keep my voice steady whenever someone we know walks in and I have to explain why we have to close down. I take Sophie to all her favorite parks in the city—Central Park, and Washington Square Park, and Bryant Park. I buy her ice cream, and milkshakes, and anything she wants, because I just can't find a way to say no to her right now.

"Come with us," she says to me one night, after we've turned off the lights and the room is filled with the soft sounds of the street outside. "Please, Mateo."

With a knot in my throat, I reach for her hand. "I can't, Sophie," I say. "Not right now. But just think about the future. Think of what your life is gonna be like in Mexico—all the new places you're gonna see, all the friends you're gonna make. And maybe, in a few years, Ma and Pa will be allowed to come back to the US. Maybe we can all be together again."

She squeezes my hand, not saying anything. I wish I had something else to offer her—something other than hope for a future we can't even imagine right now. But before I can think of anything else to say, her hand becomes loose in mine, and her breathing becomes soft and slow as she drifts off into sleep.

★ ★ ★

The day before Sophie's flight, we're all feeling a little antsy. Packing her things took less time than we expected, and now that her bags are ready and waiting by the door, there's not much left for us to do.

"I have an idea," I say to her, and she turns sharply toward me. "Let's go to the beach."

Sophie's eyes light up. We pack up a few towels, snacks, bottles of water, and then we're on our way. We don't speak much during the subway ride, and I can feel the things we're not saying lingering in the air around us. Sophie doesn't talk about Mexico. She doesn't ask me any more questions about what life will be like once she gets there, doesn't even ask me to come with her. Meanwhile, I try my best to stop thinking about how heartbreaking it was to watch Jorge sign the papers to sell the bodega earlier this week, how many times Pa almost changed his mind, how many other options he tried to come up with. I don't tell Sophie how terrified I am of tomorrow—of having to say goodbye, of watching her leave and having to start a brand-new life on my own. Today isn't about any of that—today, the only thing that matters is that we're going to the beach.

We walk for a while along the shore, our feet sinking into the sand. We move past the worst of the crowds, past the amusement park, until we get to our spot—the place we always used to come to. It's a little less busy here, so I can hear the wind and the waves above the sound of people's voices. The boardwalk is right behind us, and straight ahead is an endless expanse of water.

We lay out a couple of towels, and while Sophie runs off toward the water and starts splashing around, I soak my feet, trying to figure out how I feel. There's something about the wind and the smell of salt that helps me breathe a little easier. If I close my eyes, I can almost pretend Ma and Pa are right next to me, and that everything that happened in the last few months was just a bad dream. But when I open them again, it becomes impossible to ignore the pain that I can feel deep down—pain because this is the last time Sophie and me are ever gonna get to do this, because after all those summers of coming here, of making this our spot, the four of us will never get to be here together again.

I suddenly feel the urge to talk to Ma and Pa. I need to see their faces, hear their voices, just for a little while. I pull out my phone and start a FaceTime call with them.

"Hi, Ma," I say when she appears on the screen.

"Mateo?" she says. "Where are you?"

I lift my phone up so she can see what's around me. "We're at the beach, Ma."

She lets out a sigh, and something inside of me shifts. Her sigh says everything I can't put into words—it makes all this pain, all this nostalgia make a little more sense. It makes me feel less alone.

"I miss you," she says.

"Me too, Ma. I wish you could be here."

Sophie comes running toward me, her hair dripping wet. "Is that Ma on the phone?"

"It is, Sophie."

I hand her my cell phone, and she takes it with shaking hands.

"Mi nena," Ma says, sighing again. "How are you? How's the water?"

"Not too cold, Ma. You would've liked it."

My mind flashes back to images of Ma soaking her feet. Even though Sophie and I go swimming every single time, Ma would only join us if the water was warm.

"The beaches in Mexico are even better than Coney Island, Sophie," Pa says, coming up behind Ma. "Just wait and see."

In that moment, I realize something. We're all here together. Despite the distance, and despite the fact that Ma and Pa aren't standing right next to us, the four of us are all here, together at the beach, just as we said we would be.

I turn to meet Sophie's eyes. They're sparkling, as though she's thinking the exact same thing—as though she's realizing that this moment feels just like the old days. As she and I sit down on a towel, with Pa and Ma smiling on the phone, I can't help but think that, after all those times Ma told us to be strong and brave, that's exactly what we've become. And no matter how hard they tried to separate us, how much the distance hurt, or how it nearly broke us, we are really, truly indivisible.

★ ★ ★

We wake up at the break of dawn the next day. I cracked the bedroom window open last night because it was too hot, but now the early morning air is bringing a chill into the room, reminding me that fall is coming, that school is starting soon, that the time has come for Sophie to leave.

We have breakfast at the kitchen table. Amy went all out today and made a huge meal as a way to wish Sophie farewell, but Jorge is the only one who has the appetite to finish all his food. Sophie and I barely touch ours, partly because it's too early to eat, and partly because we're feeling a little anxious.

When we walk out of the building, there's a familiar blue car parked right across the street. Jorge borrowed Amy's parents' car again, and left Ellie with them for the day so he and Amy could drive us to the airport. He helps us load Sophie's heavy suitcase into the trunk, and then we're on our way to LaGuardia.

"But why can't you stay with me until I get on the plane?" Sophie asks as we stand at the start of the security line.

"We're not allowed to, Sophie. But Stacey here will help you. She'll make sure you get on the plane safely." Jorge smiles at the airline worker who offered to walk Sophie all the way to the gate.

"And do you promise it won't be scary?" Sophie asks me. She's been asking about this a lot since last night—what it's like to be on a plane. It's hard to believe now that she wanted to do this all on her own, that she hadn't stopped to ask herself these same questions before running off to Penn Station.

"I promise. People fly on planes every single day." I don't really know what I'm talking about, of course. I've never been on a plane either, but I just know she'll be okay.

"And will you call me?" Sophie asks. She's also asked this question a lot lately.

"Every day. And I'll see you again before you know it. I'm coming to Mexico for Christmas, remember?"

She wraps her tiny arms around me and squeezes with all her strength. I squeeze back, never wanting to let go, but I know I have to. She needs to make it to her flight.

I watch as she joins the long line to go through security, and right before she goes through the metal detector, she turns around to look at me one last time. Even though she's too far away to really make out what she's saying, I'm pretty sure I can read her lips: "Te amo."

Hoping she'll be able to read my lips as well, I mouth something at her. "I love you, too."

★ ★ ★

We drive back to Manhattan with the windows rolled down. Jorge is in the driver's seat with Amy next to him, and I ride in the back.

For the first half of the way, there's sadness in the air around us. But then, when I meet Jorge's eyes in the rearview mirror, I realize that he's smiling, and I frown a little to myself, trying to understand what he could possibly have to smile about.

But as we get onto the Queensboro Bridge and I look out the window at the Manhattan skyline, I also find myself smiling. In the back of my mind, I can't help but feel as though we've made it—even after all the fear, and the separation, and the uncertainty, we've somehow made it out on the other side. I think about my parents picking Sophie up from the airport a few hours from now, and about all the things I'm gonna do with my future—because as long as I'm here, and as long as we hold on to the hope that Ma and Pa will one day return, their American dream lives on.

I roll my window all the way down. With the wind blowing in my face, I start to imagine a day when I'll be looking at this skyline next to Sophie and my parents. I start dreaming of a life I know I'll be wishing for every single day from this moment on—one where we will all be back here in New York, together again.

ACKNOWLEDGMENTS

I DON'T REMEMBER EXACTLY WHEN OR HOW I started dreaming of becoming a published author. My earliest memories of writing are from my old home in Mexico, where I would sit in front of our family computer for hours at a time and type out short stories. I must've been seven or eight years old, and in the time that has passed since then, there have been so many people who have helped me get to where I am today.

This book is, first and foremost, for my family. None of what I have now would be possible without the hard work and sacrifice of my parents. Ma, thank you for being my most enthusiastic reader and biggest supporter. Pa, thank you for always making sure we had everything we needed and more. Thank you to my sister, Alejandra, who has always looked out for me, and to my brother, Fernando, who has always loved my stories.

My agent, Pete Knapp, read this book in one sitting and was its fiercest supporter from the start. Thank you for believing in me, Pete. I'm eternally grateful for all your passion, kindness, and guidance, and I'm excited to continue bringing books to the world together! To everyone at Park & Fine: Thank you for giving me and my stories such a wonderful home.

I feel incredibly lucky to have worked with two amazing editors on this book: Laura Schreiber and Farrin Jacobs. Laura, thank you for treating this story with such passion and care. Farrin, thank you for giving me such a warm welcome to Little, Brown, and for trusting and challenging me in equal measure. I'm so proud of what we've accomplished together!

Thank you to the wonderful teams that made everything possible, especially Hannah Allaman, Seale Ballenger, Phil Buchanan, Esther Cajahuaringa, Jody Corbett, Siena Koncsol, Melissa Lee, Annie McDonnell, Emily Meehan, Christie Michel, Clare Perret, Simón Prades, Marisa Russell, Victoria Stapleton, Neil Swaab, Hallie Tibbetts, and Megan Tingley.

To my amazing film agent, Mary Pender-Coplan, and everyone at UTA: Thank you for believing in this story.

There are so many people who have helped, motivated, and inspired me, in ways both big and small. I am forever grateful to Jacky Carrasco, Frida Quevedo, Paulina Reynoso, Vanessa Castillo, Bianca Guilbert, Valeria Mayor, Daniela Morales, Victoria Gies, Sarah Ellwood, Lucy Boyko, Dani Fayaaz, Elizabeth Grant, Brittney Clendenan, Lauren Lawson, Taylor

Steele, Renee Cervantes, Gaby Cruz, Prerna Ramaswamy, Mikyla Kay, and Lindsay Holmgren.

Karla Gutiérrez, I am so grateful to have you by my side even after all these years. Matt La Placa, thank you for listening to my endless rants, for long walks and patio drinks, and for making sure I ate real food every once in a while. Thank you to Sarah Devine, one of the first readers of this story, who tirelessly believed one day the world was going to read my work. To Luis Ernesto Guerra, who believed in me before even I believed in myself: Thank you for taking seven-year-old me seriously, for reading my stories even when they sucked, and for always thinking I could do it.

I'm so fortunate to have met so many wonderful authors and publishing professionals throughout this long, wild journey. Special thanks to Faridah Àbíké-Íyímídé, Lane Clarke, Elora Cook, Kess Costales, Jennifer Dugan, Francesca Flores, Ayana Gray, June Hur, Peter Lopez, Yamile Saied Méndez, Aida Salazar, Sarena and Sasha Nanua, Kathleen Nishimoto, Beth Phelan, Adam Sass, Liselle Sambury, Crystal Smith, Louisa Onomé, Amélie Wen Zhao, and Julian Winters.

And to all the readers who see a piece of themselves or their lives in this story: I see you, I believe in you, and your dreams matter.

Turn the page for a sneak preview of

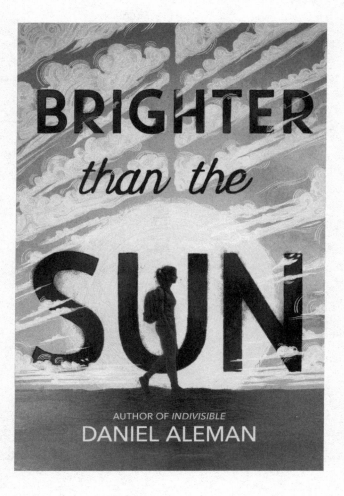

BRIGHTER
than the
SUN

AUTHOR OF *INDIVISIBLE*
DANIEL ALEMAN

AVAILABLE MARCH 2023

1

WHEN MY PARENTS PICKED OUT MY NAME, I don't think it even crossed their minds that they would be cursing me for life. Soledad—*solitude*. Or, to give them some credit, María de la Soledad, because I was unlucky enough to be born on December 18, the feast of Our Lady of Solitude.

No matter how hard I've tried, I've never been able to let go of the burden that comes with my name. My loneliness has a way of following me everywhere I go. I used to try to run away from it—I even tried to convince people to call me Marisol, but the nickname didn't stick, so I had to try with Sol instead. It was then, once people stopped calling me *solitude* and started calling me *sun*, that I almost fooled myself into believing I would become a different person.

Now, even though almost everyone calls me Sol, most of the time I feel like a Soledad. That is especially true today, while I sit at the breakfast table next to Papi, breaking off bits from a piece of pan dulce.

Sitting here in silence has become part of our daily routine, much like getting up at the crack of dawn, or rushing out the door before the clock strikes five. This is one of the few moments of peace I get to have each day, so I usually try to make the most of it. I like to breathe in the stillness of the silence, taste the sweetness of the bread, feel the warmth of my hot chocolate as it makes its way down my throat.

Today, however, there's something about the silence that's making me deeply uneasy. The bread tastes like nothing, and my hot chocolate may as well be cold, for the lack of comfort it's bringing me. Since I opened my eyes this morning, I haven't been able to stop thinking about all the ways everything's about to change. I haven't been able to shake off the realization that today will be our last day of normality, and come Monday, life will be a lot different.

From the corner of my eye, I catch Papi staring at me. He does this sometimes. It's as if he's trying to read me, as if he's trying to figure out what's going through my mind, even though it's been a long time since either of us has spoken during breakfast.

"You don't have to do it," he says suddenly. His voice is

loud, as though it came out stronger than he'd intended it to—as though he had been holding back what he wanted to say for a while, until it finally burst out of him in a near-shout.

"You could stay," Papi adds, and this time, his voice comes out weak. In the muted glow of the kitchen lights, it's impossible to ignore that there's a lot more gray in his black hair and mustache than there used to be, or that the lines on his face are now deeper, as if they've been carved into his skin.

I turn to the window, and my eyes fall on the lime tree that Mami planted years ago, when she and Papi first moved into our house. On sunnier mornings, its leaves look bright green, but the days have been getting shorter lately, and today the sunlight is nothing but a soft gleam far off in the horizon. The tree is just a dark shape silhouetted against the sky, but still, I stare at it, trying to make sense of this loneliness that's swirling around inside of me—loneliness because I wish more than anything that I could take him up on his offer, loneliness because I'm terrified of leaving home and starting a new life somewhere else, loneliness because even though Papi is sitting right next to me, there is distance between us that I don't know how to bridge.

"We don't have to talk about this, Papi," I say finally. "Not now."

I swallow hard, and a dull pain hits the back of my throat—the kind of pain that comes with holding back tears, with not being able to say the things that I actually wanted to say. Right when the tears start burning my eyes, I push my plate aside, looking up at the clock on the wall. It's almost five.

"We should get going."

The morning air is crisp as we walk out of the house and toward our old Volkswagen. I get in the passenger seat, and Papi hops in a second later, slamming his door shut with a loud bang.

Tijuana looks bleak at this time of day. Even though those of us who cross the border every morning are already awake, the rest of the city doesn't come to life until much later. It's when the sun is shining high in the sky that you can see the bright facades of the houses along the street and hear the sounds of the city—the cars beeping, the music blasting from speakers at storefronts, the street vendors yelling to attract customers. Right now, all I can really see are the red lights of cars braking ahead of us.

Papi has always insisted on driving me to the border—ever since I started going to school across the bridge, back in the ninth grade. That's the reason he wakes up at the crack of dawn and sits beside me at the kitchen table every morning. He says he wants to make sure I get to school on time, but I know he just doesn't like the idea of leaving me to have breakfast on my own while the rest of the family sleeps in, or of me walking through the city alone while it's still dark out.

The streets become more alive as we approach El Chaparral. Finding a spot to pull over is near impossible some days, with all the traffic, and taxis dropping off people, and pedestrians moving between the cars. There are times when Papi has to slow down just long enough for me to jump out, but today we get lucky. A car pulls out ahead of us, and Papi takes its spot.

"Are you okay?" he asks as I unbuckle my seat belt.

I freeze, trying not to look directly at him. I don't want to make him feel any more guilty than he already does, so I choose to lie.

"Yeah," I answer. "I'm fine."

Papi presses his lips together, nodding slowly. I know none of this has been easy for him, either. I know how badly he wishes things were different, how hard he's tried to figure out alternatives, how long it took him to accept that this was the only way—that me taking a job on the US side of the border was the only remaining option we had to keep the family afloat.

I reach for my bag. With one hand wrapped around the strap and the other on the door handle, I try my best to give him a small smile. "I'll see you tonight, okay?"

Without waiting for his answer, I step out of the car and start walking across the esplanade, toward the big sign that says PUERTO FRONTERIZO EL CHAPARRAL. This is as far as people who won't be crossing the border can go—where parents wish their children a good day at school, and where people say goodbye to loved ones who are leaving for a while. I walk past the small crowd to get onto the ramp—a long, zigzagging structure that leads up to a bridge—and hold on to the straps of my backpack as I tighten my pace.

There are countless people rushing up the ramp all around me, many of them students wearing backpacks. There's a good amount of workers, too, some of them in plain clothes, others in uniforms, and even a few dressed in suits and high heels. Almost everyone here knows exactly what they're doing. They know that you have to walk as quickly as you can, because for every person you pass, you'll end up saving a few minutes.

The pedestrian bridge begins where the ramp ends. In the two years I've been doing this commute, I've heard some people say it makes them feel claustrophobic, and it's not hard to understand why: It's an iron and glass enclosure that seems to go on for miles. I walk quickly, twisting and turning with the bridge, until I see people slowing down ahead, where the line begins. It isn't too bad today. Judging by where I'm standing, I'd say it'll be about an hour, an hour and fifteen minutes at most.

While I move slowly with the line, watching the sun rising through the metal grating walls of the bridge, I can't help but think about my brothers. A part of me suspects Luis is still asleep. Lately, his schedule seems to be the exact opposite of mine: He goes to bed late and sleeps in, but Diego might be getting up soon. He might open his eyes and begin his day without fully understanding that this will be the last normal Friday we'll get to have in a long time.

"Sol!"

I turn around to find a familiar face staring at me. Bruno Rodríguez is one of the kids at Orangeville High who also commutes from Tijuana every day. He's a year older than me, so I never really hang out with him at school, but he always joins me whenever he spots me on the bridge.

"What's up?" he asks as he comes to stand next to me. There are at least ten people who have lined up behind me since I got here, but no one protests. Joining friends in line is considered fair game.

"Not much," I reply. "Just tired."

Bruno nods once, as if to point out the obvious—that he's tired, too. He has jet-black hair, which he rarely ever combs, and round features that make him look like an overgrown child—round eyes, round chin, round nose. Most importantly, though, he has a way of reading me that nobody else does. When I'm not in the mood to talk, he stands quietly beside me, keeping me company while we move slowly with the line. Other days, when I'm feeling more lively, he keeps us both entertained by telling me stories—about his dog, a rescue bulldog who's the laziest being on the planet; about his younger sister, who's a year away from starting high school; and about his obsession with a Santa Monica–based rock band. He usually does most of the talking while I just listen, but I've also shared a few stories with him over the years—about my family's restaurant, which has been around longer than any of us can remember, about my younger brother, whom I worry about every second of my life, and about what things used to be like before Mami died.

Today, he seems to understand that I'm not in the mood to talk, so we wait in silence while my throat gets tighter and tighter. I've always resented the long hours of waiting at the border, but now that I know I won't be doing this any longer, I'm almost nostalgic. I almost miss standing in line next to Bruno, even though we're both still here, and even though I won't be officially moving to Chula Vista until Monday.

The line moves slowly while the sun keeps rising, and it's at least an hour before we reach the end of the bridge, which spirals down into a large room with shiny white floors, where the crowd breaks up into several smaller lines.

By now, I know most of the border officers by name—or by last name, at least, because that's all that's printed on the front of their uniform. I get Johnson today. He is very different from officers like López or Harris, who sometimes joke around with the students. He takes a quick look at my passport, scans it, and hands it back to me, barely even looking into my eyes.

"Welcome to the United States," he says.

I look over my shoulder to check if Bruno is coming up behind me, but he's nowhere to be seen. He must still be stuck in line, so I keep walking toward the exit, knowing he wouldn't expect me to wait for him anyway.

I swing my bag over my shoulder and follow the crowd toward the MTS station. When I get on the trolley, I look down at the time. It'll take me about fifteen minutes to travel a couple of stops and another ten to walk to school, which means I'll be early today. It's just as well. I have found myself running breathlessly into school too many times, so I've learned that it's much better to be early than late.

A bell rings softly overhead, and a woman's voice comes from the speakers.

"This is a blue line trolley, bound for America Plaza in downtown San Diego. All passengers must have a valid fare. There is no smoking or eating permitted on the trolley and—"

Leaning my head back against the window, I allow my eyes to shut just for a little while. The commute is never exactly easy, but today has felt particularly difficult. Even with the short line at the border, I'm exhausted already, and my day hasn't even started yet.

*   *   *

There are a few things about Orangeville High that surprised me when I first started coming here a couple of years ago. The first was how massive the school is—three times as big as the middle school I went to back in Mexico, where almost everyone knew each other. The second was the fact that the walls were freshly painted, the desks in classrooms undamaged, the equipment in the laboratory relatively new. The third was how lonely this place can be, even when I'm surrounded by people at all times.

"No inventes. She couldn't have said that."

"Eso fue lo que me dijo, I swear!"

"—don't think I got the answer right, porque—"

"He asked me que si quería ir a ver una movie after school, pero of course I said no."

"Well, why did he even—"

The voices that fill the hallways are always a mix of Spanish and English. At least half of the students at Orangeville are Latino, which means that if you don't have even a basic understanding of Spanglish, you might be feeling a little left out. Not that that's a problem for me—I speak both languages, but there just aren't many people I talk to on a regular basis, regardless of the language. The only person I ever really hang out with is Ari, but we aren't in any of the same classes this semester, so I mostly see her at lunch.

When I walk into the cafeteria, a feeling of dread invades my stomach. It may be easy to blend into the crowd when I'm walking down the hallways, but here, where there's lots of open space, I can almost feel a dozen different pairs of eyes falling on me the second I walk in.

"No one's looking at you, Sol. I promise," Ari said to me last year, when I told her about the way I feel exposed sometimes. "You could walk into the cafeteria in your underwear, and no one would bat an eye."

That didn't help much. If anything, the image of me standing in my underwear in front of all these people haunted me for weeks.

Once I've gotten a slice of pizza and an apple, I hold on tight to the edges of my tray and turn around to face the rows of tables. I can see Ari from here, already sitting at our usual spot and laughing at something that one of her new friends must've said.

She and I have known each other since we were both in diapers. She's tiny, probably well under five feet, but she has a loud voice, which she's always been unafraid to use—especially when I can't use my own. When we were in elementary school and a kid on the playground pulled my hair, she made sure one of the teachers found out. When a guy made a mean comment about my shoes in freshman year, she snapped back at him before I could even open my mouth. And when I've told her about all the things I can't quite understand, like the fear that people are watching me, or the loneliness that follows me everywhere I go, she's always been there to listen to me, to reassure me, to make me feel a bit more like Sol even when I'm feeling most like Soledad.

"Hey!" she says when she sees me approaching the table. In a quick movement, she takes her bag off the chair she saved for me and places it on the floor beside her.

"Hi," I say. No one else looks at me as I put my tray down. The conversation keeps going, which isn't all that unexpected. Even though we've been sitting at this table for almost two years, I still have a hard time thinking of any of these people as my friends. To me, they've always been Ari's new friends, even though they're not at all new anymore.

"Congratulations again," Ari says to me, her smile widening. "Did you do anything last night to celebrate the job offer?"

"Uh...not really," I say. "My dad and my abuela were a little shocked that it's all happening so quickly, so..."

Ari presses her lips together, smiling in a way that tells me she doesn't need any more explanation than that—she gets it.

She's the one who helped me find a job. For weeks, I sat in

front of our family computer, applying to every single opening I could find, but the furthest I ever got was with a movie theater chain in Imperial Beach, which sent me a generic email where they spelled my name as "Sole" and blandly explained I was not right for the position at that time.

When I told Ari that I needed to find an after-school job to help my family, though, she jumped into action. She spoke to one of the managers at the department store she works at, got me an interview, and then helped me prepare for it, cheering for me every step of the way—up until yesterday, when I got a call saying that I'd gotten the job.

"No way," Tony says suddenly from the other end of the table, his eyes widening. *"No way."*

Ana María nods, her lips pressed into a smile. I've never understood what she sees in Tony. She's the kind of pretty that makes people do double takes, whereas Tony is just...Tony. A bit snarky at times, a bit funny at others, entirely obnoxious always.

On my other side, Camila and Olivia are talking about this influencer that I've never heard of before.

"Oh, her eyebrow game is so strong."

"I know, but it's not like I have hundreds of dollars to spend on that shit."

Before I can open my mouth to ask who they're talking about, Ari whispers into my ear again.

"My mom told me to ask you whether you prefer a soft or a firm pillow."

"I don't—"

"She's gonna freak out if I don't come back to her with an answer."

I can't help but smile at Ari. I love it when we're able to do this—when we're able to have our own private conversations even though we're sitting at a table full of people. If it wasn't because of these whispered chats, I wouldn't normally say much during lunch.

"I guess...soft, maybe?" That's the way my pillow is at home, but it's only because I've had the same one since I was little. For all I know, firm pillows could be so much better, but I don't wanna cause Nancy any more trouble than I already am. Because Ari didn't just talk to her manager at the store. She talked to her mom, too, and convinced her to let me move in with them so I'll be able to make it to my early-morning and late-night shifts.

Ari nods once. "Soft it is."

"Are you sure your mom is okay with everything?" I ask. "I don't wanna be—"

"She is *more* than okay," she interrupts me. "And, you know...I was thinking. Once you move in, we'll be able to do fun stuff after school—when we're not working, of course."

"Yeah," I say, nodding slowly to myself. "Totally."